TOO HOT TO HANDLE

Maybe he was asleep and this was a dream. There was no way Gwen Day, the woman he'd wanted from the first moment he saw her, was here now, touching him . . . damn near everywhere. "Er . . . Gwen . . . babe, did you need something?"

"You could say that." She pushed him back a few steps before shutting the door behind her. Just when he thought this encounter couldn't get much weirder—or hotter—she leaned down, grabbed the hem of the slinky black dress she was wearing and pulled it over her head. Then she stood before him in nothing but a black lace bra, tiny matching panties, and black strappy sandals. He was completely and totally screwed.

Also by Sydney Landon

WATCH OVER ME

A DANVERS NOVEL

SYDNEY LANDON

A SIGNET ECLIPSE BOOK

SIGNET ECLIPSE
Published by the Penguin Group
Penguin Group (USA) LLC, 375 Hudson Street,
New York, New York 10014

USA | Canada | UK | Ireland | Australia | New Zealand | India | South Africa | China
penguin.com
A Penguin Random House Company

First published by Signet Eclipse, an imprint of New American Library,
a division of Penguin Group (USA) LLC

First Printing, September 2015

ISBN 978-0-451-47621-0

Printed in the United States of America
10 9 8 7 6 5 4 3 2 1

Chapter One

"Well, this officially goes down as my crappiest birthday ever. Hands down," Gwen Day moaned. She looked up to meet the sympathetic eyes of her friends, Mia Gentry and Crystal Webber. "I'm finished with men. I mean, what do you even need them for anymore?"

Crystal, who was newly divorced, nodded her head in agreement. "You got that right, girl. I have a vibrator that's always hard, doesn't talk back or leave the toilet seat up, or dribble toothpaste in the bathroom sink. I've come more in the last six months with my plastic boyfriend than all of my combined years with my ex. If I'd had one of those suckers when I was twenty, I'd have never gotten married."

Beside Crystal, Mia gave them a sheepish look. "Um . . . well . . . I like my man just fine and trust me . . . he's always hard whenever I want it."

"You suck," Crystal grumbled. "The rest of us don't have a perfectly wonderful, hottie boyfriend like Seth Jackson. You could at least share him, you know. Have you two considered broadening your horizons with a threesome? Because I'd totally be up for it." Wiggling her brows, she added, "I seem to remember you mentioning a certain threesome fantasy featuring Suzy Merimon and her hubby, Gray."

The conversation between her close friends had distracted Gwen momentarily from her pity party but she soon returned to brooding. She had no interest in her vibrator, although she agreed with Crystal that men were completely overrated. She had thought all of that was changing for her when she met McKinley Powers. His company handled the security for Danvers International, where she worked. He was drop-dead handsome with his short military haircut that he still favored even after leaving the Marines, not to mention his rock-hard body that never failed to make her heart race and knees tremble. The fact that he was a genuinely nice guy was an added bonus.

When they had first started dating, Mac had been more than content with her "taking things slow" request, which maybe should have been her first red flag. After they'd been going out for a month, he still hadn't put any type of pressure on her to move beyond kissing. By the end of the next month, she was horny and frustrated. It had seemed like he was the one now wanting to take it slow when she was ready to rip the clothes from his buff body.

They had engaged in some make-out sessions that never progressed past second base. He always pulled back when he got too close to third base, and dammit . . . crossing home plate had become just a distant dream.

Gwen knew all of the books said never to let a man

determine your self-worth, but she had been really struggling with that one after Mac's silent refusal to have sex with her. Until she finally put all of the pieces together and figured out that it might not be who she was that was the problem, but more important, who she wasn't—Ava Stone.

Mac was good friends with the Stone siblings, who also worked for Danvers. There was Declan, who had served with Mac in the military; Brant, who was Declan's older brother; and then there was Ava. She was an attractive blonde Gwen had seen around the office on several different occasions. She had come to understand that there was possibly something more than friendship between Mac and Ava when she witnessed Mac completely losing it because his coworker and good friend, Dominic Brady, had given Ava a ride on his Harley. Mac had been so upset that warning bells had gone off in Gwen's head.

From that point on, her relationship with Mac was on borrowed time and she knew it. He had become more distant than ever. He forgot to call her, didn't return her calls, and was just generally unavailable, physically and emotionally.

So, one evening she had gone to his house to talk and just to spend some time with him, and he'd taken off almost immediately after receiving a call concerning Ava. Gwen had decided to wait it out and see if he came back home. When he finally did, hours later, they had ended it. There was no fight, no ugly words, or insults. It was very civilized. Gwen might not be happy with Mac for dating her while he was hung up on Ava, but he had been honest with her in the end and she knew that it had really upset him to hurt her.

Her self-esteem had been limping along since that evening—until Mia had dropped her bombshell this morning. Mia had heard from her friend Suzy that Mac and Ava had gotten married over the weekend in Las Vegas. Gwen definitely hadn't been expecting that blow. She had figured she would be tortured for a while seeing them as a couple around the office. She had never expected Mac to break up with her and then almost immediately tie the knot. God, was she now the woman men dated right before they found "the one"?

She had been so lost in thought that she almost jumped from her seat when Mia's hand landed on her arm, shaking it excitedly. "I know—let's have a girls' night tonight! Seth's leaving this afternoon on business for a few days so I'd love to go out. How about you, Crystal?"

Gwen was secretly hoping that the other woman would veto the whole thing because she wasn't really in the mood to socialize. She just wanted to go home, eat herself into oblivion, and watch some man-hating movies on Lifetime. Of course, she'd probably run right into Dominic at the apartment complex where they both lived. *Geez, she needed to move now.* Wasn't it just her luck to live doors away from Mac's friend? Dominic was already so annoying . . . okay hot—completely, smoking hot—but still annoying.

It was no one's business if she peeked through her blinds every time she heard his boots in the hallway. Yes, dear Lord, she had to admit to herself that she could distinguish the sound of his tread from the rest of her neighbors. He just looked so good in his cargo pants and those tight shirts. And some evenings she was even lucky enough to catch him in all of his masculine glory after returning from a run. Shirtless . . . and wearing those low hanging shorts he favored. She loved the sight of his hard body with those rippling muscles, glistening sweat, the tattoos, the . . . "Hmmm?" Gwen looked around to see both Mia and Crystal staring at her.

Crystal smirked. "Honey, where was your head at? You just moaned and your eyes went crossed."

"And you have some drool on your chin," Mia pointed out helpfully.

Gwen felt her face flush as she quickly ran a hand across her mouth. Darn it, there was drool there. Freaking Dominic Brady! "I . . . er . . . was just thinking about dinner."

"Yeah, sure." Crystal grinned. "Whatever you say. So anyway, how about drinks at Hawks tonight?"

Mia rubbed her hands together. "Ohhh, going the sports bar route, I like it. Seth would hate it, so it sounds perfect to me."

Gwen found herself agreeing. Surely an evening out with her friends was better than sulking at home. After all, her ass was big enough and adding another pint of ice cream to it wasn't going to help things any. Tonight she would have fun and forget all about Mac—and Dominic. How hard could that be?

Dominic Brady sprawled back on his sofa with a big sigh of contentment. Jet lag was a real kick in the ass.

Maybe he was just getting old, but flying to Vegas and back in less than forty-eight hours was not something that he cared to do often. When he was in the Marines, he and his friends had lived for quick trips like that. They'd get a few days off and make the most of it. Sin City was a frequent destination back then. Now, just being home in his apartment in Myrtle Beach was much closer to heaven than the bright lights and the scantily clad women on the strip. Yeah, hell, only thirty-three and he officially sounded old.

The trip this weekend had been for a good cause, though. One of his best friends had gotten married to the woman he'd loved all of his life. It had been a long, rocky, and uncertain road for them, but Mac and Ava had finally worked it out and Dominic couldn't have been any happier for them. He and Mac, along with Gage Hyatt, owned a company together called East Coast Security. They monitored and provided security for many high-end companies, including Danvers International, which housed their headquarters.

For Dominic, the job and the location fit him perfectly. His family lived in Georgia, so he was close enough to visit when he wanted and far enough away to keep his nosy mother and sister out of his business. He loved them dearly, but they had been trying to find him the "right woman," since he was potty trained. If he still lived closer to home, they'd be herding single women past him like an assembly line. The fact that his sister had married her high school sweetheart and promptly popped out two kids put only that much more pressure on him.

He had just started on his second Corona and was watching *SportsCenter* when he heard a sound at his door. It was more like someone moving against the frame than knocking. Biting off a curse, he reluctantly put his beer down on the coffee table and went to check. It was likely no one coming to visit him. His neighbor at the end of the hall liked to party, and even though he always tried to keep the noise down, occasionally there were a few lost strays in the hallway.

Dominic checked the peephole, then pulled back in surprise. This was a new one. He could make out the crown of someone's head and that was about it. He stood there for a few moments, hoping that the person would just move on. When he heard nothing but silence, he came to the resigned conclusion that he was either going to have to leave them there all night or open the door and encourage them to move on.

Swinging the door open suddenly might not have been the best idea, Dominic concluded, when a soft body landed against his. He heard a feminine giggle, then a "whoops!" He froze in place when hands started roaming his chest and then his torso. "Mmmm, you are sooo hard. . . . I knew you would be."

What the hell? Just as he registered that what he thought was brown hair through the peephole was actually dark red, his interloper looked up, and he gasped in shock. "Gwen?"

"Dominic," she purred back, blinking at him with wide eyes like an owl. Her hands continued to roam and he didn't know whether to be thrilled or sorry that he was wearing nothing but a pair of basketball shorts.

Her hands on his bare skin were having a direct effect on his cock and the silky material wasn't doing much to contain it. On the other hand . . . it felt good . . . no, amazing.

Maybe he was asleep and this was a dream. There was no way Gwen Day, the woman he'd wanted from the first moment he saw her, was here now, touching him . . . damn near everywhere. "Er . . . Gwen . . . babe, did you need something?" He almost groaned aloud when her hand dropped to cover the bulge in his shorts.

"You could say that," she moaned as she pushed him back a few steps before shutting the door behind her. Just when he thought this encounter couldn't get much weirder—or hotter—she leaned down, grabbed the hem of the slinky black dress she was wearing and pulled it over her head in a move that would make a stripper proud. Then she stood before him in nothing but a black lace bra, tiny matching panties, and black strappy sandals. He was completely and totally screwed.

Still trying to be the voice of reason for some crazy reason, Dominic held out a calming hand, saying, "Babe, what're we doing here? I mean . . . God, you're gorgeous!" All right, maybe that last line had slipped out before he could stop himself, but holy hell, how was he supposed to stay calm when Gwen was standing in front of him, practically naked, with a come-hither look in her eyes that was making him pant like a dog in heat?

She began to prowl forward and he walked uncertainly backward—which he figured out was a big mistake when he tripped over his coffee table and landed in a heap on the sofa. "Oh goody," she rubbed her hands together as she stopped a few inches from where he had landed. "It looks like we're both on the same page." Then . . . she dropped down to straddle his waist, and it was all over for him. When she grinned before pulling a strip of condoms out of her bra, he almost professed his love on the spot. Who was this woman? She certainly looked like his beautiful neighbor, but that was where the similarities ended.

He'd caught her checking him out on more than one occasion, and yes, in his fantasies, he had wanted to believe that she desired him as he did her. But she'd never given him any outward reason to believe that was true. He had certainly never imagined her showing up on his doorstep like a wet dream. So he forced himself to ask one last time, "Are you sure about this?" In answer, she ground herself against him before licking his neck. Well . . . that meant yes in his book.

He put his hands on what he had come to think of as the Holy Grail . . . her ass. It was firm, round, and drove him to distraction. Dominic had never been one to desire a skinny woman. He loved soft, lush curves and to him, Gwen had the perfect body. His only problem was deciding where he wanted to lavish his attention first. "I need you inside of me," Gwen murmured as she bit his ear. As if to prove that point, she plastered her body against his chest, freeing his hips, before saying urgently, "Shorts off, condom on."

Dominic had always been something of an alpha male so this role change was not only different for him, but it was also surprisingly sexy as hell. He couldn't remember the last time he'd felt this uncoordinated as he did his best to push his shorts down and then fumble to put the condom on his throbbing erection without causing it to blow early. At this point, he was hanging on to his composure by a mere thread.

After what was probably seconds but felt like hours, he was sheathed and past ready to feel her around him. "All right, baby, let me take care of you."

"Yes . . . God, yes," she breathed throatily. "I need to take my panties . . ." Refusing to let her up, he ripped one side of her flimsy excuse for panties and then the other. She lifted her hips slightly and he pulled the fabric free, sending it sailing somewhere nearby. He ran a finger through her cleft, finding it wet and swollen. "Dom . . . I'm ready, now please!"

Putting a supporting hand under her ass, he raised her body before bringing her down onto his waiting shaft. He held himself still as she cried out, afraid that he'd hurt her by going too fast. "Okay, baby?" he asked as he stroked her hip soothingly.

Gwen rose to her knees, so that he almost slid out of her wet heat before she bottomed out on him once again. "Harder, Dom!" Her demands broke what little control he had left. He wrapped his arms around her, pulling her close enough to devour her lips, while pumping his hips at a ruthless pace into her tight passage.

Soon, they were nothing but a tangle of shifting limbs, grinding bodies. Dominic bit, sucked, and licked every available inch of her skin, and it drove him to distraction when she did the same. He'd never really thought he would enjoy having his own nipples nipped, but damned if it wasn't off-the-charts hot. He wanted to make it last for hours, but all too soon, he felt the familiar tingle at the base of his spine. When Gwen started to spasm around him, he was helpless to hold back any longer. But his orgasm seemed to go on forever as black dots danced through his vision.

Dominic collapsed backward as all of the blood that had been gathered down below finally redistributed throughout his body. He grazed his hand lazily up and down Gwen's spine as she nestled against him. He knew he needed to get up and dispose of the condom, but he figured he could do that when she inevitably freaked out and ran from his apartment. He was braced and waiting for that to happen. Hell, he felt almost like the woman in this scenario, wanting to cuddle and talk about feelings and crap like that.

When Gwen sat up, he dropped his hand, already trying to distance himself. He was floored when she licked her lips and gave him a lopsided smile. "If you don't mind, I'm going to need to do that again. Can we? Please?"

Well, hell, it was official. He had gone and lost his heart to the girl next door . . . and his best friend's ex. In true fashion, he never took the easy route.

Chapter Two

Gwen woke up and looked around the darkened room for the glow of her alarm clock. Her head was throbbing and her body was sore—in places it hadn't been in quite some time. Just about the time that thought hit home, she realized two things. First, there appeared to be an oven at her back and second, there was an unfamiliar weight across her waist.

Holding her breath, she moved her hand along the anchor holding her in place and hissed in shock when a voice suddenly sounded in her ear. "Baby, you've pretty much sucked me dry, but if you give me five minutes, I'm sure I'll have something for you." It appeared that he wasn't lying because the "something" was currently digging rather impressively into her backside.

Panicked, she jumped from the bed and promptly crashed into a hard object. "Oww, damn!" she cried as she tried to get her bearings. She was holding her injured hip in one hand and trying to locate a light switch with the other when suddenly the room was bathed in brilliance. The term "bull in a china shop" had new meaning as she flailed around, temporarily blinded.

"Whoa, darling, hold still before you break your neck," said a husky voice right before a set of strong hands encircled her hips—her naked hips. "You're going to bruise this beautiful body, and I'll be forced to lick it better."

Suddenly, it hit her with the force of a freight train. "Dom-Dominic." She blinked a few more times before letting her eyes wander down his body. Naked and big—very big. Dominic. "We had sex, like a whole lot of sex, didn't we?" she blurted out.

"We did." He grinned wolfishly, then licked his lips. "I must say, Red, you're a whole helluva bag of surprises that I would have never expected, but I'm damn sure thrilled to discover them."

Gwen felt herself flushing all the way to her roots. Oh my God, the things she'd done to him . . . the things they'd done together. She might be embarrassed now at how wanton she had been, but the memories were enough to have her squeezing her legs together restlessly. Ouch, she was sore down there in what had been no-man's-land. But it was a good feeling—no, OMG amazing was more apt.

Now, though, she wasn't sure what he expected from her. Was she supposed to get dressed, tell him thanks, and leave? She hadn't really thought this through last night when she'd stumbled to his apartment after drinking a few glasses of wine . . . Okay, maybe more like a bottle with her friends. The only thing that had been on her mind had been reaffirming the fact that someone out there wanted her. She could have hooked up with some faceless stranger at the bar, but she hadn't been able to get Dominic out of her mind. Her friends had urged her on when she'd declared that she was going to "rock his world all night long." They had called her a cab and sent her off to battle with a lot of war cries and hoots of encouragement.

And holy mother, it had been worth all of the awkwardness she was feeling now. Thanks to her alcohol consumption, things were fuzzy in a few places, but she remembered enough to know the man was a freaking sex god. He had a huge cock and he needed almost zero recovery between rounds. She was pretty sure that they'd blown through the strip of condoms that Crystal had stuck in her bra as she was getting into the taxi. Apparently, her friend, although claiming to be celibate now, didn't intend to stay that way for long.

When Dominic's hands slid soothingly over her ass, she croaked out, "Um . . . so . . . I guess I should go?" She grimaced at how pathetically hopeful she sounded. She had not meant for her statement to come out as more of a question.

When Dominic released his hold on her and turned toward the bed, she fought tears of disappointment. Before she could move though, he extended his hand and grabbed her wrist, tugging her down with him. "It's still early, babe. Come back to bed." Without protest and possibly a tad too eagerly, she followed behind him until she was settled with her back to his chest and his arms curved around her waist, anchoring her close to his warmth. "Yeah, that's better," he said huskily against her neck. Wait. . . . Did he just smell her? Oh, my . . . that was seriously hot . . . and kind of disturbing since she hadn't showered recently, but who the hell cared. She finally felt herself beginning to relax against him. Just as she was close to drifting off, he said something that had her jerking around to look at him in shock. "We need to prepare for the possibility that you could be pregnant, babe."

"What?" She gawked at him, wondering if she'd heard wrong. "I . . . we used condoms, and that's like ninety-nine-point-something percent effective. I mean, that's what they do, right?"

He ran his thumb over her bottom lip while nodding. "Of course." She smiled, thinking he was just overly cautious, when he added, "But we had the . . . mishap on the last round."

Their last round . . . Oh God, she remembered it now. They had been in a position that she'd never imagined was even possible. It involved him standing and her legs draped on his chest while he held her arms and lifted her up and down. Wow, she felt like a world-class porn star just knowing that she'd done that. Her fond memories took a bit of a dive as she recalled the "mishap" in question. Dominic had cursed when he'd pulled out and found that the condom had ripped at some point. She had been so boneless by that point that she couldn't have cared less. Until now. "Oh no," she whispered. "Oh crap, I had forgotten about that." Studying his calm face, she asked, "Do you think anything leaked out?"

The ass had the audacity to chuckle at her question. "Um, I'd say some probably got away, babe. I mean, I don't want to brag or anything, but my boys are probably kick-ass swimmers."

Gwen rolled her eyes and dug her elbow into his stomach. She felt a small glimmer of satisfaction when she heard him groan. "You're not helping, you know. Can you be serious for just a minute?"

Dominic gave a resigned sigh before saying, "I'm sure it'll be fine, Red. No need to get all worked up over spilled milk or in this case . . ."

"I get it," Gwen rushed to cut him off. She quickly did the math in her head and felt a little better. "I think I'm in a good place cycle wise. I mean, I just had my period so I haven't hit the midway point yet."

Scratching his head and looking adorably confused, Dominic said, "Babe, I have no clue about women's cycles. I'll leave that to you. Just promise me one thing," he added, suddenly looking serious. "Don't keep it from me if something should change. I can handle anything but lies."

Gwen melted back against his chest, enjoying the feeling of his arms holding her close. It had been so long since she'd had a man holding her in the early morning hours. Mac had never stayed the night with her, so she'd never experienced this with him. She had no idea what would happen between them once they left this bed and started their day, but for now she wanted to pretend, if only for a while, that he wanted her—for more than one night.

Gwen made it to her office at Danvers International with just moments to spare. It wasn't as if there was a time warden standing at the elevator to punch them in and out, but she always tried to be diligent in arriving before nine each day.

She had just put her purse away and was checking her e-mail when someone tapped on her door before swinging it open. Crystal walked into her office and leaned against the corner of her desk while Mia followed, closing the door behind her. They both had identical, expectant looks on their faces. Gwen decided to sit quietly and see who broke first. Finally, Crystal blurted out, "Well?"

"Well, what?" Gwen asked as she pretended to study her computer intently.

Mia tried her hand next. "So . . . er . . . did you do it?"

By this point, Gwen was fighting hard not to laugh as she said, "Do what?" in a bored tone.

"Hell's bells, Gwen!" Crystal snapped. "Did you get laid or not?"

"Way to blurt it right out there, Crys." Mia rolled her eyes. Pointing to Gwen, she said, "Look at her—of course she did. I've never seen her looking this relaxed."

Crystal had just opened her mouth to make a comment when there was another knock at the door. "Yes," Gwen called out, wondering who else could possibly be dropping by this early. Most of her coworkers tended to hole up in their offices with cup after cup of coffee until at least noon.

Gwen almost swallowed her tongue when Dominic strolled in looking like sex-on-a-very-big-stick. He gave her an intimate smile that had her panties melting. "Hey babe, I know you were running late this morning so I thought you might not have had time to stop for coffee." He lifted his hand, holding up a white cup. He walked past her friends as if they weren't even there and put the cup in front of her. Then, he dropped a kiss on her shocked lips before whispering in her ear, "It's decaf . . . just in case." When she continued to sit there, staring at him dumbly, he tapped her chin. "See you tonight? I'll make dinner." Without waiting for a reply, which she seemed unable to give, he straightened and nodded to Crystal and Mia as he walked past. "Ladies . . . have a good day." With that, he was gone and Gwen would have thought that she had imagined the whole thing if not for the cup of coffee sitting in front of her.

"Wait. . . . Did that just happen?" Mia asked looking shell-shocked.

Fanning herself, Crystal said, "Well, if the orgasm I just had is any indication, then hell, yeah, it did. Gwen Day, I hate you!"

Gwen felt the urge to kick herself. It wasn't as if it were the first time that a man had brought her coffee. Mac had done that in this very office before. But something about Dominic's visit had felt so personal . . . so intimate. Even with her friends looking on it had been as if they were the only two people in the room. And dammit, he had even bought decaf on the outside chance that she was to get pregnant. That thought alone should have her freaking out, but strangely, it felt too good to have someone watching over her. He had even mentioned cooking dinner for her as if it was a foregone conclusion that they would be together that evening. When Crystal huffed loudly, Gwen focused on her friends and stated the obvious, "I have no idea what I'm doing."

"You don't need to know right now, Gwen," Mia added softly. "He came for you this morning. You didn't have to wait around on pins and needles wondering if he'd call. He laid all of his cards on the table for you."

"He looked at you like he was going to eat you right where you sit for breakfast. It was so hot, I was practically spitting fire watching you two."

Gwen gave up all pretense of playing it cool and sagged against her chair. "Last night was amazing. I don't know what I was expecting, but he was so far beyond even my wildest dreams. We . . . you know . . . for hours. Every time I thought I couldn't last another moment, he proved me wrong. I—I thought it was just the one night, but now . . . I'm not so sure."

"Oh, sister." Crystal winked before walking over to put a hand on her shoulder. "It appears he's thinking way beyond that. Now, do yourself a favor and lasso that stallion and have the ride of your life."

Mia gave a thumbs up. "Yep, exactly what she said. You deserve someone who actually focuses all of his attention on your needs, and I think he's just the man for the job. It didn't bother him at all that we were standing here. He homed in on you immediately and didn't let anything distract him from his goal. Tonight, march right over to his place and take him up on his dinner offer."

"And dessert." Crystal grinned. "It's always good to take a gift, so stop and pick up a can of Cool Whip on the way home."

Gwen laughed with her friends and felt as giddy as a teenager before her first date. Somehow Dominic made her want to be that carefree again. She longed to go back to the days when she hadn't been disappointed and let down by every man she dated. Why did she always have to be the one in the relationship willing to give everything to make it work while the other person just treaded water until something or someone better came along? For once, she wanted to be number one. It wasn't as if she needed to be worshipped twenty-four/seven, but dammit, was it too much to ask for a man to just want to make her happy? She wanted to come home at the end of the day and feel like she'd actually been missed while she was away. In the past, she mostly came home to an empty apartment and a lot of excuses.

Mac had been one of her better dating experiences until the last few weeks of their time together. After that, the pattern had become all too familiar—knowing there was something going on, but wanting to believe that it was just her imagination. God, she had grown to hate those alarm bells that inevitably went off in all of her relationships. The warning bells that told her she was hanging on to a sinking ship and no amount of paddling would ever make it right again.

Crystal might be disillusioned with men after divorcing her controlling husband who always wanted her to be perfect, but Gwen had never had that problem. The men she'd dated didn't seem to care enough to try to control her. That would have involved more time than they were willing to give her. The sad part of it all was that after the experience with Mac, she had concluded that it had to be her. Men fell in love and got married every day; heck, most of her exes married soon after they dumped her. Maybe she was some type of marriage training course. They dated her and got their selfish, jerk days out of their systems, and then went on to settle down and be perfect husbands. Stranger things had happened.

Mia and Crystal left her with her thoughts. She promised that they'd try to have lunch together tomorrow so she could fill them in on her dinner with Dominic. Gwen only hoped that she wasn't a complete fool for even considering spending more time with him after breaking up so recently with his friend. She winced at the thought because it sounded so cliché. When had her life turned into something from a romance novel?

"Dude, you got laid, didn't you?" Dominic blinked in surprise at Gage's accurate assessment. Shit, was it that obvious? He hadn't said anything even alluding to his night with Gwen so he had no idea how Gage had zeroed in on it within fifteen minutes.

Dominic kept his head down and his eyes fixed on the security feed from the previous evening. Their first task each day was to read reports from their various clients and glance through the footage to ensure nothing was missed. This was something that they could assign to one of their other employees, but when time permitted, he, Gage, and Mac still preferred to keep their hands on the pulse of their business. "Don't you have something else to do?" he asked Gage when the other man continued to sit and study him.

"Well, of course," Gage scoffed, "but this is so much better. I mean, I'm pretty damned impressed that you had the energy to go out and hunt a woman after traveling all weekend. I'm just gonna admit that I went home and crashed till this morning. If I'd found a naked woman on my doorstep, I'd have probably sent her on her merry way."

When his hand slipped on the mouse and it clattered to the floor with what sounded like the force of an atomic bomb, he knew he was screwed. Gage was now in his favorite position of interrogation. His feet were propped on the desk in front of him, and he was leaning back in his chair. "No fucking way. Who did you get a door prize from last night? Crap, was it Kandi?"

Dominic had briefly dated a woman named Kandi a few months ago. When they'd met, she told him that she was a dancer but had been evasive as to where she did that dancing. He'd been surprised that wherever they went, half the men in the place seemed to know her. One night, she had finally confessed that her real name was Mona and her stage name at the strip club where she worked was Kandi. He was far from a prude, but when she wanted to share him with her friends, Bambi and Trixie, he'd called it a day. Yeah, he'd had a threesome back in his wilder, boot camp days, but it wasn't something he was interested in now. Of course, her strange need to speak in baby talk to his crotch didn't exactly make her a keeper, either. Gage had never gotten over his rejection of Kandi and her crew. He was sure there had actually been tears in the other man's eyes when he'd told him. "No, it wasn't her," he answered flatly, trying to discourage further questions.

"So, that actually happened? Shit, I was just harassing you, but some chick did show up naked last night? If it wasn't Kandi, then it must be someone new. A neighbor? I can't believe you let go of your Gwen crush long enough to sleep with someone else."

Why, oh why couldn't he keep his cool around Gage? For the love of God, he served two tours in the Marines and most of them in Afghanistan, where having a poker face kept you alive, and he couldn't bluff the man sitting next to him. Instead, he was fumbling around with his keyboard and mouse like a virginal schoolgirl being hit on for the first time. He might as well be holding up a sign saying: I HAD SEX WITH GWEN LAST NIGHT, because there was no way Gage was missing his complete loss of cool. "Can we not talk about this," he said weakly, hoping for mercy, which wasn't going to happen.

Gage's chair hit the floor with a heavy thud. "Bro," he began in a voice heavy with shock, "you slept with Gwen last night, didn't you? She showed up naked at your door, and you finally did it. How did that happen?"

Dominic was shaking his head before Gage finished his last sentence. "I'm not giving you any details, man, nor am I going to confirm that any of what you just said happened."

Grinning, Gage said, "You don't have to confirm it. You started bumbling all over the place when I mentioned the words naked, doorstep, and Gwen. It doesn't take a rocket scientist to figure out what happened. I just can't fathom why. How does she go from dating your best friend and barely acknowledging your existence to suddenly finding you irresistible? Massive quantities of alcohol?"

Dominic felt a little pang at the thought of Gwen being intoxicated. She'd admitted to having some wine with her friends, but otherwise she seemed to be aware of where she was, who she was with, and she damned sure seemed to know what she wanted. Maybe it had taken a drink to lower her normal reserve and admit that she wanted him. Stone-cold sober, he could admit that he wanted her, and he couldn't bring himself to regret the events that brought her to him so unexpectedly. Hell, he was pitifully grateful to have finally had a chance with the woman he had spent so long enamored with from afar. He wasn't even rattled over their condom mishap from the previous night.

Not that he was looking to be a daddy anytime soon, but if it happened, he was all in. Until he knew different, he planned to operate as if Gwen could be pregnant and treat her like a princess. Heck, he would have been happy to do that without a pregnancy scare. He was tired of one-night stands and casual dating. He wanted a woman in his life to love, respect, and lay the world at her feet. Something told him that woman could very well be Gwen, and he was a man who always trusted his intuition. It had kept him in one piece more than once in his life.

He could feel Gage's eyes boring into him, waiting for an answer to his rash of nosy questions. When he reared back in his seat again, balancing it on its back legs, Dominic did what he and Mac were so fond of when they needed to distract the other man. He reached out, pushed against the back of the chair, and listened to Gage scream like a girl as he tipped over. That never got old and the man never learned. Damn, he loved his job.

Chapter Three

Gwen stood apprehensively outside Dominic's apartment door, hesitant to knock. He had called her this afternoon just to check on her and to let her know that dinner would be ready at seven. So, here she was feeling like a basket of nervous anxiety at the thought of facing the man that she'd ridden to pleasure countless times not even twenty-four hours ago.

Just when she was pondering whether to make up some excuse, the door swung open and she could only stare at the picture of masculine beauty standing before her. He was wearing a black T-shirt and a pair of dark jeans that showed off his powerful thighs to perfection. She stood gawking at him, feeling like she was in danger of swallowing her tongue. He gave her a knowing grin and took her hand, pulling her inside. She barely had time to register the delicious smell permeating the apartment before she was pushed against the closed door and engulfed in a kiss that had her eyes rolling back in her head. This was no tentative brush of his lips against hers; he took control and ravished every corner of her mouth. His hands settled on her ass, pulling her against the hard line of his cock and without thought, she locked her arms around his neck and lifted her legs around his waist. God, she wanted nothing more than to feel him moving inside of her again. "Dominic . . ." she moaned, unable to get close enough. What was it about this man that set her on fire so quickly?

"Something's burning," he hissed against her neck as he ground his lower body against her.

"It is . . ." she agreed. "Oh, yes . . ."

When she felt him shaking against her, she pulled back enough to see him laughing. "I meant our dinner, baby, but I agree, you are as well, and I promise to put that fire out soon." He gave her bottom a firm squeeze before unwrapping her legs from his waist and stepping back. Instead of walking off, he took her hand, kissed her knuckles, and pulled her behind him into the kitchen. He waved her toward a seat at the bar before pointing to an array of drinks sitting to the side. "I wasn't sure what you wanted to drink. I have caffeine-free soda and tea as well as bottled water and there's milk in the refrigerator. I know a bottle of wine would be nice, but I thought for now we would skip any alcohol . . . until we know."

Gwen didn't know whether to be irritated or touched that he was making decisions about her health for her. She decided to let it go, thinking she could probably use a wine-free night after her overconsumption the previous night. Apparently, that left her choices at something without caffeine so she chose water and added a wedge of lime that he had sliced and set out. As if drawn there by some unstoppable force, she found herself staring at his butt as he bent over to remove a skillet from the oven. He seemed to be fascinated by her backside, and she was by his as well. Apparently, they were both ass people. Clearing her throat, she said the first thing that came to mind. "So, how was your day?"

He grinned over his shoulder, before grabbing a knife and cutting into what appeared to be a perfectly cooked steak. "It was good, babe. In fact, it was down-right educational."

Now *that* she hadn't been expecting. Curious, she asked, "Educational?"

With a quirk of his perfect lips, he gave her a grin that left her inner sex kitten panting. "Yeah, Gage and I were buzzing through the security feeds this morning and ran across something . . . interesting from the previous evening."

"Like illegal interesting?" she asked, thinking they had caught someone breaking the law.

"Well, maybe in some states." Dominic grinned at her, looking downright devilish. He finally took mercy on her when he noticed her confusion. Leaning back against the counter and crossing his ankles, he said, "Well, a guy who works night security at one of our properties decided to take his dinner break a little too far, which was really stupid when he knows how many cameras are on the property. Apparently, his girlfriend dropped by and they got it on in the supply closet. Not a real smart move since there are cameras in there to discourage employees from helping themselves to one too many pens. I have to say, though, if he applied even half of that enthusiasm and energy to his job, the man would own the company by now and I'd be working for him."

Gwen couldn't help herself; she started giggling just imagining Dominic's face when he saw the video footage. "What did you do?" she managed to gasp out between laughs.

Wiggling his brows, he said, "Well, I think Gage disappeared for a while to ponder the situation, but after that we had to call Chad in and let him go."

"What?" she cried, all laughter gone. "You fired him . . . for having sex on the job? Couldn't you just give him a warning or something?"

Dominic shrugged halfheartedly, but she could tell that he felt bad about it. "I wish it were that simple, babe, but we're under strict contracts with our customers. We can't have stuff like that happening on their properties. While Chad was shopping for office supplies, someone could have broken in, and literally, he would have been caught with his dick in his hand. Trust me, all of our employees are well aware of what they can and cannot do. Your reputation is the one thing in this business that you must guard above all other things."

"That sounds like a very Marine Corps motto." She smiled, thinking she quite liked that part of him. Something about those military and ex-military men was so sexy. It was almost like an inborn confidence—no matter what life tossed their way, they could handle it. Dominic, like Mac, was all man. He could cook dinner for her and bring her coffee, but there was never any doubt as to his masculinity.

"Maybe," Dominic agreed, "but I would like to think

I'd have known the importance of my good name even without Uncle Sam drilling it into me. Anyway, Gage insisted on taking him out for a drink afterward to soften the blow."

"Really?" Gwen asked, impressed. At least that was something for poor Chad.

"Yep, of course, I think he just wanted his autograph or something. The guy was quite . . . creative and the camera loved him."

"Oh God," Gwen choked, before picking up the dish towel lying in front of her and throwing it at Dominic. "You're so bad."

He laughed as he plated their meal. Her mouth was watering as he set a large steak with a twice-baked potato down in front of her. "I hope you're hungry." Her stomach growled on cue, causing her to blush.

Gwen had always felt self-conscious when eating in front of men, especially someone she was romantically interested in. She wasn't fat, but she was healthy and had a slightly bigger butt than most women her size. No matter how many diets she tried, that part of her anatomy never seemed to get any smaller, and if she lost weight, it just made it appear bigger than the rest of her. She had dated a guy in college who had cheated on her and had blamed it on the fact that he just wasn't attracted to her because of her weight. Even though she felt like it was just an excuse, the jerk had scarred her for life. When Mac had skirted having sex with her, she had wondered if maybe he felt that way as well. With Dominic, though, she had felt like he loved her body. His hands had been constantly touching her as if she were perfect and he couldn't get enough. "This looks great." She smiled shyly, as she cut off a small piece of the meat. She found herself moaning in appreciation when the steak literally melted on her tongue; it was so tender.

When he was suddenly quiet, Gwen looked over to find his fork suspended in midair. She looked down at her plate, wishing she'd managed to control herself. The last thing she ever wanted to do was to call attention to herself while she was eating. When she glanced back up and he was still staring, she dropped her fork, suddenly having no appetite.

"You have no idea how badly I want to swipe everything off this counter and fuck you on it."

Startled at his quiet declaration, Gwen's head jerked up to find his eyes smoldering and locked on to hers. "Wh-what?"

"When you drew that fork slowly out of your mouth, moaning in bliss, I could picture you sucking me off in exactly the same way. We need to finish here because I'm not gonna last much longer. If you lick that fork again, I'm going to have your panties around your ankles in two seconds flat."

Her breath hitched in her throat and her nipples fought to escape the confines of her bra at his words. She was ready to stand up and shove everything out of the way herself. She didn't think he'd have to bother with removing her panties, though, because they were fast becoming a puddle beneath her. Dominic made a gesture with his fork for her to continue eating and she did, almost in autopilot. She couldn't look away from his big hands as he cut his steak with neat precision. She needed him to touch her now. Her pride was completely out the window and for the second night in a row, she was going to initiate sex with him. *Who was she and where had boring Gwen Day gone?*

Dropping her fork and pushing her plate aside, she stood and stepped over to him. Without saying a word, he put his fork down and turned until she was standing between his spread thighs. "I want you," she admitted huskily.

He settled his hands on her waist and pulled her closer. "How do you want it, babe?" he asked as he stared into her eyes.

She shocked herself when she admitted, "I want you in my mouth." He groaned in reply, before taking one of her hands and lowering it to the front of his jeans. Her fingers fumbled as she unbuttoned, then gingerly slid the zipper past his erection. He had on a pair of sexy blue boxer briefs with a black waistband that said Ralph Lauren. Somehow, she'd pictured Dominic as more of a Hanes man, so this was almost like a naughty surprise.

He raised his hips slightly while she worked the fabric down until his cock sprang free. Gwen hadn't been sure how this position would work with him still sitting on a barstool and her standing, but when he moved his hips forward slightly, she found that it worked . . . quite well for her. Things had been so rushed and out of control the previous night that she hadn't taken time to appreciate Dominic's large asset. She'd never really found a man's penis beautiful, but his looked like a work of art. As she ran her palm up and down his length, she marveled that something so hard could also be so velvety smooth. She smeared the moisture gathering at the tip around the thick head and felt him twitch within her hold. "This is going to be embarrassing if I don't even make it until I reach your mouth," Dominic groaned as she pumped him in her hand.

His words jolted her into action, and without thinking, she lowered her mouth and attempted to take his whole length. He was only halfway in, and she was in danger of gagging as his tip pushed against her throat. She pulled back slightly until she was comfortable with his presence. Dominic laced his hands through her hair and helped her establish a rhythm. He was careful not to push too far, leaving it to her to deepen the penetration as she wanted.

Gwen had never been a big fan of this part of a sexual relationship. She knew that it was something that men enjoyed, but it wasn't something that turned her on . . . until now. Dominic's moans of pleasure were like a direct zap to her sex. Unbelievably, she was close to orgasming just from sucking his cock. She knew that it would take only a couple of swipes against her throbbing clit to push her over the edge. When he suddenly shouted a warning that he was close, instead of pulling back like she would have in the past, she continued to suck him, savoring his essence as he spurted over and over down the back of her throat. She greedily licked the last drop of moisture from the end of his cock before releasing him with an, "Mmmm, you taste good."

Things were a whirlwind after that. Before she could

even register that he had moved, she was splayed on a kitchen counter with her legs over his shoulders. She didn't even recall losing her pants or panties. She was coherent enough to register the sound of the buttons from her blouse hitting the floor as Dominic jerked it apart. Left with only her bra, she couldn't do much more than gape at him in surprise when he pulled the material on either side of the clasp until it ripped causing her breasts to spill free. "Sorry, baby. I'll buy you another."

He used one hand to pinch her sensitive nipples while he sucked and tongued every inch of her dripping sex. As her orgasm was thundering through her body, she yelled, "Screw the clothes!" Dominic chuckled against her neck as he sucked the smooth skin there. He pulled her from the counter and set her on her feet. She wanted to dissolve into a post-coital coma until she noticed that he was growing hard again. Her body, which had seemed completely sated only seconds before, was now humming with renewed interest.

Dominic pulled her closer as he filled his hands with her ass. "I want to take you from behind," he rasped, lightly squeezing her cheeks.

Gwen froze for a moment, remembering an ex-boyfriend who had been obsessed with deflowering her back door. She wasn't a prude, but she wasn't ready to go there . . . not to mention, he was so big. She'd never be the same again after something like that. "Er . . . I've never done that . . . and I just . . . I mean, I think we should keep things—in the front area, okay?"

"The front area?" Dominic repeated, sounding adorably baffled. "I bent you over a chair last night. Did you not like it or do you just have a thing for face-to-face action? I can work with either, baby, but I love looking at your ass."

"You mean just looking, right?" she asked warily.

Dominic's mouth turned up, displaying a set of adorable dimples that had her completely distracted. "Well, I'd like to touch it, maybe even smack it if you're a bad girl. Oh, and definitely squeeze it. You have an epic ass, babe, and I can't keep my hands off it. Which part don't you want me to . . . ?" When her face flamed red, he halted in the middle of his sentence before bursting into laughter. "You thought I was talking about anal, didn't you?"

"Oh my God, this is so embarrassing," Gwen whispered as she turned to hide her face. "What was I supposed to think, though?"

"It's okay if you're into kink, babe; I'll try to accommodate you. I hadn't been thinking of that myself, but I'm game if that's what you really have your heart set on."

Gwen flew around at his matter-of-fact statement. She knew her mouth was probably flapping like crazy as she sputtered, "No! That's not— I wasn't asking for— I thought you— Oh, shut up!" He had finally given up trying to look serious as she struggled to get herself out of the hole her big mouth had dug. He pulled her into his arms and laughed softly against the top of her head.

"You are so fucking adorable when you're all worked up." She was getting ready to elbow him in the ribs when she felt his cock nudging against her butt. She thought he deserved an award for staying hard through their whole awkward conversation. As if to emphasize the fact that he was still eager and ready, he pushed his hips against her teasingly. "Just an FYI, I'm going to take a condom from my wallet, bend you over right where you're standing and put my cock in your preferred 'front area.' Do you have any problems with that plan?"

"No," she whimpered with need as he grabbed a condom and quickly sheathed himself. He put his hand on the small of her back, bending her forward until she grabbed the foothold of a barstool to steady herself.

"Just to be clear," he said huskily, "this is my target." With that, he circled a finger around her wet slit, before burying it inside of her. She jerked forward, moaning embarrassingly loud.

"That's it," she panted. He pushed his finger in and out a few more times before removing it. A protest was forming on her lips when she felt the big head of his cock lining up with her slick opening. She locked her arms, preparing for his thrust. He took her hips in his hands before burying his shaft deep inside of her. "Awww, yes!" she shouted as he stroked across her clit before rubbing against her G-spot. She wasn't sure if she was light-headed from her vertical position or the fact that her body was nothing but one big mass of arousal.

When she began pushing her hips back to meet his driving thrusts, he moaned, "Damn, Gwen, you feel so good. You're taking everything I give you and coming after more. Fuck!" The more he talked, the hotter she became. Hearing him talk about her body so intimately was sexier than she could have ever imagined. She felt like a supermodel as he praised her. She had never been happier to have a big backside because Dominic couldn't seem to keep his hands off of it. In what was probably one of the most vocal sexual performances of her life, Gwen threw her head back and screamed like a banshee when her orgasm hit. Dominic thrust a couple more times and shouted his release as he continued to glide in and out of her, bringing them both down slowly. She could only imagine what his neighbors must be thinking. How thick could these apartment walls be?

Dominic pulled out of her and disposed of his condom, all the while keeping one hand on her waist. "I don't think I can walk," she said as she slowly straightened, attempting to work the kinks from her back. When he suddenly swung her up into his arms, she was speechless for a moment before stuttering out, "Dom, put me down. I'm too heavy." *Way to bring that to his attention, you idiot!*

He shook his head as he looked down at her. "You're not even remotely heavy, babe. I'm going to run us both a bath so we can relax. How does that sound?" Now he was truly something straight out of a romance novel. He cooked dinner, gave her multiple orgasms, said she was skinny—well, close enough—and now was carrying her to the bath. How was this man still single? Had no other woman discovered the hidden gem that was Dominic Brady? What was she missing? There had to be something wrong with him. Maybe he hogged the covers, farted in bed, and watched sports obsessively. Of course, she'd probably even be willing to overlook all of that. Just his sexual skills alone were worth a lot. Heck, if he took out the garbage and put the seat down on the toilet, she would marry him in a minute.

"That sounds amazing," she murmured as he carried her effortlessly into the bedroom and sat her gently on the edge of the bed while he continued into the bathroom. She heard him whistling under his breath as he started the bathwater. She couldn't resist getting to her feet and edging toward the open door to watch him. Oh myyyy, his firm ass was bent over the bathtub as he poured in something that looked like bath salts. He lowered his hand to check the water temperature and then turned to grab two towels from the cabinet behind him. When he also pulled out some candles and a lighter, she felt herself swoon until a thought occurred to her. There was no way he had known they would end up in the bath tonight. So, he was lighting another's woman's candles for her. Okay, maybe it was unreasonable to think that, but somehow it just felt wrong.

She had no idea that she had been scowling at the offending wax until he cleared his throat and held the fat candle up for her to see. "These are new, babe. My ever-hopeful and completely inappropriate sister left them the last time she visited. She claimed that if I were more romantic, I might find 'the one.' I tossed them in here so I would be prepared for the next power outage and that's where they've been until now." Suddenly, he looked achingly shy as he asked, "Do you like stuff like this? If you don't, I can put them back."

Gwen felt like a bitch as he looked away nervously. What was wrong with her? Wasn't she always complaining about the men that she dated never putting her first or thinking of her needs? And here was Dominic, trying to do something sweet to please her. Only how had she handled it? Practically reduced him to vapors with the glare she had leveled on him. She was so used to being the one trying to make an impression that she didn't know how to handle it when the other party was actually making an effort.

She reached him in a couple of quick strides, wrapping her arms around his taut middle. Wow, this night was just full of surprises. She and Dominic were both still nude and she was comfortable with that as she hugged him. Normally, she would never have made it this long without at least putting a shirt on. With him, though, things were just easy. It was as if they'd known each other intimately for far longer than two days. "I love candles," she whispered against his chest. "I think it's a great idea."

Gwen felt him relax against her as he ran a hand up and down her back soothingly. "Good, I'm glad." They stood there locked together for another few moments until he stepped away to turn the water in the big Jacuzzi tub off. He tested the temperature again before reaching for her hand and pulling her gently forward. She bit off a moan as she settled back into the warm, scented water. She closed her eyes in bliss, almost forgetting where she was until she felt a tug on her hair. "Mind if I join you?" Dominic quirked, smiling down at her indulgently.

"Oh crap, sorry." Gwen moved suddenly to her knees to give him some room, which was a big mistake in a slippery bathtub. She had just enough time to squeak out, "Yikes," before her knees went out from under her and the silky water engulfed her. Before she could panic, hands were pulling her up and he was gently pressing a towel against her face.

"Baby, are you okay?" Dominic asked, sounding concerned. "Shit, I didn't mean to startle you. Do you need to get out?"

"No, no," she stammered as she pushed her damp hair out of her face. Dominic kept a hand on her shoulder while he stepped in carefully behind her before pulling her gingerly between his legs. She sighed against him before letting a giggle escape. "Oh, dear Lord, that was so ugly, wasn't it? I think Justin Timberlake can relax because there's no way I'm ever 'bringing sexy back,' ugh."

His chest vibrated against her back as he laughed along with her. "It was quite a sight, but I disagree with the sexy part. You don't need to bring it back, babe, because it never left."

"You're pretty sexy yourself," she joked, running a hand down his thigh. "I mean, where did you get a body like this? I know you run because I see you when you're coming back all hot and sweaty. But, you've also got serious muscles so you must spend a lot of time at the gym."

Chill bumps covered her body as he lazily moved her hair aside and kissed the nape of her neck. "We have a workout room at the office that we use in the mornings. It's easier to get it out of the way early instead of waiting until the evening. Running is just something I enjoy doing to de-stress. How about you? You're tight in all of the right places so you obviously exercise."

Gwen shifted around nervously, not wanting to answer his question. There was no way a hard-core fitness buff would be impressed with her brand of exercise. He would probably laugh her right out of the bath. "I . . . um . . . take classes at the gym next to the office."

"What kind of classes?" he asked, sounding genuinely interested.

"Er . . . water classes," she replied, still trying to keep her answer short.

"You mean like swimming?"

"Well . . . not quite." Good grief, the man was like a drill sergeant. Couldn't he just let it go?

He turned her sideways until he could look at her and asked, "If you're not swimming, then what kind of water classes could you be taking?"

"Senior Swingers, okay? Are you happy now?"

"Senior Swingers?" Dominic parroted as if testing out the words on his tongue. "What's that?"

"It's a water class for active seniors. We do jazz exercise, Zumba, water ballet, and water spinning. It's completely awesome," she finished defensively.

He studied her for a moment before saying hesitantly, "You know you're not a senior, don't you?"

"Duh," she snorted, "of course I do. I just thought it would be fun to join a gym and all of the other classes are full of nothing but a bunch of Lycra-wearing Barbie dolls who look down on those of us who are less than . . . coordinated. I always felt so self-conscious that I found myself not wanting to go. One day in the locker room, I met a nice lady named Marion who was sitting next to me on the bench in a swimsuit. She was really friendly and urged me to bring my suit the next evening and take a class with her. Well, I did and I loved it. Yes, I'm the youngest one in the class, but everyone is so friendly that I look forward to going. And . . . I never feel bad about wearing a swimsuit."

Gwen hadn't realized how worked up she had become until he rubbed her arms, instantly calming her. The man probably thought she was a nut-job after that rant. She had not meant to give out so much information, but after feeling like some of the women were so judgmental at the gym, she got easily riled over it.

"Baby, I think it's great," he said earnestly. "It sounds as if you've found a group of friends that you really enjoy spending time with. Who cares what their ages are? I've been a member of some health clubs before where I wasn't comfortable and I didn't go for long. As for other women not treating you well—honey, it's just pure jealousy. You're a beautiful woman with a body that men dream of. You have curves where they're supposed to be. Contrary to popular opinion, most guys want a woman to look like a woman, not a stick-figure drawing. I'm not an artistic man, but I could write poetry about your ass. It makes me weak in the knees and hard in the cock. Never . . . ever . . . even consider getting rid of it."

This man was driving her crazy. Every word that

WATCH OVER ME   43

came from his mouth was more perfect than the last. Both her head and her heart were ready to explode from the abundance of compliments that he bestowed on her, and she didn't think he was the type to spout meaningless flattery. Heck, what would be the point; she was already having sex with him. She was almost sure that he meant everything that he was saying. He liked her body just as it was and heaven knows she loved his. Actually, she wanted to love it some more, like right now, and she had noticed how he had thickened in the last few moments as well. "Dominic?"

"Hmmm?" he drawled against the top of her head.

"Could you take me to bed, like immediately?"

"Tired, babe?" he asked as he began to release her.

"No. I want more . . . sex?" She cringed briefly at her choice of words. It had come out as more of a question than a firm statement of fact.

"Do you now?" he asked, sounding as if he were choking on laughter. "Well, as you said last night, I'm glad we're both on the same page." Standing behind her, he stepped out before turning to help her. "Let's get you all dried off, babe, so I can make you wet again. . . ."

And did he ever.

Chapter Four

"You did it how many times?" Crystal asked in disbelief.

"Um . . . three not counting the—other stuff," Gwen replied, knowing her face was probably redder than her hair by now. She wasn't one for sex talk; well, mainly because she never had any good enough to share . . . until Dominic.

"I love the 'other stuff,'" Mia purred, fanning herself.

"That's such bullshit," Crystal pouted. "My ex told me it was bad for a man's system to come more than three times per week. He never—and I mean never ever—did it more than once per night and even that was a letdown."

"How about other men you've dated?" Gwen asked, curious.

"What other men? My parents were so strict with Ella and me that we really didn't get to date much. Bill attended our church and was a carbon copy of them so they were constantly pushing us together from the moment I turned eighteen. I swear I think they secretly arranged the whole marriage. I was so desperate for freedom that I went along with it, and before I knew what was happening, I was married to the male version of my mother."

"Oh wow," Mia winced. "I've heard a few stories about her from Suzy. She's . . ."

"Batshit crazy," Crystal offered. "Yeah, you can say it. I love the woman, but she acts freaking nuts most of the time. She has barely spoken to me since I divorced Bill. To her, I'm completely in the wrong, and she wants me to beg him to take me back."

"Do you miss him?" Gwen asked, noticing an underlying hint of pain in her friend's voice.

Expelling a breath, Crystal said, "I miss the idea of him. For so many years, I did everything I could to make him happy. I thought if I could be the perfect wife then our relationship would improve. Only that never happened. Both he and my mother had been pressuring me to have kids, and I just couldn't go along with it. I knew if I did, then he would have me trapped forever. It forced me to finally accept that I was miserable. I gave him an ultimatum to change and he tried for all of five minutes. A few months later, I packed my bags and left him. So . . . in answer to your original question, I have no experience outside of my relationship with him."

Mia threw an arm over Crystal's shoulders, giving her a brief hug before saying, "Well, I'll go ahead and tell you that men are definitely capable of coming more than a few times a week without breaking their plumbing. You just need to find the right guy."

"Hey, how about the one you kneed in the crotch a few weeks ago? Didn't you say he was cute before you emasculated him in the parking garage?" Gwen joked.

Dropping her head, Crystal shuddered. "Oh God, you mean Gage."

"Doesn't he work with Dominic?" Mia looked intrigued.

"Wait. That was Gage?" Gwen asked in disbelief. She remembered Gwen telling them all about the incident but didn't remember her mentioning the man's name.

"Yeah, that's him," Crystal groaned. "He had asked me out a few times before I shoved his balls up around his neck. I mean, it wasn't on purpose or anything. I had worked late that evening and was walking through a mostly empty parking garage when someone suddenly grabbed my shoulder. I thought I was being mugged so I did one of my self-defense moves and kneed him right in the baby-maker. That shit works, too, because he dropped like a stone. I looked down right before I took off and recognized him instantly." Looking dejected she added, "He's avoided me like the plague since then."

"Well, duh," Mia laughed. "No man wants his dick chopped off."

"Who got their dick chopped off?" asked an interested male voice from behind them.

Gwen whirled around in her seat to see Dominic standing behind her, looking equal parts curious and amused. "I . . . oh . . . hey."

"Hey, babe," he said in reply before dropping a kiss

on her upturned lips. "Hi, ladies," he turned to greet her friends.

Crystal kicked her under the table, snapping Gwen out of her daze long enough to introduce her friends. "Dominic, this is Crystal and Mia." He shook each of their hands, and she noticed both of her friends swooning under his handsome gaze.

Returning his attention to her, he said, "I dropped by your office on the way out to see if you needed anything. Sorry. Things were a bit hectic this morning and I missed bringing you coffee."

"That's okay." She fidgeted under the watchful eyes of her friends.

"How about dinner tonight?" he offered as he rubbed lazy circles on her shoulder. She wished he would stop touching her because she was only seconds away from panting with desire for him. He had magic hands with a direct link to her clit.

"Oh, I can't. I'm babysitting for Shannon tonight." Shannon was a neighbor, as well as a single mom. She worked at a local hospital and sometimes had problems finding a sitter when she worked the evening shift.

"The Shannon who lives a few doors down from you?" Dominic asked, which surprised her. She should have known that someone in his line of work would make it his business to know the people he lived next to.

"Yes, that's her. I help her out with Megan and Maddy occasionally."

"I know," he said, again surprising her. "I've seen you with them on the complex playground. How about

I pick up some pizza and come along? Do you think the girls would like that for dinner?"

It was on the tip of her tongue to warn him about how rambunctious the kids were when she suddenly thought better of it. Maybe he needed a reality check on how tough it could be to spend the evening with a couple of little girls who looked like angels yet acted more like devils most of the time. The poor man would probably run screaming for his life after the first hour. Trying to hide her smirk she said, "I think that's a great idea. The girls just love pizza. I'm supposed to be at Shannon's at six so why don't you come on by when you get home?"

"Sounds great, babe," he said as he dropped another kiss on her lips. "I'll see you this evening." With those words, he walked toward the front of the restaurant and picked up a couple of to-go bags before waving a final time on his way out the door.

"You totally just set him up." Mia shook her head. "I've heard you talk about those kids before."

Leaning back in her chair, Gwen couldn't stop the evil laughter that escaped her throat. "Ladies, it's time to separate the men from the boys before I go any further. If he makes it an hour tonight, then I'll know that he's got more staying power than my last three boyfriends combined."

"And if he doesn't?" Crystal asked, playing devil's advocate.

"I'll just use him for sex, without relationship potential." Gwen rubbed her hands together, suddenly looking forward to babysitting more than she ever had before. *Come on, Maddy and Megan, don't let me down now.*

"Do you have a penis?" asked the little blond-haired cherub standing in front of him. Dominic couldn't remember if this was Maddy or Megan, and he wasn't sure it mattered at this point.

"How about another piece of pizza?" He attempted to derail her train of thought without answering her question.

"I got a gina," she continued, completely ignoring his food offer.

The older of the two put her hands on her hips and rolled her eyes. "It's a V A G I N A," she carefully enunciated. He almost sagged in relief when Gwen walked into the room, shook her head at the conversation she had obviously overheard and then did the unthinkable—she turned and walked away, leaving him in hell. The older girl continued in a scary, matter-of-fact voice, "A penis is like a stick and a vagina is a hole. You gotta be careful so nothing falls in there, you know." *Fucking shit, how could Gwen have left him? He wasn't supposed to be having a conversation like this.*

"Who wants to watch a movie? I think *Frozen* is on. I bet you love that movie." The remote shook in his hand, and he tried desperately to find the correct channel.

One of the little fountains of horrifying information blurted out, "Jimmy Miller told me that I have cooties and boobies." The remote fell from his nerveless fingers and clattered to the floor. He looked helplessly away, not knowing what to say when the younger rammed her finger almost to the knuckle in her nostril before pulling it back out and sticking it in her mouth.

Dominic felt his stomach rolling as the little girl made sucking noises. "Um . . . do you need a tissue?" he asked.

The older one shook her head. "She eats her boogers all the time. I told her she should just wipe them on her shirt like I do."

"Yeah, 'cause that's much better," Dominic said to himself.

"Do boys wipe their pee?" the older one asked as she pointed to a spot near her sister on the floor.

He was getting ready to run for the door when the little one walked up to him and tugged on his hand. "I had an accident. I forgot that I had to pee pee." He looked down to see a puddle that seemed to be following her. Dear Lord, how many gallons had she been holding in her small body?

"Pee comes from your hole," the older one said nonchalantly as she picked up a slice of pizza and stuffed half of it into her mouth. "How do babies get in your stomach?" she managed to ask between bites. Right in the middle of eating another piece of pizza, she suddenly tossed it aside and stood, waving frantically. "I . . . ate . . . too fast. My flux is coming!"

"Your what?" Dominic shouted in alarm as he jumped to his feet. He was afraid she was choking, and he started doing what his mom had always done for them. He held one of her hands in the air, for what he had no idea, and began patting her between her shoulder blades. In retrospect, not the best move for someone with reflux because she spewed like a fountain not thirty seconds later. "Son of a . . ." He stopped himself before he could release the last word as he looked upon the scene before him. There was puke all over her and everything in the nearby vicinity as well as what looked like an even bigger puddle of urine covering the floor under the little one. The puker—who he now knew was Megan, thanks to her sister Maddy screaming her name when she got vomit on her—looked right as rain despite the chunks clinging to her clothing.

He was stunned when Megan turned to the nearby pizza box and resumed eating as if nothing had happened. "My uncle Mason has a boyfriend. Did you know that boys could have boyfriends?"

He was trying to process Megan's statement when Maddy added another level of alarm as she started dancing in place. "I've got to poop."

"Gwen!" he shouted in desperation. She came skipping into the room with a smirk on her face that disappeared as soon as she looked around.

"Wh-what happened?" she croaked out, wrinkling her nose at the foul smell.

"Maddy had an accident," he answered, indicating the nearby puddle, "Megan ate too fast and triggered her reflux"—he pointed to vomit and then pointed back to Maddy—"and she's got to poop, stat!" Gwen took Maddy's hand and rushed her down the hallway. He looked over at Megan, who was munching away and shook his head in resignation. He went to the kitchen for a roll of paper towels and a bottle of cleaner. He grabbed the trash can on his way back to the living room and then dropped to his knees and got to work. He'd seen some nasty shit in the military, but this was right there at the top of the list.

When Gwen returned from the other room with a freshly changed and hopefully bathed Maddy, Dominic had just finished mopping the floor and wiping down Megan as best he could. She smelled so bad that he'd even considered spraying her with the 409 cleaner and hoping that it helped. In the end, he did his best with damage control until Gwen could change her clothes. "You cleaned up," she said, looking at the once again tidy room.

"Yeah, I think I got it all. Now, if you've got this, I'm going to run the bag of trash to the Dumpster and then go shower and change myself."

"Sure," she agreed as she motioned Megan toward the bathroom. "I guess I'll see you tomorrow," she threw over her shoulder as she turned to follow the little girl.

"I'll be back as soon as I shower," Dominic assured her as he held the foul-smelling garbage bag in front of him. She just waved as if she didn't believe him, which made him feel a bit guilty. Truthfully, he'd love nothing better than to go to his place, take an extra-long shower, and pop the top on a cold one, but Gwen needed him. Look at how out of control things had gotten in just a few minutes tonight. There was no way he was going to leave her there alone. Those two little girls could probably take down an entire team of Army Rangers without breaking a sweat. No, they were in this together, and regardless of how much he wanted to run, he wouldn't do that to her. She needed to know that she could depend on him and that meant even when he had puke squishing in his shoes. Holy shit, Linda Blair had nothing on that kid.

Gwen couldn't believe that he'd come back. Earlier she'd sat in the kitchen, dying of laughter as Maddy and Megan had tortured him with their favorite topic of discussion, body parts. Actually, that one was pretty mild. Apparently, their grandfather was quite a character and they picked up a lot of not-so-great tidbits of wisdom from him. Poor Shannon, she had her hands full.

"What are you doing back?" she blurted out in surprise. He looked puzzled as he walked through the doorway, shutting the door behind him. *Oh, sweet mother, he looks and smells so good.* She was pretty sure he had just caught her sniffing him as he threw an arm over her shoulders.

"I told you I'd be back, babe. I would have stayed, but I figured you'd appreciate me washing the stink off. Where are the girls?"

"I . . . I was just tucking them in," Gwen murmured, still in shock that he was here. The man was certainly a glutton for punishment. He had not only cleaned up a mess that would have had most parents gagging, but he had returned for more. She had to admit that Dominic Brady now officially had more staying power than any man in her past. Then he further impressed her by following her down the hall instead of dropping into a chair and leaving her to it.

He walked to the center of the girls' room and put his hands on his hips. "All right, you little monkeys, which one of you threw all of the super slime on Uncle Dominic earlier?" The sound of giggling filled the room as both girls broke into fits of laughter. Then Maddy and Megan started pointing at each other. *So much for having your sister's back under fire.* Dominic teased them for a few more minutes before walking to the bookshelf and thumbing through the books there. "I don't know about you ladies, but I'd love to hear a story. Anyone else?" Gwen raised her hand along with a very enthusiastic Megan and Maddy. Dominic settled onto the floor with his back against the nightstand and began reading *Cinderella.* Looking at the two small girls, Gwen could tell that she wasn't the only female in the room completely riveted by Dominic.

When he shut the book, both girls were asleep, and she was yawning. He held out a hand, pulling her to her feet before putting the book back on the shelf. "Thank you," she whispered, after shutting the door quietly behind her. "You've gone above and beyond tonight."

He pulled her against his chest, dropping a kiss on her head. "I'd say it was my pleasure, Red, but you might not buy that."

She giggled against him, remembering the scene she had walked into earlier. "I can't believe Megan threw up on you. I never expected that."

Dominic pulled back slightly, looking down at her with raised brows. "So, you expected the other stuff?"

"Um . . ." She squirmed, trying to get away. "Of course not. I've never heard them talk like that . . ."

"Gwen." Dominic stared her down, and dammit, she had to look away, unable to contain her grin.

She took off running, trying to quiet her shrieks of laughter as Dominic gave chase. He finally cornered her in the kitchen, tickling her with one hand, while putting the other over her mouth. "Keep it down before you wake the girls, babe. Now . . . I believe there's a little matter of some payback for your earlier evilness."

"What?" she croaked out against his hand.

"Drop the innocent act. You totally set me up, didn't you? You knew good and well that they would eat me alive."

"No . . ." She giggled, unable to keep a straight face. Dominic's hand was just beginning to slide down her ass when the sound of someone clearing their throat sounded behind them.

Shannon stood leaning against the kitchen counter trying hard to keep a stern expression. "Is everything okay in here, Gwen?"

Gwen felt her face heat up as she looked into the amused eyes of her friend. "Yep, Dominic was just helping me . . . clean up."

Shannon's eyes dropped to where Dominic's hand was still wedged in the back of her jeans. "Really? Just what kind of cleaning does he do and where can I hire someone like him?"

Dominic jerked his hand out, and Gwen was surprised to see him actually flushing as well. He recovered quickly though and gave Shannon a lazy grin. "Just a little retribution. Hi, you must be Shannon. I'm Dominic." Gwen noticed that he kept the hand that had been in her pants to his side and offered the other one to Shannon, who by this time was literally swooning.

"Hi, Dominic, nice to meet you. I've seen you around the grounds before . . . jogging."

Gwen wanted to roll her eyes. Geez, apparently every woman in the building watched him jog. Maybe she should suggest he start wearing some loose-fitting sweatpants and a shirt. He needed to stop displaying so much of his man candy to the world. Gwen quickly filled Shannon in on Megan's reflux issue but left the rest out. She knew how much it embarrassed the other woman when her girls went into detailed discussions of their body parts. She figured after a long evening at work, she didn't need any added stress. Dominic seemed to be of a like mind and didn't mention it, either. They all talked for a few more minutes before they left.

Once outside in the hallway, Dominic took her hand, leading her to his apartment. She pulled against his hold, causing him to stop. "It's late and I really need to get some sleep tonight."

"I know, baby," he said, before pulling her forward once again. "I'm tired too so we'll just go home and crash."

"But . . . I should go to my place," she protested. "I don't have any clothes to wear to work tomorrow."

He stopped again, turning to face her. "Gwen, do

you want to go home tonight? I want you to stay with me, but I'm not going to force you."

She stood there uncertainly, wanting to be with him, but feeling like she needed to put some space between them. They barely knew each other and already they were spending every available moment together? What would she do when he was gone? She needed to keep some distance; it would be easier in the end, right? "I'm just going to go on home."

Without another word, he turned them toward her apartment and waited while she fumbled with her keys. "See you tomorrow," he whispered huskily against her lips as she stepped in the door. "Lock up," he instructed.

She stood in the entryway of her lonely apartment and wanted to kick herself. *Way to go, Gwen, this is so much better than going home with Dominic.* There was no changing her mind now, though. She'd made a decision, and she had to live with it. Dammit, she was already way too attached to a man who would walk away soon.

Chapter Five

Gwen felt a hand touch her shoulder as she stepped into the lobby of Danvers International. "Good morning, babe. You look gorgeous today." Spinning around, she felt her heart knock in her chest as she looked up at a grinning Dominic. It should be illegal for a man to look that good before nine in the morning. He was wearing his usual work uniform of cargo pants and a company shirt, but holy wet panties, was he a sight to behold. Speaking of hotness, Gage stood behind him, watching them with interest. She wished at that moment that she had worn something other than the snug, black wrap dress that seemed to stick to her butt like a second skin. Fashion did not cater to women with a big booty. It was always a challenge to find clothing that didn't make her look like she was on her way to a street corner.

"Good morning," she managed to reply as she tried to get a handle on her out-of-control body. Did he seriously have to be that hot? Mac had been one handsome guy, but her body had never reacted to his closeness with the same intensity as it did with Dominic's. He pulled her close, dropping a kiss on her surprised lips.

"I missed you this morning," he whispered for her ears alone.

"Me, too," she admitted before she could stop herself. God knows it was true. After sleeping over at his place only twice, she was addicted. She had been at loose ends at her apartment this morning as if she hadn't lived alone for years.

Gage, seeming tired of waiting to be included in the conversation, walked closer and gave her a mischievous grin. "It's good to see you again, Gwen. Dom's right, you do look great this morning. I like the dress."

Dominic scowled at his friend while Gwen smiled. "Thanks, Gage. It's good to see you as well."

Gage looked nervous for a moment before asking, "So . . . I saw you with Crystal the other day. Are you two friends?"

Gwen tried desperately to keep a straight face, remembering Mia's story of how Crystal had kneed Gage in the balls in the parking garage. Was it just a coincidence that Gage's hand was hovering close to his crotch? Maybe he remembered what had happened as well. "Er . . . Crystal Webber?"

"Yeah, that's her." Gage nodded. Dominic just stood between them, shaking his head.

"Yes, we're friends. She's an amazing person." Oh crap, maybe she should have left that part out. It sounded a bit like a sales pitch. Gwen didn't think Crystal needed that because Gage appeared to already be sold on her.

"Hmmm," he muttered, "do you think that maybe we could . . ."

Before he could finish his sentence, Dominic put his hand against the nape of her neck and began leading her toward the coffee shop at the other end of the lobby. "Pick up women on your own time, bro. My woman needs her morning coffee." Both Gage and Gwen were gaping at Dominic as he ushered her to the rapidly forming line. "Sorry, honey. I didn't want him to put you on the spot. I'm certain he was going to suggest a double date and I think we should spare ourselves that." He gently tucked a strand of her wayward hair behind her ear. "Now, what kind of coffee do you want this morning?"

Clearing her throat of the sudden lump there, Gwen said huskily, "Vanilla latte—skim." Dominic ordered an Americano for himself and a decaf vanilla latte for her with skim milk.

"I don't think you need to avoid whole milk, babe. You're sexy as hell just as you are."

"You might actually be the perfect man," she said before she could stop herself.

Quirking a brow at her, he asked, "Why's that?"

Blushing, she haltingly said, "Because . . . you don't think I need to lose weight or that my . . . backside is too big."

He took her elbow, leading her toward a quiet corner. "Whoever told you that you weren't perfect as you are must be blind. And your ass, sweetheart . . . my cock was damn near coming out of the top of my pants watching you walk to the coffee counter." Before she could stop herself, Gwen looked down, immediately spotting the truth that he wasn't able to hide. The bulge in the front of his pants was readily apparent for all to see. He inched closer to her, whispering against her neck, "Your ass has been the star of many of my fantasies. . . ."

"Dominic . . ." she moaned shakily. "You're killing me."

"Ditto, baby," he replied flashing his signature grin. "I'm going to need you to walk me to my office."

"Why?" she asked, confused. Surely, he didn't want a quickie in his office with Gage somewhere near. The thought thrilled her more than she cared to admit. Apparently, she had a bit of an exhibitionist in her.

"I'm going to need a little cock cover. . . ."

Following his gaze down to the tent that remained in the front of his cargo pants, she said simply, "Oh." So, in what was a first for her, she provided a human crotch cover for the man who was becoming an alarmingly important part of her life.

When they reached his office, she stopped outside the door, knowing that she was going to be late if she didn't leave now. She wanted nothing more than to have the right to throw her arms around Dominic and kiss him good-bye. They had had sex quite a few times now, but it was still too soon to consider it a relationship. She'd learned better than to assume anything like that where men were concerned. Heck, the last man she thought she was in a relationship with had just gotten married to another woman in Vegas. Maybe casual sex was what she needed to focus on now. No strings equaled less pain when things ended. Men, it appeared, understood that concept much better than women. It wasn't that she was desperate to get married and have a family because she wasn't. She was just tired of being let down and disappointed. Maybe Crystal was right— a good vibrator was the only thing that a single girl could depend on.

Yet Dominic, it appeared, had no problem moving in for a good-bye kiss. He embraced her as if he had done it every day for years. His lips met hers with no hesitation, and he kissed her senseless right there in front of East Coast Security. No doubt, Gage was somewhere close by enjoying the show. "I'd love to take you out for dinner tonight if that's okay with you?"

"Mmmm K," she muttered as he released her. So much for trying to be tough. One good swipe of his tongue against hers and she was agreeing with everything he said. Damn, she was in so much trouble.

Gwen was relieved when Dominic led her toward his black Silverado pickup truck. She was late getting home and had just enough time to change into a belted, green sheath dress and strappy, black sandals. She hadn't considered the fact that he might drive his motorcycle until they walked toward the parking lot.

She couldn't help but admire how he looked in his perfectly pressed black dress pants with a blue button-down dress shirt. She had always thought him all rugged male, but seeing him dressed up tonight showed her that he fit in perfectly well, no matter what the surroundings.

He took her hand, helping her up into the truck before pulling the seat belt around her. He kissed her lightly, then ran his hand down her thigh. "You look beautiful tonight, baby."

"So do you," she said honestly. She didn't bother to hide her admiration as she openly stared up at him.

"Don't look at me like that," he growled, "or we'll never make it on time." She grinned as he adjusted himself before stepping back and shutting the door.

He held her hand as they made their way through the Myrtle Beach traffic. "Where are we going?" Gwen asked, realizing that she had no idea. She would have been just as happy having dinner at his apartment again. Yeah, that resolve to keep her distance wasn't working at all.

She almost thought she had imagined the quick grimace that crossed his face until he said tightly, "You're probably going to be pissed off at me so I might as well give you fair warning."

"What? Why?" she asked, confused and a little unnerved by his prediction. Where could he possibly be taking her that would make her mad? She didn't care if they went to McDonald's; she just wanted to spend some time with him.

"We're . . . kind of having dinner with my sister at Ivy."

"Oh, I like Ivy." Gwen smiled before the word "sister" sank in. "Um, your sister?" she squeaked, fighting the urge to open her door and roll out into traffic. She and Dominic had been doing *things* for only a few days and she was meeting his family? Oh my God, she'd never made it that far with a man before. She felt herself beginning to panic when the truck suddenly stopped.

Dominic had pulled off the road and was looking at her with a worried expression. "Shit, I'm sorry, Gwen. It's just that my sister, Meredith, is in town for some convention. She's a blogger for a romance book site. She had told me originally that she'd be going home right afterward, but then today she called and said she was staying overnight. I wanted to see her, but then you and I had already made plans and I didn't want to break those. I just kept putting off making a decision all day and then it was six and it was too late to change anything. So, fuck, please don't be angry. I just didn't know what to do." At any other time, Gwen would have found Dominic's unusual rambling funny. He was normally so calm and self-assured, but it was obvious now that he was afraid she was going to freak out and dammit, she was about to.

"Maybe you should just take me back home," she suggested tightly. "Your sister is expecting to just see you tonight. You don't want to spend your time trying to entertain me when you could be catching up with her." Why were men so completely oblivious to social situations that made women cringe? Meeting a man's family was something that usually didn't happen for quite some time—or in Gwen's case, never. She certainly hadn't been expecting to meet his sister the first week they started dating.

Dominic took both of her hands in his, forcing her to look at him. "Babe, I really want you with me tonight. I know you'll like Meredith. She's a lot of fun and you two will get along well. Please do this for me. I wouldn't ask if I thought you'd be uncomfortable around her."

Oh shit, he was giving her the sad puppy dog eyes. How was she supposed to say no? He'd included her in his life tonight as no other man ever had. Maybe it was way too soon, but if she turned him down, it might set the tone for the rest of their possible future relationship. How bad could it be? She'd have a glass—or three—of wine and enjoy a meal at a restaurant that she couldn't often afford herself. It was a win-win. She just needed to pull the big-girl panties up and say yes. "All right," she agreed softly.

"Really?" A look of relief crossed his face as he squeezed her hands tightly. "Thank you, Gwen. I promise you'll have a good evening." She nodded in reply, already regretting her decision. As they walked through the parking lot, Gwen saw a dark-haired woman rushing toward them. Dominic leaned down and said something that struck fear in her heart just before his sister launched herself into his arms. "Meredith reminds me a lot of Maddy and Megan. Heck, she could be their mother. You don't embarrass easily, do you?"

Surely, he was just kidding . . . "Dom!" his sister yelled as she hugged him tightly. Suddenly, she turned in his arms and noticed Gwen standing at his side. "Holy shit, did you actually bring a woman with you?"

"Very funny." Dominic laughed, pulling on his sister's hair. "Mer, this is Gwen Day. Gwen, this is my sister, Meredith, and she's the rude one in the family."

Gwen extended a hand to the other woman only to

find herself pulled into a hug instead. "What a surprise! Wow, my brother brought a woman to dinner!" Gwen looked helplessly at Dominic as Meredith slung an arm over her shoulders and steered her toward the restaurant. "Now, how long have you known my brother?"

"Um . . . a few months," Gwen replied. She might not have been sleeping with him that long, but she had known of him. Surely, that counted for something.

The other woman pulled back enough to look her up and down. "Honey, don't take this the wrong way because I'm totally loyal in my love of men, but you are hot. I can see why Dom would like you. It's so nice to see him dating someone with a little staying power."

"Staying power?" Gwen asked uncertainly. She wasn't sure she even wanted to know what that meant.

Meredith made a vague hand gesture before saying, "You know, a normal girl who has more on her mind than planning her next tattoo or body piercing." They had been walking toward the glass doors of Ivy when Meredith stopped and spun around, causing Gwen to pull up sharply to avoid a collision. "Please tell me that you didn't meet my brother at a strip club."

"What?" Gwen gaped at her, thinking she must have heard the question wrong.

"You don't collect dollar bills in a G-string for a living, do you?" Meredith asked, looking completely serious.

"N-no," Gwen managed to get out, thinking Dominic was right. His sister was every bit as bad as Megan and Maddy. And what was it with the stripper questions. Was that Dominic's usual mode of picking up women?

As if sensing her thoughts, Dominic closed the distance between them, resting his hand on the small of her back. "What are you two talking about?" he asked, looking just a tad too concerned.

"I was just assuring your sister that I didn't work a pole for a living. She seemed to think that we might have possibly met that way."

Looking not the least bit surprised or even upset, Dominic rolled his eyes at Meredith. "Could you at least wait until we're inside before you run Gwen off?"

"Come on," Meredith laughed, "it's a valid question. Gage told us all about Kandi. He's still upset with you, by the way, for dumping the poor girl." Before Dominic could comment, they were seated at a table in the corner and a waiter had taken their drink orders. Gwen, though, found that she couldn't let his sister's earlier comment go without finding out more. She figured Meredith would happily satisfy her curiosity even if her brother did kill her afterward.

Flashing a brilliant smile, Gwen turned to the other woman and asked, "So, who's Kandi?" She pretended not to hear the groan Dominic emitted beside her. Meredith, however, looked thrilled by her question.

"Well, I never met her personally, but according to Gage, my brother here thought she was some kind of ballet dancer who was quite popular with the men everywhere they went. She finally confessed that she performed her particular brand of 'ballet' to Beyoncé's "Naughty Girl" most evenings at midnight . . . so he dumped her."

"That's not why we stopped seeing each other," Dominic jumped in quickly.

Turning in her seat to stare at him, Gwen asked, "Oh really? Then why?"

He seemed surprised by her question before slumping down in his seat. "You don't want me to answer that, babe. Trust me. Hell, neither of you want to hear it."

Gwen was more determined than ever now to know the reason and his sister seemed to be right there with her. "Come on, brother dear, you can't leave us hanging like this. Gage said it was just because you were a prude and didn't like her profession."

He shook his head, looking like a deer in the headlights. It was obvious that whatever the reason, he didn't want to talk about it. She really should just let it go. He was more than likely right, and she was better off not knowing, but geez, it was going to kill her now. His sister continued to needle him until he finally cracked, saying something that Gwen hadn't been expecting. "All right! She called my . . . package her lollipop, and she talked to it in some weird baby talk. It freaked me the fuck out, and I just couldn't . . . do it and could you please stop being BFFs with Gage!"

Meredith burst out in laughter while Gwen just stared at him. Did he mean that he never slept with Kandi or that he couldn't do it that last time before they broke up? She was helpless to deny the twinge of jealousy working its way through her system. No doubt, she had been no older than twenty-five, with the perfect, small ass, unlike herself. "Dear Lord, Dom." Meredith giggled. "I can just imagine your face when that happened."

"I'd rather you not be able to picture any of it, Mer. You are my sister, remember?" Gwen felt his eyes on her before his hand slid over her leg. "I told you that you didn't really want to know," he said quietly. "She didn't mean anything to me, and she damn sure didn't hold a candle to you."

Meredith watched them from across the table, seemingly surprised by this softer side of her brother. If her smile was any indication, she completely approved. "Anyway, now that we've covered that, let me tell you what your nephews have been up to. Caleb got pissed at Jacob because he broke his iPad. Therefore, in retaliation, he flushed Jacob's goldfish down the toilet. Then Jacob freaked out, took Caleb's favorite Georgia Bulldogs T-shirt, and attempted to flush it. Well, needless to say, they clogged the upstairs toilet and flooded the bathroom and the hallway. Derrick was so pissed off I thought he would stroke out. He had the whole throbbing-vein-on-the-side-of-his-face thing going on."

Dominic winced, laughing softly. "Those boys are something else. I guess that's why Derrick said in his last e-mail that he'd been up to his knees in shit."

"Trust me, he meant that literally." Meredith shuddered. "We'd been meaning to have the carpet taken out and install hardwoods so that project got a major jump start."

"How old are your boys?" Gwen asked, enjoying the easy banter between Dominic and his sister. It was obvious that he loved his nephews a lot and took great interest in their lives.

"Caleb is eight, and Jacob is six. Derrick's holding down the fort while I'm gone, but hopefully he hasn't set them out on the side of the road by now."

Dominic smirked at his sister, saying, "I can't believe you haven't figured out how Derrick keeps the kids under control when you're away. I mean, have you never noticed those muzzles in the hall closet?"

Meredith laughed, pointing her finger at her brother. "Hey, I'm smart enough not to question what happens when Mom's away. As long as they are in one piece when I get home and Derrick's not handing me divorce papers, I let it go." Turning to Gwen, she added, "In case you're wondering, my hubby's a veterinarian." Fanning herself she said, "The damn sexiest one you'll ever meet. He has nerves of steel and a body for sin. I'm a very lucky girl!"

Dominic made a choking gesture at his sister's words. "Can we please not turn this into an hour of talking about your husband's . . . attributes. I feel like I know the man's body much better than I should. Let's leave it at 'he's a hell of a guy' and deserves some kind of gold medal for all that he does."

Meredith raised her glass of wine, smiling fondly as she said, "Here, here. No complaints there. So, Gwen, what type of work do you do?"

"I work at Danvers International as a senior accountant." With a rueful grin, she admitted, "I'm a numbers nerd; I always have been."

Giving her a look hot enough to melt the clothing

from her body, Dominic growled, "You're the sexiest nerd I've ever met."

Meredith grabbed her wineglass, taking a gulp. "You do remember I'm here, right?"

Dominic looked at her as if surprised. He actually seemed to have forgotten that there was anyone else in the room other than the two of them. "It's not like I haven't heard worse from you," he tossed back. Gwen could see a telltale blush on his face that was totally adorable. She loved that he could get so caught up in her that he blanked out the rest of the world. Again, that was something that had never happened to her with another man and it felt far too good.

As if just remembering Gwen's earlier words, Meredith snapped her fingers, saying, "Hey, your office is at Danvers as well, right, Dom? Is that how you two met?"

Before thinking better of it, Gwen answered first. "Nope, we live in the same apartment." Then realizing how that sounded, she was quick to clarify. "I mean we live in the same complex, but a few doors away. I noticed him there a long time before we actually crossed paths at Danvers."

"A long time, huh?" Dominic eyed her across the table. "Exactly how long had you been watching me before we officially met, babe?"

Oh great, now she was the one turning red and stumbling over her words. She knew the guilt was written all over her face. Dammit, she had watched him for months. Even when she'd been going out with Mac, she hadn't been able to resist ogling her hot neighbor. It made her feel as if she was a cheater when she realized that he and

Mac were not only coworkers, but best friends. She'd like to say that she'd never looked at him again from that point on, but it would be a lie. "Well, um . . . I mean, of course I saw you coming and going sometimes. And, when you returned from your runs in the evening or in the summer when you were using the pool." With both Meredith and Dominic now openly staring at her, she became even more flustered. God, she had admitted way more than she'd intended. Now she sounded like some kind of crazy stalker lady. She made matters even worse when she hastily added, "It was hardly ever, though. Not every day or anything."

Meredith took advantage of her pause to wink at her. "Ah, girl, it's okay. I don't want to stroke his already overinflated ego, but my brother's smoking. Even I can admit that. If I had a neighbor, not blood-related, of course, who looked like him, I'd be glued to my window every chance I got. Derrick thanks his lucky stars that we have only senior citizens living near us because he knows what would happen otherwise. I'm afraid being a book blogger has given me a new appreciation for the male body."

"Thanks for that, sis. You managed to kill the thrill of Gwen's words by sharing your inner pervert with us once again." He looked around the table before shaking his head in shock. "We're on our second bottle of wine, and we haven't even ordered yet. How did that happen?"

Looking sheepish, Meredith admitted, "I kept waving the waiter away. The conversation was way too good for us to be interrupted. I guess we should eat now, though, because I'm buzzing just a little bit."

Dominic picked up one of the wine bottles, then looked at Gwen. Before she could stop what she knew was coming, he grabbed her glass and said far too loudly, "Baby, are you drinking wine?"

"I . . . didn't even think anything of it." And that was the truth; nothing had entered her mind other than having a glass to relax. She figured by this point, though, she was a few past that. Putting her hand over his, she tried to reassure him covertly since they had an audience, "It's fine."

He lowered his voice to match hers, sounding concerned. "I still think you should be on the safe side until we know for sure."

Gwen felt like a cross between a scolded child and an unfit mother or mother-to-be, which only served to piss her off. She didn't like being questioned; she wasn't used to having to defend herself against something like this. Before she could make the snarky comment that was hovering on her lips, Meredith dropped her hand loudly onto the table and said in a whisper-shout that was mainly the shout part, "ARE YOU PREGNANT?"

And it was at that point that the evening went to hell. Gwen barely tasted what she knew was probably the best seafood of her life while Dominic tried to convince his sister that she had misunderstood things. For the rest of the meal Gwen spoke only when she was asked a direct question and then felt horribly guilty for being so rude to Meredith. She was determined to get her e-mail address from her ass of a brother and apologize.

A heavy silence hung over them as Dominic drove them home. He put his hand in the small of her back when they left his truck, and she childishly wanted to step away, but let it go. When they reached her door, she stopped and quickly found her keys in her purse. He took them from her hand and opened her door, as if he planned to come inside. She stepped up, blocking the doorway. Good manners kicked in, and she said stiffly, "Thanks for dinner. I'll see you . . ."

He didn't let her finish her brush-off. Instead, he put his hands on her hips and pushed her gently forward enough for him to enter behind her and shut the door. "Not so fast, baby. I'm not letting you go to bed and stew on how pissed off you are at me all night. We need to talk about this now."

Gwen clenched her hands at her side to keep from wrapping them around his neck. Instead of yelling, though, she said sweetly, "Don't you think I need my rest? I mean . . . we need to be cautious right now, just in case."

He ran his hand through his hair, causing the spiky strands to stick up even more. She hated that she was so riveted even by his damn hair. It was hard to stay mad at him, when she just wanted to stare at his masculine beauty. Meredith was right; her brother was all things hotness. "Gwen, fuck, I'm sorry. I know I shouldn't have said anything in front of my sister. I embarrassed you and made an ass out of myself."

When he paused, she pointed her hand saying, "Keep going." She was still mad, but he was on the right path. At least he could admit that he was wrong.

"I don't have any excuses. I just panicked when I realized how much wine we drank. Hell, I think I even poured one of the rounds and it never entered my mind. I've been insisting that you drink decaf coffee, yet I plied you with alcohol tonight."

For the first time since the mess at dinner, Gwen noticed how upset he was over it. She had been so mad at him at the table that she hadn't thought about anything beyond that. But, now he just looked scared and guilty. Like he was the one who had done something wrong. Moving closer, she laid her hand on his chest, trying to give him some measure of comfort. She was fast learning that he was a natural caretaker—he felt like he had failed with her tonight, and it was tearing him up. "Dominic, I'm an adult and it's my job to remember things that concern me and my body. I've done some research on the Internet and there's no reason to change my habits until I take a pregnancy test and know for sure. But if it makes you feel better, I will cut way back on caffeine and alcohol while I'm waiting to take a test."

He still looked upset as he stared down at her. He dropped a kiss on her nose before curling his arms tightly around her waist. "I want to take care of you, babe. It's not a job for me—it's a privilege. There's never been a woman who I've wanted to keep close and protect like I do you, and I'm probably going a little overboard with it. I can't seem to help myself, though."

Gwen found herself relaxing into his embrace, enjoying the feel of his strength surrounding her. He made her feel delicate and petite, which was unusual for her. "It's okay. I think we can both agree that there are things we could have handled differently." Poking her finger playfully in his ribs, she added, "But if you ever spring a family dinner on me again without any warning, I won't be responsible for my actions, capisce?"

He had the good grace to look shamefaced. "That was a dick move," he agreed. "I already had plans with you that I was looking forward to when Meredith called me at the last minute. I hated to tell her no, but I wanted to spend the evening with you. Yet another thing I know that I could have handled better." When his hand moved lower to caress the curve of her ass, she started to squirm against him. "I'd love to make my bad behavior up to you," he breathed against her ear as he pulled her close enough to feel his hardening length.

She knew she should at least put up a token protest. Instead, she was all but panting against him while he ground lightly against her. Her voice was horribly wobbly and husky as she moaned, "Dominic . . ." She was ready for him to push her against the nearest wall and take her, but despite urging him in that direction, he resisted, trailing gentle kisses across her throat.

"I want you in a bed tonight, babe. We're always so crazy for each other that it's hard to make it that far. I want to touch and kiss every inch of your delectable body before I take you."

"Oh yes, please," Gwen shuddered before she could help herself. Just hearing Dominic say something like that in his rough, sexy voice was more of a turn-on than any of her sexual experiences with other men. When he looked at her, it was as if he couldn't get close enough. She felt like the center of his universe when they were together, which should have been strange, considering they hadn't actually been together for long. He was taking all of her walls and breaking right through them. To be the sole focus of a man like Dominic was heady and intoxicating. She was drunk off the feelings he ignited inside of her. "I want you—so much," she admitted, helpless to deny him.

At her admission, his eyes locked on hers, showing her a tenderness that made her breath hitch in her throat. "I want you too, baby, more than you could possibly imagine. I have for so long." Her mind registered surprise at his words, but she was powerless to focus on the significance of them. He reached for his pants and pulled a condom from the pocket before growling, "Your bedroom . . . now." She turned on wobbly legs and led him down the hallway. She wanted to protest when he walked to the bedside and clicked on the lamp there, but managed to stay silent. She preferred to make love in the dark, but maybe change was good and necessary. He gently turned her to face the wall, while he eased the zipper of her dress down, kissing each new inch of skin that he exposed.

She was incredibly grateful for her last trip to Victoria's Secret as he hissed his appreciation for her blue bra and matching thong. She wasn't one to splurge on many things, but she never passed up a sale at her favorite lingerie store. She liked to think of it as wishful thinking. As in someday, someone might actually see some of it again. His almost reverent touching of her body gave her the confidence to undress him without trying to cover herself. When he kicked away his pants, she cupped his cock through his silk boxers. Stroking his hard length, she marveled, "Are you always this hard?"

His hand dropped to cover hers, showing her how he liked to be stroked. "If you're within a mile of me, I'm hard." Rubbing a finger against the wet silk covering her slit, he confessed, "I seem to be obsessed with your body, Red. I can't think of anything but how it feels to be inside of you."

She was reeling from his words when he pushed her underwear aside and slid a big digit into her wet heat. "Ohhh, yesss!" she cried, already close to coming. He used his thumb to rub her clit while he continued to glide one, then two fingers in and out of her.

"Ride my hand, baby," he instructed as he steadied her with his other hand.

Gwen held nothing back as she rocked against him, taking everything he gave her and moaning for more. Her orgasm was an avalanche roaring closer, and she pursued it with everything she had. As she sought that one final movement that would push her over, Dominic curled his fingers, hitting her G-spot, and time stopped before the world shattered around her. She clasped her legs closed, trying to remove his hand from her sensitive tissues as she fought to recover. "Too much," she gasped, as her core continued to flutter.

Dominic took mercy on her, releasing her sex, before nudging her a few steps backward until the bed met her legs. "I don't think you can handle my mouth on you right now, no matter how much I want to taste you."

Boldly, Gwen pushed his boxers down, sighing in pleasure when his heavy cock bobbed against his stomach. She rubbed her finger over the moisture gathering on the mushroom top. "Can I have this instead?" She licked her lips to emphasis her point, causing him to sway on his feet.

He gave a pained laugh. "I don't think I can handle you tasting me, either, when I'm this close to the edge. I know I said we'd take things slow, but I've got to be inside of you now. I promise the next time will be more leisurely." Gwen had the crazy urge to laugh, thinking about how strange it was to be discussing having more than one sexual encounter on a work night. *My God, when had she gotten so old? The only thoughts a girl should have about having sex with a man like Dominic were *yes* or *hell, yes*!*

He grabbed the condom he had thrown on her bed and quickly sheathed himself. When he settled her on her back and came up over her, Gwen was amazed to discover that there was nothing quite like the missionary position with him. Just being able to look into his eyes while he thrust inside of her was the most erotic feeling. He urged her to wrap her legs around his hips, pushing him impossibly deep. Even though he had claimed to be on the edge, he still took the time to build her toward her next orgasm. They licked and sipped at each other's mouths while their desire raced higher. Sweat dotted Gwen's brow as she felt the familiar tingle of her orgasm cresting. As if knowing she was close, Dominic's control snapped. He used a hand under her hips to pull her closer and took her hard. "Ahhh, Dominic, ohhh!" Gwen cried as she convulsed around his shaft.

"That's it, baby. Come all over me," he grunted. He thrust a few more times before she felt him stiffen and release with her name on his lips. A little later Dominic left her to dispose of the condom before returning to curl his body around hers. As she fell asleep to the steady sound of his heartbeat against her ear, Gwen tried to tell herself that she couldn't possibly be falling in love with a man that she barely knew.

It was just the sex—that had it be it. Really good, amazing sex was just that . . . it was not love—and it would never be.

Chapter Six

"Where are you going, babe?" Dominic groaned as Gwen shimmied out of his arms. The room was still dark, and it seemed way too early for her to be leaving for the office. A quick look at the bedside clock confirmed that it was only six in the morning. Thinking she must be going to the bathroom, he threw an arm over his pillow, wanting to catch a little more sleep. "Hurry back to bed," he called over his shoulder as his eyes drifted shut. He was almost asleep when the sound of the shower running from the adjoining bathroom got his attention. After only a few minutes, Gwen was back in the bedroom dressing. He turned onto his back, rubbing the sleep from his eyes.

"I'm going to the gym before work," she said as she sat on the side of the bed, putting on her shoes. Her damp hair was pulled back in a ponytail, and she was wearing a pair of sweatpants and a T-shirt. He wanted nothing more than to pull her back into bed and cuddle with her. *Holy shit, when had the word cuddle become part of his vocabulary?* "Just lock the door behind you when you leave." She sat looking down at him as if wondering how to say good-bye. He took her arm, pulling her against his chest and gave her a slow, leisurely kiss. If her answering whimper was any indication, she wasn't even cursing his morning breath.

"Which gym are you going to?" he asked as he licked her bottom lip. When she mentioned the name of the big facility near Danvers, he smiled inwardly. He might work out most days at the office gym, but he also had a membership to Gwen's gym. Even though he'd prefer to have her underneath him this morning, he would take the other option available to him and join her for a workout. He surprised her by jumping from the bed and pulling her to her feet. He quickly pulled his jeans on and grabbed his shirt and shoes from the floor. "Give me five minutes to change clothes and I'll be ready."

"Ready for what?" she asked, sounding confused.

"I'm going with you. I have a membership there as well. We can work out together."

"You're going to work out with me?" She seemed to be having a hard time wrapping her mind around that concept for some reason.

"Yeah, babe. Whatever you want to do, I'm game." He dropped another kiss on her lips and steered her through her apartment, flipping on a light so they could see to navigate. "I'll be right back, and then I'll follow you to the gym."

He jogged to his door, opening it and making a bee-line for his bedroom. After packing a change of clothes for work, he put on a pair of athletic shorts and a fresh T-shirt. Just minutes later, he walked back to where

Gwen was now waiting outside her door for him. "Ready?" She nodded and let him take her hand.

When they reached their cars, he opened her door and waited until she had started her car before getting into his truck and following her out. It would be nice if they could take just one car, but Dominic's work hours were unpredictable, and he didn't want her to have to wait for him. When they arrived at the gym, he again threaded his fingers through hers and walked to the brightly lit entrance of the Sports Complex. Gwen stopped outside the locker room doors grinning mischievously. "You know that I take the water classes here. Are you sure you want to work out with me?"

She stood grinning at him, waiting to see him squirm. He cocked a brow, as he unzipped his gym bag and pulled out a pair of swim trunks. Her mouth dropped open in shock, and he pushed it closed gently. "Checkmate, baby. I'm sure if you like the class, I will as well. Now, let's get going." With that, he pushed her toward her locker room door, and he walked into his. Hell, this would probably be his easiest workout in years, and he'd get to see Gwen in a swimsuit. There didn't seem to be a downside at all.

His first trickle of unease came a few short moments later when he walked out to the pool area and found Gwen waiting for him in what most would consider a conservative, black, one-piece swimsuit. All he could see however were perky breasts and an hourglass body showcased flawlessly by clinging spandex and dear, sweet Christ, when she bent over to put her water shoes on, he felt light-headed. He had been so busy ogling her that he was oblivious to his surroundings until someone yelled, "Hey, Gwen, is that hunk with you?"

Dominic jerked around to find a group of what looked like twenty women staring at him with more than a little interest. As if that wasn't horrifying enough, he realized that there was no way they'd missed him staring at Gwen's ass like a horny schoolboy. The only positive he could see in the situation was the avid interest in him had effectively killed the hard-on that Gwen had brought to life with her sexy swimsuit. "He sure is, Gladys." Gwen laughed as she straightened to look at him. "Ready, sport?"

She didn't verbally issue any kind of challenge, but he could see it in her eyes. She thought he was going to run. Hell, he wanted to, but there was no way that was happening. He was ex-military and worked security. He refused to be intimidated by some smirking women treading water in a pool. He straightened to his full six-foot-two height and motioned toward the steps. "After you, Red." Gwen walked past him, and he almost groaned in misery. Letting her go first had been a mistake. Now all he could focus on was the sway of her hips as she took the steps into the pool. Dammit, he was sure she was moving slower than usual. He had no doubt that she knew exactly what she was doing to him.

When they finally took their place in the water, everyone went around saying their names. There was one other man in the group Dominic estimated to be in his sixties. He came over and clapped Dominic on the back, saying, "Hey, glad to see another man here."

They exchanged names and made small talk until the class started.

After the first fifteen minutes, Dominic knew two things with certainty. First, he wasn't cut out for water dancing of any kind, and second, if drinking pool water killed you, then he was a dead man. He flailed, he fell, he splashed and generally made a complete ass out of himself. The only bright side was that Gwen had probably laughed more during the thirty-minute class than in the entire time he had known her. He was just getting back into place after an embarrassing side kick gone wrong when the instructor, Dolly, called out, "Dominic, why don't you come to the front and be my partner for the next song." Was she fucking kidding him? He looked at the gray-haired woman calling him out and wanted to curse over the attention that she had brought on him.

"Actually I think I should just stay back here," he began, trying to gracefully decline.

She put her hands on her hips and shook her head. "Honey, you need to come on up here before you drown. It's easier for a beginner to dance in shallow water. The deeper water is only for those who are more advanced." Turning to Gwen who was trying her best to give him an innocent look, she added, "Gwen, didn't you tell him how much harder it was in the deep end?"

Gwen shrugged her shoulder before patting him on the back. "I . . . must have forgotten that."

He circled behind her on his way to the shallow end of the pool, reaching out to covertly pinch her butt as he passed. She yelped, splashing around less than gracefully. "You know what they say about paybacks, right?" he asked lightly as he moved away from her.

Dominic might not be *Dancing with the Stars* material, but the rest of the class was much easier in three feet of water. He still couldn't believe that Gwen hadn't told him. She must have been laughing her ass off as he splashed next to her, looking like Jaws on steroids.

He had to admit afterward that he'd actually enjoyed himself, for the most part. Dolly even told him that she hoped he'd come back. He thought most of the women had enjoyed the comic relief that he'd unwittingly provided. He shook hands with everyone as they exited the pool, waiting for Gwen, who seemed to be taking a long time to make it to the front. When she finally drew even with him, she had the good grace to look just a bit guilty. "Did you, um . . . enjoy the class?" she asked, as she studied the bottom of the pool.

He decided to have a little fun with her instead of drilling her about what she'd done. "I had a great time, baby. I can't wait to do it again."

Her head flew up as she sputtered, "Yo-you did?"

Throwing his arm around her, he hugged her against his side before helping her up the stairs and out of the pool. "Oh yeah, it was awesome. You're right. It's a great way to exercise and have fun. Maybe we'll start coming together every morning."

He took her arm, pulling her along when she stopped to stare at him. "We better get ready for work. I'll wait for you out front if I finish first." He dropped a kiss on her cheek and strolled into the locker room. A quick look back showed her still standing outside the door, looking stupefied.

Dominic took a quick shower and dressed in his standard work clothes. He saw no sign of Gwen as he made his way to the front lobby to wait. He was just checking his e-mail on his iPhone when a hand landed on his shoulder. He looked up with a smile expecting to see Gwen standing there. Instead, he was faced with two blond-haired women who looked as if they ate too little and exercised too much. He was also fairly certain that the overabundance of breasts barely contained by their skimpy tops were fake. Men knew that shit just by looking. Only his good manners kept him from jerking away when one of them rubbed her fingers along his biceps, purring, "Well, hi there, handsome. You must be new here because I would have remembered seeing you before."

Dominic took a step back, trying to dislodge her hold on him. He had no problem with women taking charge from time to time in the bedroom, but an overly aggressive attempt at getting his attention did nothing for him. "I've been a member here for a while now," he said politely.

The woman who continued to stroke his arm stepped closer to him while saying, "My name is Brandy, and this is my friend Misty." He nodded his head at both women. When they looked at him expectantly, he grudgingly answered the unspoken question. "I'm Dominic. Nice to meet you." He didn't mean a word of it, but again, his mother had raised him to always be respectful of women if possible. Misty seemed content to let her friend Brandy do the talking while she stood twirling her hair and looking at him like he was her last meal.

"So, what time are you usually here, Dominic?" Brandy asked, seeming far too interested in his answer.

"I don't have a usual time. I'm not here that often," he replied, beginning to tire of the unwanted attention. Where in the hell was Gwen? He was past ready to get out of here.

Brandy giggled in a way that made his hair practically stand on end. She reached up to squeeze his arm. "Oh, come on, there's no way you are in such great shape without hitting the gym every day. Maybe we could work out together. Misty and I also take some of the spinning and Zumba classes if you're interested in those."

Just as he was debating leaving and texting Gwen, he saw her walking slowly toward them. She took in Brandy's hold on his arm, and he saw her mouth tighten and her eyes narrow. She looked like she was ready to kick someone's ass, and he had a bad feeling it was his. Surely, she couldn't believe that he would have the slightest desire for the stick figures standing far too close to him. She was the perfect woman to him. Her face was carefully blank as she stopped a few feet away. He had the feeling that she had been considering walking past without stopping. He gave her a soft smile over Brandy's head. "Hey, baby. I was wondering where you were."

Both Brandy and Misty swung around, staring at Gwen in shock. Dominic took the opportunity to step away from Brandy's suddenly limp fingers and walk around to Gwen's side. He dropped his arm around her waist, pulling her to his side. "Who—how do you know each other?" Brandy wheezed out, looking faint.

When Gwen remained silent, Dominic gave Brandy an easy smile, saying, "This is my girlfriend, Gwen. Have you met? She's a regular here. She prefers the water classes though since everyone is so much . . . nicer there." He dropped his hand to her hip, caressing her skin. "You can't argue with the results, can you?" He turned to look into Gwen's eyes, asking, "Ready, baby?" She nodded in reply, and he put a hand in the small of her back as they began walking toward the door. Over his shoulder, Dominic said, "Nice meeting you, ladies." Yeah, like hell, but they looked too shocked to register the insincere tone of his voice.

When they cleared the doorway, Gwen pulled out of his hold and threw her arms around his neck. He had no idea what had prompted this unusual display of affection, but he wasn't above taking advantage of it by pulling her even closer. "Oh, my God, thank you!" she squealed against his neck before dotting kisses there. "It was so nice to see those two speechless!"

Pulling back, Dominic looked down at her beaming face. "You know them?"

Still smiling, she replied, "We're not friends, trust me. I used to go to one of the Zumba classes that they were in. It was horrible. Th-they made fun of me and were always so mean. I almost quit coming here at all because of them."

"They're the reason you started going to the water class," Dominic mused, remembering her earlier comments about how uncomfortable she had been before making her new friends. He could easily see both Brandy and Misty being jealous of someone as beautiful as Gwen. They might not be able to admit it, even to themselves, but that was exactly the reason for their behavior. No matter how much they dieted and exercised, they could never hold a candle to the woman in front of him. She was a natural beauty—healthy, and luminous. No amount of money could buy those things. He couldn't imagine any red-blooded man picking the other two over her.

"Yeah, the terror twosome," Gwen said dryly. "They hated me from day one, and I never did anything to them other than be nice. I tried staying in the back of the class and off their radar, but it didn't help. They always found a way to throw a tacky comment or insult at me. I've never hated anyone in my life, but I came close with them. I joined the gym to exercise and feel better about myself, but I found that they were actually causing the opposite to happen."

"Baby, I told you that it was all jealousy even before I met them. They were choking on it when they saw you. You're everything that they've always wanted to be. Never, ever let someone like that change how you see yourself because that's what they want."

"They were only jealous because you were with me," she said softly as she absently rubbed his back.

He kissed her softly, keeping it somewhat PG-rated since they were still standing in the front of the gym. "That was just the final straw for them, sweetheart. They've been green with envy over you all along. How

about I run by Starbucks and get us coffee on the way?
I'll bring yours to your office when I get there."

"Oh, that sounds amazing," Gwen moaned. Her
breathy sound had his body twitching in an uncomfortable place as he helped her into her car. He followed
her out of the parking lot and they parted ways at the
light for his stop at the coffee shop. When he reached
his destination, he sat in his truck for a moment, taking
a deep breath.

He was in over his head with her, and a part of him
was terrified. He'd shamelessly used the condom mishap to get close to her and stay there. Yes, there was an
off chance she might be pregnant, and if she was, they
would cross that bridge then. He would have wanted
to take care of her regardless, though. She brought that
out in him. He'd wanted her for so long that now that
she had let him in, he wanted to shift from taking it
slow to running like he was in a fucking marathon. In
some crazy way, he had known that she was "the one"
for him almost from the moment he saw her. He had
never had that feeling before, not even close, which
was why it had gotten his attention. He wasn't a man
who believed in nor had he experienced love at first
sight. There had been moments of desire or lust, but
that was it. With Gwen, he had been close to obsessed
from the beginning. The feeling had been so strong that
it had scared the hell out of him for a while. Hence,
why he'd waited to make his move and almost lost her
to his best friend. He wouldn't make that mistake
again. This last week with her had shown him that no
matter how strong his feelings had been for her from

afar, they were nothing compared to how he felt now that he knew her intimately.

He was terrified of a possible pregnancy, but for completely different reasons. He was afraid that she was letting him close only because of it. What would happen when and if she found that she wasn't expecting his child? Would she push him away and move on? He couldn't lose her now that he finally had her. Each day with her only solidified the depth of his feelings for her. He was trying to pace himself to keep from scaring her. He knew that she wanted him, but she was skittish. She seemed to almost believe that she wasn't good enough for him, which was a joke. He wanted to drop to his knees and thank God for bringing her into his life because she was perfect.

He didn't know that much about a woman's cycle or timing, but he knew one thing for sure. He had to make her fall for him, and he figured he had a couple of weeks to do it before they found out if their night of passion had consequences. He wanted to be with her, but he wanted her to want it too, and for the right reasons. It was time for him to show her that there was something real between them. If he had to take a water aerobics class and make a fool of himself or give her orgasms until she couldn't walk, then so be it. From this moment forward, he would be her dream man because she had been his dream woman from the start.

Gwen was on a call with the purchasing department, requesting some purchase orders for invoices when Dominic knocked on her door and walked in. God bless the man, he was carrying a drink tray with two huge coffee cups and . . . a bottle of water? Maybe that was for him. Right now, even though she knew the damn thing would be caffeine free, she needed that steaming cup more than her next breath. She ended her call and clapped her hands together enthusiastically. "Gimme." When he raised a brow, she batted her eyes and added, "Please."

He laughed softly as he took a cup that was marked decaf on the side and handed it to her. While she was taking a sip, he took the bottle of water and put it on her desk. Okay, so maybe it was for her after all. Then he surprised her further by setting his own coffee down and pulling a small bottle from his pocket. "I bought these for you yesterday. All of the baby articles say that you should be taking extra folic acid so I picked up some. You already take a multivitamin, right?"

She knew she was staring at him, but she hadn't seen that one coming. If someone had told her a month ago that she'd feel weepy over the gift of vitamins, she would have thought they were insane. Now, though, she was fighting the urge to melt into a puddle in her seat over his care of her. How could the man whom she had only a short time ago thought of as such a tough guy be such a tender caregiver? He thought of things that would never have even crossed her mind and she was the woman. Almost on the heels of that thought came the pang of fear that this would all be over if she wasn't pregnant. She had never imagined that men like Dominic existed and now that she knew, she wanted to wrap her arms around him and never let go. She cleared her throat when he shook a tablet into his hand and handed it to her. "I . . . thanks," she murmured as she took the water bottle he offered her.

Touching her arm briefly, he said, "Sure, babe. Anything else before I go?"

Boy, what she wouldn't give to answer that question honestly. He probably wasn't expecting her to beg him to never leave when he asked, so instead she smiled and shook her head. "I'm good. Have a great day."

Dropping a kiss on her upturned lips, he replied, "You too, baby. I'll touch base with you later on." As he walked out of her office, she knew that unlike other men that she'd known, he would contact her at some point during the day. Dominic didn't make false promises. Her head slumped back against her chair. She had a few weeks to form a relationship with him that didn't involve the prospect of a baby. Maybe giving up now before she was further under his spell would be better, but she couldn't. She had tried to keep some distance between them, but it had proved futile. She was just too drawn to him and was powerless to deny herself his company.

She was still wallowing in misery when her office door slammed and she jumped in her seat. Mia stood with her hands on her hips and a concerned expression on her face. "For someone getting laid on a regular basis now, you sure do look miserable."

"That's because I want to keep my new amazing sex life," Gwen groaned.

Mia perched on the chair in front of Gwen's desk,

giving her a questioning look. "Has something happened between you and Dominic?"

Rubbing at the headache that was beginning to form at her temples, Gwen said, "No, he's more perfect every day."

"Then what's the problem?" Mia asked quietly.

She couldn't hold the truth from her friend any longer, and she was in dire need of support. "He'll leave when he finds out that I'm not pregnant."

Mia had nodded once before her eyes bugged out as Gwen's words sunk in. "Why would he think you might be pregnant? You've only been together for what, a few days, haven't you? Unless . . . ?"

"No, we didn't have sex before that." Feeling strangely embarrassed, Gwen told Mia all about the condom mishap, as she had come to think of it.

Mia put her hand on her chest. "Oh, my God, he brings you decaf coffee and folic acid? Where in the world did this man come from? Don't get me wrong. Seth is usually beyond thoughtful, but I can't imagine him thinking of vitamins." Noticing Gwen's despair, she added, "And now you're afraid that he's only Mr. Perfect until he finds out you aren't pregnant, and then he'll turn into an asshole?"

"I don't think Dominic has the asshole gene," Gwen defended him. "I'm just scared that he'll take all of himself and his awesomeness and move on to someone else when there is no longer anything holding us together."

"Gwen," Mia said gently, "no matter what you want

to believe, it was the attraction between you two that brought you together in the first place. If he hadn't felt the same way he would have shown you the door. You might have had some liquid courage that night, but he's the one you went straight to. I've got a strong hunch that he has been hoping something would happen between you two for a while—and maybe you have as well."

"It was just sex—men never turn that down," Gwen argued weakly, afraid to get her hopes up. "And I was dating Mac until very recently."

"Honey, don't be dense," Mia snapped. Gwen braced herself for the tough love she knew was coming. "I've seen you and Dominic together a couple of times now and trust me, he doesn't act like a man just going through the motions until he can move on. He looks at you like there's no one else even on the planet but you two. I'm not bragging or anything, but I consider both Crystal and myself at least glance worthy, and he only gave us the barest bit of polite interest. We could have been naked and fondling each other's breasts and the man wouldn't have noticed or cared. He was centered on you completely. Plus, if Mac was really thinking of Ava while you two were together, I'm pretty sure you were thinking of Dominic as well."

Ignoring her comment about Mac, Gwen said, "He did take me to dinner with his sister, but we had made plans to go out already when she contacted him. I think he hated to cancel on me."

"Oh, bullshit." Mia snorted. "A man just killing time would not have cared about canceling plans with you, and he damn sure wouldn't want you meeting any family members. Men guard that like some national security secret. He is showing you in every way possible that he's more than interested in you so don't go running scared. Nothing has to change between you if you aren't pregnant."

Gwen took a few sips of her rapidly cooling coffee while she pondered Mia's reassurances. Finally, she admitted, "I'm afraid to believe that something this good could be happening to me. I haven't exactly had much success with my past relationships. Usually, I end up doing everything I can short of proposing to make it work and it just always seems to go into a downward spiral that I'm helpless to stop."

"We've all had relationships like that," Mia grimaced. "You just have to realize something that takes that much energy to hold on to wasn't meant to be in the first place. You know I went through some tough things when Seth and I started out, but from the beginning, he was always different. I felt it, and I'm betting you do here as well. I'm not suggesting you go and profess your love today . . . but stop acting as if someone is holding a stopwatch over your head and just enjoy getting to know Dominic. I have seen nothing from him to indicate that he'll be packing his bags if two pink lines don't appear on that white stick in a few weeks. Heck, you'll probably both have a drink and a big laugh over the scare before having some amazing sex to celebrate."

Gwen felt her heart lighten for the first time in days. Could Mia be right? Who said that a relationship had to begin in the typical first date dinner and a movie manner? She had to believe that fate had led her to this point in her life, and it was up to her to embrace the opportunity. She needed to put all the fears from her mind and just focus on how much she loved being with him. They had jumped the gun a bit on that part with the whole sex even before the first date, but she couldn't pretend to regret that. She might love his company out of bed, but dear Lord, the man could do things with his body that she had only dreamed about.

She had no idea what the future held, but he was hers right now and maybe that was all that mattered. Looking ahead and trying to avoid a relationship disaster had never helped her before, so trying to live for the day might be worth a shot.

Chapter Seven

Dominic walked through the door of East Coast Security on Monday after a lazy weekend spent largely with Gwen. He had left early that morning to get a start on looking through the security feeds from the weekend. He planned to take a break in an hour and pick up a coffee for her. He looked forward to that stolen moment in her office each morning. If he was being truthful, he had more than a couple of fantasies involving bending her over the desk and burying himself deep inside of her while he palmed that amazing ass.

His head was still in the clouds—or on Gwen's ass—when the sight of Mac sitting in a chair in front of the row of monitors brought him up short. "Please tell me that Ava hasn't already kicked you out," he asked warily.

Mac looked up, giving him a lazy grin. The bastard looked entirely too content for this early in the morning. Mac turned his chair to face him, crossing his ankles, and reclining backward. "Nah, I'm still in her good graces. I decided to go ahead and come in when she said something along the lines of 'have mercy.' "

Dominic chuckled, knowing full well what the woman

must have meant with that comment. After waiting for years for the woman he loved to finally return his feelings, Mac probably hadn't let her out of bed much in the last week. He was damn glad it had finally worked out for his friend. Now, though, he needed to tell Mac about the new development in his relationship with Gwen. The other man had given him his blessing on pursuing her, but he might not have expected it to happen so soon. Heck, he hadn't expected it himself, but he sure wasn't complaining. "We could have swung another week here without you, man. I hate that you had to come back from your honeymoon so soon."

Mac took a sip from the cup sitting at his elbow while Dominic settled into a seat beside him. "Ava had some meetings scheduled this week that she hated to cancel without more warning. Everyone really helped her out by taking over for her on short notice last week. We figured we'd take some time off in a few months when things are a little less hectic." Looking blissfully happy, he added, "It's all gravy anyway because I have my woman in my home and in my bed for good this time. I could give a shit if we never take a vacation because every day with her is paradise to me."

"Go ahead and leave your man card on the desk because that is the most pussified statement I've ever heard from a dude before." Both Dominic and Mac jerked around in surprise to see Gage smirking in the doorway. "If you getting married means we have to take up knitting and just generally turn into chicks, then I'm gonna need to do something drastic at night to get the testosterone flowing again."

Dominic had to turn away until he had his laughter under control. Gage was loud and irreverent, but damn, he was funny, for the most part. He had always provided the comic relief in their group, even in the hellholes of Afghanistan. He'd seen very few things through the years that could bring Gage down for long. He was a glass-half-full kind of guy.

Mac cupped his hand over his cock, making a rude gesture before saying, "I've got your man card right here, pretty boy. If you ever find a woman you don't have to pay by the hour, you might have some feelings to discuss."

"Yeah, it's still not looking too good with Crystal, either. So, the pay-to-play route is pretty much all he's got right now," Dominic added helpfully.

"Who's Crystal?" Mac asked as he kicked a chair out for Gage to sit in.

Before Gage could answer, Dominic said, "That's the girl with the tramp stamp from the parking garage who kneed him in the family jewels. I will add, though, that I've since discovered that she's Ella's sister and is not a tramp."

Gage propped his feet up on the desk in front of him, letting the chair rear back on two legs. "And tell us, Dom, how did you find out that information? Are you friends with Crystal—or maybe you have friends in common with her?"

Dominic gritted his teeth, knowing he had asked for

the sarcastic innuendo from Gage. He should have kept his mouth shut and minded his own business. Problem was, all of them were so close that they stayed entirely too involved in one another's lives. A fact that he usually liked. Mac was looking back and forth between them, clearly trying to figure out what he was missing. He refused to sit here and squirm while Gage continued to throw out hints. "Crystal is friends with Gwen, okay?"

"Um . . . Okay," Mac drawled out. "So, you've been talking to Gwen then? Have you guys been on a date yet?"

Dominic studied his friend carefully but saw only curiosity in his gaze. He knew Mac was crazy about Ava and had dated Gwen for only a short while, but it still made things rather awkward. He was absurdly grateful that they'd never slept together because that would have been hard to get past. From what both Gwen and Mac had said, their relationship had barely progressed past kissing. Even that made him feel crazy jealous if he dwelled on it. He might not own Gwen's mouth, but he felt pretty possessive of it.

Before he could answer Mac's question, Gage jumped in. "Oh, I think you could say that those pesky first date nerves are all behind them now. In fact, I believe they are quite . . . blissful together . . . Almost orgasmic. Wouldn't you say, Dom?"

Dominic popped up his middle finger, giving the other man the universal go-to-hell symbol before turning back to Mac's questioning stare. "Boy, that was fast," he said, unable to mistake Gage's meaning. "I was only away for a week, so when did this new development occur?"

He saw Gage open his mouth to speak so Dominic hurried to answer first. "The evening I returned from Vegas." He winced knowing how that sounded. He wasn't sure why he wanted to be the one to answer. Hell, Gage probably couldn't have made it sound much worse.

Mac's mouth dropped open in shock. "Really? How did that happen? I thought you were waiting until the opportunity presented itself?"

"Oh, it presented itself all right," Gage chimed in, looking vastly amused.

Dominic glared at Gage. "Just a little advance notice, I'm going to kick your ass when we're done here. And at least I have a new development in my love life. Last I heard, you were no closer to getting a date with Crystal." Turning back to Mac, he added, "Gwen . . . approached me. I don't want to go into a lot of detail here because frankly that would be strange, but we're sort of together now."

"Don't forget the kid part," Gage tacked on. At any other time, Dominic knew that Gage would be scanning through the security feeds without paying the conversation around him much attention. He seemed to tune into his surroundings only when he could spill the beans on either Dominic or Mac. Lately it seemed to be Dominic's life that provided all of the office entertainment. He hoped like hell at some point in the future the other man had a serious relationship because Dominic planned to rain hell down upon him.

Mac's eyes looked like they were going to pop out of his head at this new piece of information. "Kid? Man,

I've only been gone a week," he reiterated. "Even you, Dom, couldn't have had a kid that fast."

Dominic grimaced as he shook his head. "No, I haven't and I'm dearly regretting unloading on the mouth-of-the-South over there in a moment of weakness. I swear you two had better never mention that you know any of this to Gwen."

"No danger of that," Gage huffed. "I only got the highlight reel. You wouldn't answer any of my important questions."

"No one answers the questions you ask, brother, because they always involve some part of our woman's body or if she's a screamer," Mac added dryly.

"We had a condom mishap," Dominic finally answered Mac's original question. "I don't think we need to be worried about a pregnancy, but I can't be certain. If it does, then I'm one hundred percent in."

"And if she isn't pregnant? Then what?" Mac asked as he studied him.

"It doesn't make a difference to me," Dominic answered honestly. "I don't think it would be the best way to start a family, and I'd like to wait and let things take a more traditional route, but either way, I want Gwen in my life. I told you after you broke up with her how I felt, and now that we're seeing each other, my feelings have only grown stronger. It's crazy, I know, but she's it for me, man. I knew it in my gut from the first moment I saw her. I screwed around dealing with a case of denial, but that's over now."

"I'm happy for you, bro," Gage said sincerely, surprising both Dominic and Mac. "I think we've all grown tired of finding a stranger in our bed the next morning."

"Since when have you ever let anyone stay the night?" Mac snorted.

Gage tossed a pen at Mac's head, laughing when he hit his mark. "Listen fucker, I was just trying to be supportive and not call both of you a bunch of whipped pansies." Then in a perfect feminine voice, he sang out, "Boohoo, I love you honey. Do you love me? Can you hold me while I cry? I'm feeling so sensitive today, and I just want to share all of my thoughts with you. Baby, I bought us matching Christmas sweaters to wear and my gift-wrapped balls are under the tree for you."

Dominic tried to keep it together, but the laughter exploded from him. He laughed until tears were welling in his eyes. He could hear Mac's booming voice as he succumbed to Gage's obnoxious brand of humor as well. "There's something wrong with you, man," Dominic managed to gasp out as he tried to catch a breath.

"I hate to even ask what's so funny." They all swiveled quickly to find an amused Ava holding a coffee tray and shaking her head.

Mac jumped to his feet, almost tripping in his haste to reach her. Yeah, Gage had one thing right—Mac was whipped and didn't care who knew it. "Hey, baby," he said as he took the tray from his wife. When the coffee was safely on the desk, Mac pulled her into his arms and dropped a kiss on her smiling mouth.

Dominic had really grown fond of Ava when he had helped in her quest to win Mac from Gwen. Yeah, it sounded like a total asshole move now, but they'd both been desperate at that point. He'd always thought that Ava was an unfeeling ice queen who had put his friend through years of hell, but he soon found out that he was wrong. In reality, she was so damaged by her past that she'd been afraid to admit that she loved Mac as much as he loved her.

The collateral damage, when the dust settled, had been Gwen. Dominic knew at some point if things continued to move forward with Gwen, that he needed to admit his role in Ava's pursuit of Mac to her. He didn't want to begin a relationship with secrets between them. Gwen had assured him that she hadn't loved Mac, but he knew that she had been hurt in the crossfire and that made him sick.

"So, what was so funny?" Ava asked, looking at Mac indulgently.

"Just Gage and his usual insults." Mac rolled his eyes.

Ava pulled away from Mac to distribute the coffee that she had brought for them. Dominic looked at his watch and stood. Gwen should be in her office by now. Seeing Mac and Ava so affectionate and happy made him want to steal a moment before the day began to see his woman. Without thinking, he started toward the door throwing over his shoulder, "I'm going to take Gwen some coffee. I'll be back in a few." As soon as the words left his mouth, he cringed. A look at Ava showed her staring at him in surprise before giving Mac a questioning look.

"Go ahead, bro." Mac waved him on. "I'll fill her in." Dominic gave his friend a grateful look before opening the door and stepping out into the hallway. He was too close to Mac and now Ava to keep his relationship with Gwen a secret from either of them. He knew it might take some adjustment on all of their parts, but they needed to accept that Gwen was in his life now, and if he had anything at all to say about it, she was here to stay.

It had been a hectic morning as was typical for the end of the month. For the most part, all the divisions of Danvers ran like a well-oiled machine, but that didn't mean there were no problems to address. Gwen had been so busy analyzing budgets for purchasing that she had been ignoring the growling of her stomach for the last hour.

When a knock sounded at her door, she figured it was either Crystal or Mia wanting to go to lunch—or if she was lucky, Dominic. She almost fell out of her chair in shock when she looked up to see Ava standing uncertainly in her doorway. Tension sat heavily in the small space as they stared at each other. Finally, Ava broke the silence by saying softly, "Hi, Gwen. I . . . er . . . know I'm probably the last person you were expecting, but I wanted to see if you would have lunch with me?"

Gwen moved from shock to completely flabbergasted at Ava's invitation. *What in the hell is her game?* Wasn't this a bit like kicking someone's dog after you'd already run over it, and then backed over it for good measure? Expelling a breath that sounded as loud as a bomb in the quiet room, Gwen said, "I have no idea why you would want to do that."

"I think we should talk," Ava replied, looking extremely uncomfortable. Gwen felt a perverse sense of pleasure that the usually poised Ava Stone seemed ill at ease. She always felt frumpy compared to the other woman and this was like a small, although petty, victory for her.

Pinching the bridge of her nose, Gwen doodled on her desk pad as she said, "I don't see what we would need to talk about. We've never been friends or even acquaintances so there's not really anything to say."

Ava took a few steps into the room until she was in front of her desk. Gwen was surprised to see her hands trembling as she clasped them together. "Please, Gwen. I realize that you don't owe me anything and that you probably hate me, but I would like a chance to clear the air with you. Dominic and Mac are best friends, and I don't want anything to change that. I owe you an apology and an explanation, and I hope that you'll give me the opportunity to do both. Please . . ."

Gwen studied the other woman for a moment before getting slowly to her feet and pulling her purse from her desk drawer. She had no idea why she was agreeing to this. Maybe, at the very least, she was curious as to what had happened to end her relationship with Mac so abruptly. She had told Dominic that she didn't love Mac and that was true, but Ava was offering her something that she'd never had in past relationships—an explanation. A reason why things had ended. "Okay, how about the sandwich shop around the corner?"

Ava waved Gwen in front of her saying, "I'll just follow you. I'm not sure which place you're talking about." Gwen clenched her jaw as she preceded the other woman down the hall. No matter how much Dominic seemed to admire her ample ass, she still felt self-conscious knowing the thin blonde was behind her. The jersey dress that had seemed like a good idea this morning suddenly felt too tight. When she heard Ava clear her throat and say, "I like your dress," Gwen had to fight the urge to run away. She also had to wonder if Ava was being sarcastic even though she heard nothing but sincerity in her voice.

"Um . . . thanks," she replied grudgingly. She was grateful to see the usual crowd of people on the elevator, which made it possible to avoid further conversation. In fact, not another word was uttered between them until they were seated at a table in the sandwich shop.

Gwen ordered a bowl of vegetable soup and a turkey sandwich while Ava, damn her, ordered a chef salad with the dressing on the side. Was it too much to hope that she'd at least have some carbs in her meal? Seeing Ava's hand shake as she lifted her water glass to her lips gave her a moment's pause. Apparently, they were both nervous about this unexpected lunch. Finally, Ava took a deep breath before saying, "I . . . God, this is so awkward, isn't it?"

Relaxing just a bit, Gwen nodded before admitting, "Yeah, it sure is. I don't guess there is much of a way around that, though, considering the circumstances."

"No, I don't suppose so," Ava agreed. "Gwen, I had planned to seek you out even before I found out that you and Dominic were seeing each other. If not for discovering that this morning, I would have probably chickened out for at least a few more weeks before I worked up the nerve to speak to you."

Gwen couldn't contain the reluctant smile that curved her lips at the other woman's candor. She had fully expected to dislike her forever, but found that she seemed more down-to-earth than she had imagined. Curious, she asked, "What does my seeing Dominic have to do with this meeting?"

"I care about Dominic—as a friend." Ava smiled fondly. "Also, he, Mac, Gage, and my brother Declan are extremely close. I don't want my actions with Mac to drive a wedge between them." Gwen could see Ava mentally bracing herself before saying, "I love Mac—I always have—but I'm not proud of my recent behavior, especially where you are concerned. In order for you to understand the relationship that I've had with Mac for years, I need to tell you a little about our past. It's difficult for me, but it's the only way you'll hopefully understand some of our history."

Seeing how hard this was for Ava, Gwen held up her hand, saying gently, "You don't have to tell me anything. Yes, I was hurt by what happened with Mac, but I'm a big girl and I'll recover."

"Please," Ava begged, "just let me try to explain myself." After a moment, Gwen nodded for Ava to proceed. "Mac's family lived next door to my grandfather, so we knew each other most of our lives. I've loved him for as long as I can remember, but he treated me more like a sister. Fast forward several years and I went to my first prom with a guy who I'd been seeing for a bit. That night he . . . he raped me."

"Oh, my God," Gwen gasped out, hardly able to believe what she had just heard.

A single tear tracked down Ava's cheek before she quickly wiped it away. "Afterward, I managed to make it to Mac's house, and he found me. I—I wasn't the same after that. My grandfather didn't report it to the police and made me feel like it was my fault. Mac . . . he tried to be there for me, but I pushed him away. Eventually, he joined the Marines along with my brother, Declan. He still wrote and visited me anytime he could. After he was discharged, we formed a friendship again, spending a lot of time together, and I knew that he wanted more from me, but I wasn't capable of giving it to him. I did everything I could to push him away and to make him believe that I was normal, when I was anything but. Finally, he had had enough and decided to move on with his life. When he started dating you, I panicked. I knew Mac slept with other women, just as he believed I slept with other men. But, he never dated anyone—until you."

"It made you realize how you felt about him, didn't it?" Gwen asked, even though she already knew the answer. After hearing what Ava had been through, she couldn't even bring herself to hang on to any of the bitterness that she had directed toward her since losing Mac.

Looking shamefaced, Ava whispered, "I always knew I loved him. I just didn't feel like I deserved him. When I met you, though, I knew I would lose him if I didn't do something. You were so beautiful and exactly the type of woman Mac would choose to settle down with. I guess I thought that we would be frozen in time forever with neither of us ever leaving the other behind. Suddenly the reality hit me hard when I had to face the fact that he was pulling away from me."

Gwen laid her hand atop Ava's, giving it a squeeze of sympathy. "I'm sorry for what happened to you, truly I am. And I know it must have been hard for you to tell someone who is essentially a stranger to you something so personal. I'm touched that you care enough about my feelings to put yourself through that, and it does help me to find some closure knowing the reasons behind what happened with Mac."

Ava gave her a timid smile, still looking more than a little guilty. "Mac really thinks a lot of you, Gwen, and the fact that we both hurt you has been hard for him to handle. I know that it's too soon and maybe you'll never be comfortable with it, but eventually I hope that we can all be friends. Dominic spends a lot of time with Mac, and I don't want anything to change their relationship."

"I know that they're close," Gwen agreed, "and I would never do anything to get in the way of that. Truthfully, I assumed that it would make both you and Mac uncomfortable to have me around."

"No, we don't feel that way at all," Ava assured her. "In fact, I think Mac would be relieved to keep you in his life. He's not the type of man who cares about someone and then walks away. He will always look out for you—that's the type of man that he is." Chuckling,

Ava added, "He's probably already lectured Dominic about what will happen if he doesn't treat you well."

"I'd hate to be a fly on the walls of that office." Gwen laughed. She thought about how strange it was to be laughing with the woman she had despised just days earlier. Maybe she should still be holding a grudge, but she found that there was no way she could feel about Dominic the way that she did and have lasting feelings for Mac. She knew now that she liked the idea of Mac more than anything. To her, he had represented stability in one hot package. He was the ideal husband material, just not for her. After the hell that Ava had gone through in her life, she deserved to be with the man who had been by her side the whole time. It was their moment to be happy, and Gwen just couldn't begrudge them that. It might take some time before they could all comfortably enjoy one another's company, but she felt confident that if she continued her relationship with Dominic, it would happen. Ava was correct; they were all too closely connected to have tension between them.

Gwen grimaced as she took a taste of her now cold soup. Her sandwich looked equally as unappetizing. Beside her, Ava picked at her salad before wrinkling her nose. "Now that we've talked and you didn't stab me with your fork, I'm starving. I'd kill for a big greasy burger from Jack's across the street."

Knowing she should probably be embarrassed by her eagerness, Gwen still grabbed her wallet from her purse and threw enough money on the table to cover both of their meals. "I'd much rather have that, but I was afraid you were dedicated to the salad route."

"Ugh, no." Ava stood quickly, almost knocking her chair over. "I just ordered the first thing on the menu. I was too nervous to even think about food."

Gwen stood and quickly rounded the table. "By all means, lead the way," she motioned as she followed Ava out the door and across the street.

Maybe the other woman was okay, after all. She seemed far removed from the ice queen that Gwen had thought her to be. No one who enjoyed a good hamburger could be all bad.

Chapter Eight

It was early Saturday morning and Gwen was buried beneath her comforter when someone knocked at her door. She opened one eye to look at the bedside clock. It was just after eight so a visitor this early in the morning couldn't be good news. She was afraid that it was Shannon needing a babysitter, which would make for a long Saturday. Or it could be Dominic. There had been a security issue at one of their locations last night, and he had left around midnight to check it out. He had said he would go to his place afterward to keep from waking her again. She had wanted to argue that he should come back since she was now pitifully spoiled and accustomed to waking up to his handsome face, and sweet heaven, he almost always put his morning wood to new and creative uses. He was most definitely a morning person. But she didn't want to force the issue.

When another round of knocking reached her ears, Gwen reluctantly crawled from her warm cocoon and stumbled to the door. A quick look through the peephole showed a handsome man and made her heart skip a beat. Without a thought about her appearance or smoothing down her mass of hair, she unchained the door and threw it open. She unconsciously licked her lips at the sight of Dominic on her doorstep in faded jeans and a close fitting T-shirt. Black boots perfectly complemented his outfit, as did the day's growth of scruff on his face. "Morning, baby," he drawled as his eyes slid down her body. She knew that her tank top and skimpy sleep shorts left little to the imagination, but she saw nothing but approval and lust in his stare.

He crossed the threshold, forcing her to move backward as he closed the door behind him. His hands reached over, pulling her flush against his chest. He dropped his head, licking the seam of her lips until they parted for his tongue. He tasted her until her legs were weak, and he was all but supporting her weight. "Mmm," she hummed against his lips. When he pulled back, she purred, "Good morning to you, too." All she wanted to do was pull him to the nearest surface and beg him to fuck her. He had turned her into something of a sex fiend. He was her drug, and she was beyond addicted. She had gone from never having an orgasm during intercourse to having multiples each and every time. Oh, the things he could do with his cock. Heck, she'd even slipped around Mia and Crystal and admitted that she called it the "miracle cock," because that was just what it was. Of course, those talented fingers that he used along with it were the proverbial icing on the cake.

Dominic cupped the cheeks of her ass, squeezing them lightly as he ground his hard length against her. He made no bones about the fact that he was an ass man. He constantly assured her, though, that it was just her ass that got him going. Whatever the reason, for the first time in her life she was grateful to the big butt gods for giving her more than her share in that department.

They were both primed and ready to move this party to the bedroom when he murmured against her neck between licks, "I've got something for you, babe."

Reaching a hand between them to grip his steely length, she moaned, "You sure do—and I'm ready for it."

He made a sound that was somewhere between a laugh and a groan. "Not that, Red, although it's all yours as well." He pulled back, dislodging her wandering hand and picked up a bag that she hadn't noticed from the floor. "This is the first part of your surprise."

She blinked like an owl before taking the bag that he thrust into her hand. She recognized the name of a popular store in the mall and wondered what he could have possibly bought for her there. "Why are you giving me anything?" she managed to get out before she opened the bag and began pulling out the contents.

"It's a belated birthday gift. Don't get me wrong," he said, grinning, "I love how we celebrated your big day the night of your first . . . visit to my apartment, but you did most of the gift giving. I think it's my turn to do something for my girl today."

Her mouth dropped as she pulled out a new pair of boot-cut jeans, a white tank top, which looked about a size too small, a black leather jacket, and finally a pair of black boots that resembled the ones he was wearing.

Bemused, she looked at the items now lying on the entryway table and then back at Dominic. "What's all of this for?"

Gwen couldn't help but think that he looked like an excited little boy as he rubbed his hands together. "I want us to take a trip on my bike today. I've been using the truck because I didn't know if it was safe for you to ride on the bike until we knew if you were pregnant or not. So, yesterday I called my brother-in-law and asked him."

"Er . . . isn't your brother-in-law a veterinarian?" Gwen pointed out. "There are probably different rules for animals versus people." Although she was touched that he had put that much thought into watching over her. She had never felt as cared for as she did with him. He treated her like a fragile piece of glass, and instead of it being annoying, she found that she quite liked it. It was a nice change from the men in her past who didn't even open doors for her. She had felt like the man in most of those relationships.

Dominic tweaked her nose before dropping a kiss onto it. "Yes, smarty pants, but he's quite knowledgeable. Plus, his best friend is a . . . you know, a doctor who deals with women and their . . . issues, so he asked him to confirm."

Quirking a smile, Gwen couldn't resist teasing him. "What kind of 'issues' does this doctor handle exactly?"

She was utterly charmed to see his face flush as he began to stammer. "Well . . . I . . . you know—stuff below the belt, I guess."

Oh, this was just too good to stop, so acting deliber-

WATCH OVER ME   119

ately obtuse, Gwen wrinkled her nose and asked, "Below the belt? You mean a woman's legs or feet?"

Her confident, alpha male's face was now full-on flaming as he struggled to find the words. "No, babe, like your private business." He pointed to the area between her legs before looking quickly away.

"Ohhh, you mean my vagina!" Popping a hand to her forehead dramatically, she said, "Duh, I'm slow today."

He studied her for a moment, seeming to comprehend that he'd been played. Prowling toward her, he shook his head, saying, "Oh, I don't think you're slow at all, baby. I believe you were having a blast yanking my chain, weren't you?"

Shaking with laughter, Gwen took a step back for every one he took forward. "Of course not, honey, I just didn't know what you were talking about. I'd never try to intentionally embarrass you, now would I?" As she suddenly sprinted down the hallway, she yelled over her shoulder, "Vagina, vagina, vagina!"

She gave a squeal of surprise when he swung her up into his arms inside her bedroom door. He turned to absorb the impact of their fall as they tumbled onto her disheveled bedcovers. She felt his chest move against her head as he rumbled with laughter. "You're a little minx this morning, aren't you?" he said against the top of her head.

She lifted her head to give him a lopsided grin. "Aw, come on. You've been below my belt quite a few times now. I can't believe you'd have a hard time talking about a female body part. You seem to know your way around them very well." Instead of responding to her teasing, his hands began to roam her body. He pushed inside the elastic band of her sleep shorts, palming her ass and kneading it. The skin-on-skin contact had her quickly squirming against him. Her moan was swallowed by his mouth as he crushed his lips to hers.

Gwen was busy trying to unbuckle his belt to release the bulge that was driving her crazy when Dominic removed his hands from her shorts and clamped them onto her wrists. "No, no, baby, that's not part of your birthday surprise. If you're a good girl, I'll let you unwrap that present later, though. Right now we need to get going." He sat up, pulling her with him. "Now, go dress that gorgeous body of yours in what I brought you."

Gwen let out a huff of frustration as she stood. Scowling, she said, "Do we have to be somewhere at a certain time or something?"

Dominic left the room, only to return with the clothing he had bought for her. "Nope, we aren't on a set schedule for today. We'll just relax and enjoy ourselves."

She looked from the bed to the front of his jeans where the evidence of his arousal was still pressing against his zipper. "Oookayyy." Pointing to the bed, she snapped, "Well, if that's the case, then why can't we finish what we started there?"

Dominic bit his lip as if trying to keep from smiling. "Are you pouting because I'm not fucking you?" Dammit, Gwen wanted to stomp her feet. He had managed to challenge her with his last sentence, and there was no way she was begging him. Everyone knew that women had more self-control than men did when it came to sex. No matter how horny she was at this moment, she would be damned if she would give him the pleasure of knowing it. *Game on, Mr. Brady . . . game on.*

Grabbing the clothing he was holding, she sashayed toward the bathroom making sure she put more swing in her hips than usual. If his quick intake of breath was any indication, he had noticed it. She shut the door behind her with a soft click and then locked it for good measure. She wasn't sure if she was trying to keep him out or her in.

She took a quick shower—cold—and then quickly dried her hair before realizing that she would need to go back into the bedroom for a bra and panties. Unless . . . did she dare to go bare today, just to torture him? It might take a while for him to clue in to her lack of panties, but going braless would be readily apparently in the thin tank top. She could always keep her jacket on if they stopped anywhere in public. She stood there trying to decide until he pounded on the door, hurrying her along. With an evil grin, she pulled the jeans on, marveling at how soft they were and how well they fit. She figured he had to have looked through her clothes to know the correct size. Men were usually completely off in the guessing department on women's sizes in one extreme direction or the other.

Of course, as she had suspected, the top was very form fitting and about a size too small. Probably on purpose since the pants were perfect. The jacket as well could have been tailor-made for her. The rich, buttery leather was as comfortable as wearing an old bathrobe, but way more stylish. The man did have good taste. She knew without even guessing that the boots would fit as well. Dominic wasn't a man to leave much to chance.

Gwen stood studying her reflection in the mirror. It wasn't a style that she was used to, but she had to admit that she looked good—sexy even. Her breasts had never looked as impressive as they did now pressing against the too-small top. One glance was all it would take for him to know that she wasn't wearing a bra. Her nipples were practically shouting, "check me out!"

She pulled her hair back into a ponytail to keep it out of her face, and then she was ready. She'd ridden a motorcycle once before, but that had been back in college. She was excited by the thought of sharing something with Dominic that she knew he loved. And having him between her legs wasn't exactly a hardship, either. Maybe the vibrations from the bike would give her some relief from the slow burn that she'd been experiencing since the moment he had shown up looking so damn sexy.

Gwen debated leaving the jacket off so that Dominic would notice her braless state but decided it would be more fun to spring the girls on him later.

He was patiently waiting on her sofa when she stepped into the living room. She walked in front of him and did a slow twirl. When she was facing him again, he swallowed audibly before getting slowly to his feet. "How do I look?" she asked, even though the answer was written all over his face. It seemed that Dominic liked her in leather. He reached out to pull her to him, and she sidestepped him, walking toward the door. "No, no, none of that, baby. We need to hit the road." She wanted to burst out laughing as she repeated his earlier words to him. He gave her a strained smile in return, and then attempted to discreetly adjust himself as they walked out the door. His eyes were glued to her ass, and Gwen couldn't help but think that one man's big butt was another man's nirvana.

When they reached his gleaming Harley, he took a few moments to go over the basics of riding before handing her a helmet. She grimaced at it, knowing that her sexy factor was going to go down a few levels with the hat hair she would soon be sporting. Dominic chucked her chin, saying, "I'm sorry, baby, but I won't take chances with your safety. I need for you to wear it."

Gwen did something she rarely did after that. She stood on her tiptoes and pressed a kiss to his mouth. He was just so darn cute in his concern for her. "Okay," she whispered as she pulled back. He looked thrilled at her show of affection, that she had taken the lead, and she vowed to do it more today.

He threw his leg over the bike and settled on the seat. He motioned for her to do the same. She hadn't taken the weight of her new boots into account, though. As she held on to his arm to get on the bike, her leg went wide when she tried to put it over and she kicked him in the side. He let out a pained grunt, but simply said, "Easy, babe, you'll hurt yourself." The poor man was entirely too nice for his own good. She could probably kick him in the balls and he would warn her about breaking a toe.

"Whoops, sorry," she murmured, glad that he couldn't see the blush that she knew was on her cheeks. She had lost a few more sexy points with that less than graceful move. Luckily, she still had her unfettered breasts to bring him back around.

Soon, they were coasting through the streets of Myrtle Beach. Gwen relaxed her death grip on Dominic as she got more comfortable with the feel of the bike. Having him nestled between her thighs had been a little distracting at first, but now she was able to enjoy the wind in her hair and the freedom of the road. They hadn't been riding for long when he slowed to make a turn. She looked around in interest and was surprised by what she saw. When he parked the bike in a busy lot, she hugged him excitedly. "We're going to the zoo?" God, she couldn't remember the last time she had been. She had tried to take Maddy and Megan, but they always begged for Chuck E. Cheese instead.

He turned in his seat, looking at her over his shoulder. "Yeah, is this okay with you?"

"Oh, yes! This is wonderful." She laughed. "I can't believe you thought of it."

Dominic got off the bike and helped her up before answering. "I was just here last week. They're interested in hiring us to replace their current security company. There's also a park and some nature trails. I hoped it might be something you'd like."

"Thank you," she beamed. "I haven't been to the zoo since I was in college."

Dominic stored their helmets before clasping her hand in his. "I take my nephews almost every time I visit." Looking amused, he added, "I think the zoo there is about ready to pay me never to bring them back again. Last time we were there, they had the monkeys all pissed off by trying to impersonate the sounds that they made. I thought we were going to get kicked out."

Gwen laughed, imagining the scene he had described. It sounded like the perfect day to her. "I'm afraid things weren't that crazy when I went. My sister got me a yearly membership for my birthday because I liked spending the day there studying when I was in school. It might not sound ideal, but I would find a bench in one of the quieter areas and spread my books out. It was much better than sitting in a dark corner of the library for hours."

Dominic stopped to purchase their tickets before asking, "Where did you go to school?"

Snuggling into his side as he dropped his arm around her, Gwen said, "I went to the University of South Carolina." Pointing to her chest, she added, "You've got a loyal Gamecock fan right here. Hey, how about you? Did you go to college or straight into the military?"

Pulling her close as they walked toward a bird exhibit, Dominic said ruefully, "I was fully educated by Uncle Sam. It's what I call a degree in life."

They stopped for a few moments to laugh at the parrots before Gwen asked softly, "Was it hard? Your time in the Marines?"

He was quiet for so long, she was starting to wonder if he'd heard her. Then he began speaking slowly as if searching for the right words. "It was—tough some days. It taught me the true meaning of unity and trust because I would have died to save a brother or a sister and I know that they would have also, without thought. We were a family, and as such, there were days you would want to choke one another and would give anything for just some peace. But none of that mattered when we were on patrol. Then we just watched our partner's back no matter what." His voice thickened as he continued. "As careful as we were, we still lost people, and that's something you never forget. I considered being career military, but when Mac and the others left, I just didn't have it in me to stay. I missed my family, and I needed a change."

Running her hand soothingly up and down his back, Gwen said, "So, here you are."

"That's right," he agreed, "and I can't think of anywhere else I'd rather be."

"Me, either." Thinking they needed to change the subject to something lighter, she stepped out of his arms and grabbed his hand. "If I don't see those penguins now, I'm just going to freak out!"

Dominic's face, which had been so somber a minute earlier, now carried an easy smile. "Well, we certainly can't have that. And it's funny you should mention that because it's one of the surprises I have for you."

Gwen had jumped up and down before she caught herself. Yikes, she must look like a sight, bouncing bra-less in a zoo full of children. When she glanced down, she was grateful to see her jacket still covering enough to keep her PG-rated. "What is it?" She tugged on his hand as he looked at her indulgently.

He checked his watch before answering. "In about fifteen minutes, we have an appointment to help feed the penguins." When she could only stare at him in shock, he added, "That means you get your own bucket of fish."

Squealing loud enough to pop a few nearby eardrums, Gwen launched herself into his arms, wrapping her arms around his neck and her legs around his waist. He staggered for a moment from her surprise attack before wrapping his arms around her and pulling her even closer. "I can't believe that," she shrieked. Her heavy boots started to lose purchase, and she would have slipped down if not for his hands tightening on her hips and holding her steady.

"Me thinks my baby likes," he teased as he dropped a kiss on her upturned mouth before putting her gently onto her feet. "If I'd known it was this easy to impress you, I'd have had you here months ago."

Gwen gave him a skeptical look. "I don't know what my response would have been had you shown up on my doorstep offering to show me some penguins."

Leering, he asked wolfishly, "How about if I'd asked to see your monkey instead?"

Biting her lip to hold in her laughter, she swatted his arm before taking it and pulling him forward. "Come on, pervert, I don't want to be late." Suddenly, she halted in her tracks and looked around. When she saw that no one was near, she stopped a few inches from his body and pulled her jacket open. He looked confused for a moment before he zeroed in on her taut nipples pushing against the thin material of the tank top. "As a special thank-you for this trip, I might show you my monkey later . . ." Pulling her jacket closed, she took off, walking quickly to the penguin habitat. Dominic was still standing where she had left him, looking like a man battling for control when she turned back. When she waved and motioned him forward, he narrowed his eyes at her and put his hands in his jean pockets. She figured he was trying to make some more room in his boxers as discreetly as possible. "Problem, honey?" she teased as he reached where she was standing.

Through clenched teeth, he growled, "Not at all, baby. Of course, you might have a problem tonight when I extract my revenge upon you."

Doing her best to look innocent, she asked, "What do you mean?" When he pointed to her chest, she gave what she hoped was a dumb look. "But you didn't buy me a bra—or panties. You told me to put on what was in the bag. Did I miss something?"

The poor man flinched before asking in a strained voice, "You aren't wearing panties, either?"

She gave up all pretenses and just smirked. "Nope, afraid not. I guess I follow directions too well. You should have specified that I needed to include my own undergarments along with the clothes you supplied."

Dominic put his hand on her neck, probably resisting the urge to strangle her. "At any other time, this would be like Christmas come early. Unfortunately, having to walk around in a zoo full of kids with a painful erection seems wrong on many levels."

Gwen slid her arms under his jacket and wrapped them around his waist. "Awww, I'll keep everything covered up. You won't even know."

"Oh, I'll know," he promised as he squeezed her tight before releasing her. "Let's go feed some damn penguins. I need a change of focus fast."

Dominic bit back a smile as Gwen waved good-bye to Max and Sam. When she had decided that morning to go braless, she probably hadn't reckoned on going to the zoo and having a very hands-on session of feeding penguins. She had sent his blood pressure through the roof earlier by flashing him a view of her braless breasts in a tight tank top and adding the tidbit that she wasn't wearing panties. His cock had gone into overdrive and he'd been ready to find a secluded corner and have his way with her.

She had thought his reaction was hysterical, but as they say, paybacks were a bitch, and she got hers fairly soon after that. She had looked a bit uncomfortable when she had discovered that there were two twenty-something-year-old men who would be showing them around the penguin habitat. Dominic had grinned when she'd pulled her jacket closer around her body in an attempt to cover her breasts. Soon after that, Mark told them that it could get messy during feeding time so they should remove their jackets and pull on one of the smocks located nearby.

Dominic had made a big production of taking off his coat and then all eyes turned to Gwen as she stood there, shifting nervously. "Hurry up, babe, so we can get started," he'd called to her. Her eyes had shot daggers at him before she stiffened her spine and took her jacket off. His jaw had dropped because truthfully, he hadn't expected that. He figured she'd make up some excuse about being cold. That laugh was on him because Max and Sam couldn't stop staring at her chest. Damn, why had he thought it was a good idea to buy a shirt that he knew was too small?

She had taken her time putting the smock on and by the time she was finished, all three of the men in the room were sweating profusely. After that little show of defiance, though, she'd folded. Max and Sam had fawned all over her, and she'd been uncomfortable with their attention. Hell, it had started to get under his skin as well after a while. He just knew the little horny bastards were plotting ways to stage an impromptu wet T-shirt contest with Gwen as the sole contestant. Maybe there hadn't been too much payback, after all, because he'd ended up suffering as much or more than she had. Luckily, feeding the penguins had almost been enough to make up for it.

When she reached him, he took her hand and led her toward the park. "Please tell me that you didn't give them your autograph or phone number."

She blushed adorably, before pulling her jacket close. "Ugh . . . no. I think Sam was working up the nerve to ask, though. They're not exactly kids; haven't they seen a woman's breasts before?"

"Not like yours," Dominic teased. "I get a little crazy myself when I look at them." Gwen laughed softly beside him as they walked toward a crowded deli. He had already arranged earlier for a picnic lunch so they were able to bypass the bulk of the line. He carried their food toward a quiet, grassy spot under a big tree, and they settled there.

When they were finished with their sandwiches, he leaned back against the tree trunk and motioned for her to sit between his legs. He exhaled in contentment when her back met his chest and he curved his arms loosely around her. "This is nice," she sighed, seeming to melt against him.

"It is," he agreed, thinking that this had been one of the best days he'd spent in a while. Having sex with Gwen was amazing, but just spending leisure time with her also felt so damned right. "So," he added, "I know you went to college in South Carolina and that you have a sister who bought you a zoo membership but tell me more. Does your family live near here?"

Gwen stretched lazily against him and he tried to block out the fact that she wasn't wearing panties beneath her jeans. He wanted to enjoy this time with her without having his cock digging into her ass. There would be plenty of time for that later.

"My family lives in Columbia, which I'm sure you know is a couple of hours from here. My dad has his own landscaping business, and my mom handles his bookwork. My sister, Wendy, is married but has no children yet. She teaches the fifth grade and her husband, Peter, also works at the same school."

"Hmmm, I'm sensing a pattern here," Dominic mused. "If you follow in your family's footsteps, you'll be marrying someone that you work with."

He had felt her tense against him for a split second before she relaxed. "Well, my immediate supervisor is kinda cute." Now he was the one tensing until she added, "I wonder how he feels about having two wives."

As she giggled against him, he started tickling her, which led to other things . . . Before he knew it, she was lying under him, and he was sipping from her plump lips. Things were beginning to get out of hand when he heard a voice that was as effective as a cold shower. "Mommy, is he putting a baby in Gwen's tummy?"

He jerked away from Gwen and sprang to his feet so quickly that he overbalanced and crashed backward. "Holy fu— fudge," he corrected at the last moment as he looked up into the curious eyes of Maddy, Megan, and Shannon.

While they were staring at him, Gwen made her way to her feet, zipping her jacket discreetly. "Hey, guys, what are you doing here?"

"Mommy said she needed to get out of the house before she tore all of her hair out," Maddy said matter-of-factly.

Megan fingered her own hair before looking at Gwen in confusion. "Why would she want to pull her hair out? Do you think it's because Cameron keeps playing with it?"

When the adults looked around awkwardly without answering, Maddy spoke up. "I think that it's 'cause he made her scream last night. I was in my bed and she yelled 'don't stop.' He must not have listened the first time, though, because she kept saying it. Doesn't he know that Mommy doesn't like to repeat herself?"

"Oh, my God," Shannon moaned, looking horrified. "Maddy!"

Gwen walked over to put her arm around a rattled Shannon. Dominic heard her asking the other woman under her breath, "Who is Cameron?"

As Maddy and Megan walked a few feet away to chase a butterfly, Shannon said, "Cameron is a doctor I work with. We've been having dinner together some nights at work, and he came over last night. I should never have—I thought the girls were asleep."

Dominic was trying hard not to listen to the conversation between the two women. He knew Shannon was probably embarrassed enough by now. When he felt a tug on his jacket he looked down to find Maddy staring up at him. "Do you play with Gwen's hair, too?"

The question was innocent enough, but he knew this was a train heading off the tracks. He should have run when he had the chance. "Er . . . sure. There's nothing wrong with that."

Maddy, ever persistent, continued her interrogation. "Is that why you were lying on top of her? Did you have to get close 'cause you thought she had something in her hair?" Shit, if this kid didn't grow up to be a lawyer, she was missing her true calling.

He had no idea that Megan had been following their conversation until she suddenly popped up next to him, saying, "I bet she's got lice. Caroline's little brother, Bastard, had that. It's when you have bugs crawling around in your hair and you gotta get a special brush and shampoo to get them out."

Dominic was trying very hard not to laugh. Surely, there wasn't a kid named Bastard out there. "I don't think Gwen has lice," he tried to assure the girls. "She was just cold, and I was warming her up." Maybe it wasn't a great excuse, but that's the best he could come up with on the fly.

Wrinkling her nose, Megan asked, "Are you sure? 'Cause Bastard didn't know he had bugs, but he couldn't stop itching."

Gwen's burst of laughter clued him into the fact that she'd overheard Megan's statement. Shannon looked at her daughter, shaking her head. "Megan, I've told you that his name is Baxter."

"No, I think it's Bastard, Mommy," Maddy added, "just like Daddy's other name."

Dominic tried, he really did, but he couldn't keep it in any longer. He took a few steps away and bent over laughing. These girls were all kinds of crazy, and it should scare the hell out of him to think that he could have one anytime soon. Megan poked him in the side and asked, "Do you gotta go potty? The bathroom's over there."

After that, Shannon was more than ready to get the girls out of there before they embarrassed her any further. Dominic thought he'd heard it all from his nephews, but Megan and Maddy could teach them a few things. God help the world if those four ever got together. Gwen walked up to him as he stood grinning and slid an arm around his waist. "Is it wrong that I'm still a little turned on from earlier?" she whispered against his neck.

He felt his cock stirring back to life at her question. He would have thought that the girls had killed any chance of a hard-on for hours, if not days, but it seemed that it took only a few words from her to undo the recent buzzkill. "Maybe, but it appears that I've got some work to do since Cameron had your neighbor screaming last night. I refuse to be outdone. When we get home, I'm going to need to seduce you until you scream. Don't be afraid to be creative, either. 'Don't stop' has already been done. I'm thinking of the words harder, harder, and something about me being so big. The good doctor's probably never heard anything like that."

Gwen giggled against his chest, then almost made him swoon when she lowered her voice to a sexy growl and purred, "Oh God, Dominic, harder—harder. Oh baby, you're sooo big. Yes . . . oh . . . yesss!"

Using her as a cover, Dominic adjusted himself for the second time since arriving at the zoo. This so wasn't the place for that. "I can't believe you did that to me again," he growled into her ear. "I'm really regretting riding the bike today." Putting an arm around her, he began guiding her toward the exit. "We've got to get out of here before one or both of us is arrested, or even worse, Megan and Maddy return and ask me if I have a squirrel in my pants." When she started laughing again, he said, "If we run into them, I'm taking your jacket off and then you can explain why your boobies are sticking out." Her laugh turned to a nervous chuckle as she zipped the leather jacket up farther. "That's right, baby. If I go down, you follow closely behind."

"You're not scaring me," she assured him, but her pace quickened to where he was almost the one running to keep up with her. When they reached his bike, she settled behind him as if they'd been riding together for years.

"Anywhere you need to stop?" he asked, although he desperately hoped the answer was no.

"Nope, home please—and don't waste any time." He said a silent prayer of thanks and took off through the streets. He wanted nothing more than to break all the speed limits to get home faster, but he'd never risk her safety.

When they made it home, he pulled her toward his apartment without asking. He couldn't wait any longer or risk Gwen not having condoms. He'd bought a new box yesterday, and they were still sitting in a bag on the living room table. Obviously, he didn't entertain much. As soon as they walked through the door, he shut it behind them and started removing his clothes. "This is gonna be fast, baby. I need you naked—now." Her mouth fell open as he began unbuckling his jeans. He had to give her credit because she recovered quickly and had her boots and jacket off in the blink of an eye. It would be amazing if they could spend a night in bed together just touching and discovering, but there was always the need to take the edge off first. He wanted her too badly to go slow.

Soon, she was naked and attempting to cover her breasts with her arms. "Where . . . ?"

His cock bobbed stiffly against his stomach as he considered her question. "Over the arm of the couch," he instructed. His obsession with her ass was something he couldn't control. His hands wanted to be on it every second they were together. Strange he had made it to his thirties without ever knowing he was an ass man. He had always thought his interests in the female body were pretty evenly distributed until Gwen. He loved her body in general, but her ass held a special place in his heart.

He grabbed a condom off the nearby table and quickly sheathed himself. Gwen had gotten into the position that he'd requested, and her glorious backside was taunting him. He stepped between her spread thighs and dropped a hand onto one of her firm globes. "Dominic—please," she begged as she pushed against his hand. He parted her gently until he could see her glistening pink slit pulsing for him. He ran a finger through the slick heat, spreading her juices from end to end. "I need you inside me," she hissed as he continued to tease her.

In answer to her plea, he drove his middle finger into her channel, feeling her ripple around him. "Is this what you want, baby?" he teased, as he worked his finger in and out of her slowly.

"No," she whimpered, although her hips circled urgently.

He was fast losing control but tried to hold on to torment them both a while longer. "Then what do you want?" Adding another finger, he asked, "Is this it?"

"No!" she snapped, although her breathing had

quickened along with her movements. He knew she was getting close, and he was selfish enough to want her first orgasm of the evening to be on his dick. "I want you-your cock inside of me . . . please."

Her need struck a match inside of him, and he had barely removed his fingers before his cock was pushing inside of her. They both moaned as this position made her impossibly tight. He took his first few thrusts slowly, letting her adjust to his intrusion before he began moving in earnest. He used a hand on each of her ass cheeks to keep her parted, affording him a view that he could barely tear his eyes from. His cock glistened as it moved smoothly in and out of her sex. "You look and feel so amazing," he gasped out as his pace quickened.

"Dom—harder!" she yelled, almost making him blow. "You're so hard—so big—and hard," she said with something between a wheeze and a shout.

What little control he had left was gone as he raised her hips to meet him. His balls smacked against her ass with each thrust until he felt her clenching and releasing around him. He was helpless to stop her orgasm from triggering his own. His body released until he couldn't imagine having anything left inside of him. "Damn, I think your ass has supernatural powers or something," he mused against her damp back.

"What?" she asked as she tried to turn her head to look at him.

Kissing the soft skin between her shoulder blades he said, "I'm serious, babe. I lose my freaking mind when I get my hands on your behind."

She sounded a little nervous when she asked, "Do you have some kind of anal fantasy or something?"

Dominic chuckled as he pulled his heavy weight from hers. As she stood, he drew her into the loose circle of his arms. "Babe, I hate to break this to you, but every man has some kind of fantasy about that, whether he'll admit it or not. It's just that caveman desire to own all of you. Add to that the fact that it's so close to the pleasure pool in front of it, and hell, it's just a natural thing."

Resting her head against his chest, she asked curiously, "Have you ever—done that before?"

He seriously wished he had kept his mouth shut now. In his experience, no good had ever come out of discussing past sexual encounters. He didn't want to brush off a direct question, though, so he just simply said, "Yes," and hoped she'd leave it at that.

Instead, she fired back a question immediately. "With more than one woman? I mean, was it just with one person, or were there others?"

Well fuck, he really needed to stop with the chattiness after sex. This whole awkward conversation could have been avoided if he hadn't mentioned his ass hang-up. She didn't sound upset, though, still just curious, which he could live with.

"There were others through the years—but not everyone I dated," he added hastily least she think that he was only interested in that. If she was never comfortable with anal sex, then that was fine with him. She had more than enough to keep him satisfied.

"So—you want to do that—with me?" she asked,

starting to sound nervous. What he wanted to do was run away from this conversation like a coward, but he was screwed now. He'd let it go on too long.

Sighing, he just went the honest route and hoped he didn't scare the hell out of her. "Babe, of course I'd like to, but that doesn't mean that I need it. If you're ever curious and feel that it's something you want, then let me know. Otherwise, it's off the table. I'd never try to force that on you because not everyone enjoys it. You set the boundaries here, Gwen. I have nothing but respect for you, and if you're not comfortable, then neither of us would enjoy it. I own your pleasure, baby, and you own mine."

When she sagged against him, he knew he'd given her the answer she needed to hear. "I—thank you. No one has really cared about my—needs before."

Dominic felt his hair standing on end at the thoughts of her with another man. He led her into his bathroom for a shower before commenting on her last statement. "Honey, anyone who could neglect you isn't a man. If your needs weren't being met, and he didn't care, then he never deserved you to start with. I lose my mind when you're near. If I didn't make you come, the experience would fall flat for me. I need your orgasms more than I need my own and I'd never stop until it happened."

In what seemed like a lightning change of mood, Gwen stepped away from him and turned on the shower. Giving him an impish grin, she said, "I'm going to need another of those orgasms you just promised me because I'm hopelessly turned on again."

Doing his best to sound annoyed, Dominic huffed

dramatically before he moved under the warm spray and extended a hand to her. "Woman, don't you ever get enough?" When she stepped into the shower and dropped to her knees to grip his rapidly hardening length, all thoughts scattered to the wind as he threaded his hands through her hair and gave himself over to the mind-numbing pleasure that only she seemed to invoke in him.

Chapter Nine

Gwen hit the SNOOZE button on the annoying and relentless alarm clock. She rolled over, seeking Dominic's warmth only to find the other side of her bed cold. Then she remembered him saying that he had to leave early for a trip to Charleston today. She must have been more tired than she realized because she hadn't woken up when he left.

He had gone into the office for a few hours yesterday morning as was his usual routine and then they'd spent the day on the beach just being lazy. It had been a perfect weekend and she'd been sad to see it end. She was on the verge of dozing off when her alarm went off once again. She grudgingly left the warmth of her bed and stumbled into the bathroom to start the shower.

When she stripped her clothing off and tossed it on top of her already full laundry hamper, something caught her eye. Her heart pounded when she saw some spotting on her sleep shorts. Didn't she have a few days until her period was due? She was normally always a few days late and rarely ever early. She dropped down onto the closed seat of her toilet and dropped her head in her hands. It seemed so silly that she was upset when she should be only relieved. She wasn't ready for a baby, and she doubted that Dominic was either.

So why then did she feel such a crushing wave of sorrow rising up to choke her? She had a nagging feeling that it was very little to do with not being pregnant and a lot to do with her fear of losing Dominic. He seemed to genuinely enjoy being with her and the sex, well, it was nothing short of earth-shattering. But what if he had just been making the most of their time together while waiting to see if he was going to be a father? Gwen didn't think she could handle him telling her something along the lines of, "It's been great. I'll call you sometime." Despite her misgivings, she had allowed herself to become attached to him. How could she not—he was every woman's dream.

Unlike other men she had dated, she'd never once caught Dominic looking at another woman when they were together. Even on the beach yesterday, when scores of women walked by in skimpy bikinis, he'd acted as if no one existed but her. Then there were all of the little things he did each day to make her feel special. The morning coffee delivery, the texts checking to see how her day was going, his Googling of baby information to see what was and was not safe for her to do, and of course, the water class that he had taken a few more times in the morning with her. A sob escaped her throat as she imagined all of that going away as if it had never existed.

He was going to be gone until late this evening so she had a small reprieve from talking to him, and she needed every minute. She wasn't sure what his reaction would be if she broke down crying when he would probably be swooning in relief. She had to keep it together and not look like some clingy basket case. They were mature adults and if he moved on, then she would have to accept it. After all, she'd done it before—many times. The problem was that she had allowed herself to care for Dominic more than she had other men whom she had dated much longer.

Wiping her eyes, she got into the shower with a heavy heart and then dressed with much less care than usual for work. Actually, that was being kind. Her slacks were wrinkled, her hair a disheveled mess slung in a lopsided ponytail, and to top it off, she hadn't realized until she reached work that she had put on her tennis shoes instead of dress shoes. Oh well, she could hide behind her desk and no one would be any the wiser, or so she thought.

That hope was shot-to-hell when she saw Mia leaning against the door of her office, looking more polished than usual. Without preamble, the other woman looked at her in surprise before asking, "What in the hell happened to you?"

Gwen looked down quickly and noticed that her blouse was hanging out of her slacks, except for one small corner. Without answering, she quickly opened her door and flipped on the lights before running for the cover of her desk. Mia moved into the office as well and shut the door behind her. Gwen was surprised to find herself blurting out, "My period is coming early."

Mia looked momentarily confused before asking, "Isn't that good news?"

"Yes." Gwen sniffed as she dropped her head to her desk.

She felt a hand on her shoulder before Mia asked tentatively, "Did you want a baby, after all, Gwen, or is something else going on? Are things okay with Dominic?"

To her horror, tears began falling as she sobbed, "Fine—for now . . ."

Mia stuffed a tissue in her hand, giving her a minute to collect herself before continuing. "Honey, I'm not sure I'm following you. Tell me what's got you this upset. If Dominic has done something, I'll go down and put these four-inch heels to good use. His ass will never be the same again."

Gwen gave a choked laugh, grateful for Mia's attempt at humor. Of course, she was pretty certain that the other woman wasn't making empty threats either. She could easily see her nailing Dominic to the wall. Wiping her nose, she took a couple of deep breaths, and then settled back into her seat. "I know this is going to sound crazy," she began, "but I started spotting this morning and instead of being relieved, all I could think was that now I'll lose Dominic."

Mia took her hand, and then grimaced as she ended up with a wad of wet Kleenex. "Has he said something to lead you to believe that your relationship will be over if you aren't pregnant?"

Shaking her head, Gwen said, "What relationship? We've only been doing whatever we're doing for a couple of weeks, and that all began because of a bottle of wine and a broken condom."

"That's total bullshit," Mia scolded. "The man wouldn't have had you on every surface in his apartment if he wasn't attracted to you. And he sure wouldn't be spending every available moment with you since then just to find out if you are pregnant or not. He could have just as easily told you to let him know. You've been the happiest that I've ever seen you since that night and the man who I've witnessed bringing you coffee and speaking to you in a restaurant didn't look like someone desperate to run. Has he even asked you when you're taking a pregnancy test?"

"No," Gwen admitted, "he hasn't mentioned it."

"Well, there you go." Mia smiled. "If he was so desperate to end things, he'd be counting the moments until he could break ties with you. Has your period officially started?"

"There was just that spotting this morning. I'm sure it's coming."

"Why don't you buy a pregnancy test so you'll know?" Mia suggested. "Then you can go ahead and tell him and you can stop torturing yourself."

"I will," Gwen agreed. "I just need a day to get myself together. I'm glad Dominic's traveling on business today because I'd probably make a fool out of myself otherwise."

With an impish grin, Mia said, "You, my dear, need a distraction. I'm going to lunch with Suzy and a few of her friends, and I want you to come with me."

"No," Gwen shook her head frantically. "I can't do that. Isn't Ava friends with Suzy?"

"I'll check to make sure she's not coming first," Mia

conceded. "If I get the all clear, you're coming. They're a lot of fun. Crystal's probably going since her sister Ella will be there."

Gwen looked down at her clothing before looking back at Mia. "I can't go like this. I look like a mess. I even wore the wrong damn shoes."

Mia looked her up and down before saying, "I'll come to your office a few minutes early and we'll get you all spiffed up. I've got an extra pair of shoes in my desk."

Gwen could only imagine what kind of shoes those were, but teetering around in impossibly high heels had to be better than the pair of New Balance shoes she had mistakenly picked to wear with her dress clothes. She knew by the determined set of her friend's shoulders that it was useless to argue. Nothing short of divine intervention was going to get her out of lunch today. "All right," she conceded, "but you better have a miracle in your makeup bag, because I'm going to need it."

True to her word, Mia had transformed her into someone more presentable in less than fifteen minutes. But the shoes that Mia had lent her were about a size too small, so she was grateful when they reached the restaurant. Her toes had lost feeling shortly after she had squeezed them into the too tight leather pumps. Sometimes you had to suffer for fashion and this was one of those times.

When they walked through the door, Crystal ran over, seeming surprised, but happy that Gwen had come along. "You came! When Mia told me that you'd agreed to our group lunch, I didn't think you'd show up." Lowering her voice, Crystal added, "Ava's not coming, I already double-checked that."

Gwen felt herself relax, glad for the confirmation from Crystal. After her lunch with Ava, she didn't harbor any bad feelings toward her, but it still felt uncomfortable. Plus, these were Ava's friends and Gwen didn't want to barge in on that. "That's good," she said under her breath as the three of them walked over to the four women waiting a few feet away. Gwen recognized Suzy Merimon and Claire Danvers immediately. Anyone who worked for Danvers had seen Suzy with her gorgeous husband, Gray Merimon. She was also willing to bet that many of the females at the office had been heartbroken when their CEO Jason Danvers had married his assistant Claire. Both men were powerful and gorgeous, but also approachable and friendly.

She had also seen Crystal's sister Ella and Suzy's sister Beth around the office, although she'd never formally met any of them. Ella was married to Ava's brother Declan, who had also served in the military with Dominic. Beth was married to Nick Merimon, who was the brother of Suzy's husband, Gray. It seemed that Gwen's family wasn't the only one who liked to live and work together.

Before the introductions could be made, the host announced that their table was ready. They all took a seat around a large, round table. Gwen was grateful to be sitting between Mia and Crystal until she realized that it put her directly across from Suzy and Claire. They both seemed friendly but curious.

When they had ordered their drinks, Mia cleared her

throat, saying, "Let me introduce you guys to Gwen." Pointing to each woman, she said, "This is Beth, Ella, Suzy, and Claire."

Everyone said an enthusiastic hello, allowing Gwen to relax even further until Suzy spoke up. "I'm really sorry about what happened with Mac. Sitting here with you now, I, for one, feel kind of like shit-on-a-shoe for not considering your feelings in the whole scheme of things." As all of the other women gave her guilty looks, Gwen found herself trying to swallow a lump the size of a robin's egg.

When no one added anything further as if waiting for her to speak, she finally cleared her throat and said, "I . . . um . . . don't really know how to take that." Under the table, Mia squeezed her knee in support. Gwen had no idea what she could possibly say to Suzy. She was certain that as friends, the other women had known about Ava's attempts to win Mac when she thought she was losing him to Gwen. Sitting here now as the woman scorned, she had two choices. She could tuck her tail between her legs, make an excuse, and leave, or she could show them that she was more than okay and didn't need anyone's pity. Before she knew it, she found herself saying, "I'm with Dominic now—we're sleeping together."

Every mouth around the table dropped as her words seemed to hover larger-than-life in the air. Even Crystal and Mia, who knew about her relationship with Dominic, seemed surprised. They'd probably never expected her to announce it so abruptly to near strangers. God, why had she done that? Wouldn't a smile of reassurance have been better than a summary of her love life? The silence was broken as Suzy started grinning. "Good for you, girl. That man has a body like a big ole tree that you just want to climb."

Claire started fanning herself before chiming in. "If any of you mention this to Jason, I'll swear you're lying, but I go the long way around the office sometimes just to walk past East Coast Security's door. Those guys are just so *hot*." When everyone stared at her in shock, she wagged her finger. "Don't you dare judge me. I've run into all of you at one time or another in the same area, and none of you have an office near there."

Looking demure and innocent, Ella said, "I just drop by sometimes to say hello to Declan's old military buddies."

Holding a hand over her mouth, Beth let out a cough that ended up sounding like "Bullshit!"

Suzy rolled her eyes, saying, "Oh, come on, there's nothing wrong with appreciating a fine piece of prime hottie. I guarantee our men do it. I'm more than happy with my hubby, but the day I stop noticing a hot guy is the day I give up on life."

Crystal shook her head, looking as if she was pouting. "But look at the men you're all married to or dating. I was married to a man who wore knee socks for years and had perpetually pale, white skin. If I'd have been married to a man who looked anything like yours, I'd have been so happy I would have never looked twice at another man."

Ella gave her sister a look of sympathy before saying, "You'll find your Mr. Perfect, and then you'll just be a married pervert like Suzy."

Instead of being offended, Suzy seemed to take Ella's statement as a compliment. "Ah, my little innocent one, you've come so far. It seems like only yesterday you were carrying around the big V-card and praying that Declan would punch it for you. Now, you're ogling other men and insulting your friends—honey, I couldn't be prouder."

Their conversation was interrupted by their server and they all placed their lunch orders. Beth, who had been one of the quieter ones so far, looked over at Gwen and asked, "So, Dominic, huh? Is he as good as he looks like he would be?"

Claire, who had just taken a drink of her tea, ended up spitting it out as she started coughing. "Beth— God," she groaned as she mopped up the mess in front of her.

"My sister was a bit blunt, but we would like to know," Suzy smirked as if not really expecting Gwen to answer.

Gwen, however, surprised herself yet again by saying, "He's unbelievable." Knowing her face was probably on fire, she added, "I never knew a man could go like that. He never seems to get tired or—lose interest."

Just then, a female voice behind them said, "I made it! Ava's a PMSing ball of female attitude this morning. Even out of the office she's still torturing me." The woman slipped into an extra chair at the table and looked around. "Okay, what'd I miss?"

Claire spoke up, running through the introductions again.

"Holy sexy ass," Emma groaned in Gwen's direction. "You're dating one of the GI Joes? The things those men do for cargo pants should be illegal."

Gwen was grateful when Suzy changed the subject by turning her attention to Beth. "Hey, sis, you remember Mia's boyfriend, Seth Jackson, don't you?"

Instead of looking embarrassed, Beth looked down at her watch and then held her hand out to Ella. Everyone at the table watched as Ella scowled before handing Beth ten dollars. Beth tucked the money in her wallet before looking at her sister. "I bet Ella ten bucks that you wouldn't make it twenty minutes without mentioning Seth."

"Thanks a lot, Suzy," Ella grumbled. "I didn't think you'd bring it up after all this time."

"All right, what am I missing here?" Emma asked when she finished ordering her drink.

Mia and Beth started laughing as if the conversation didn't bother them. Finally, Beth said, "I had gone out with Mia's boyfriend a few times before I married Nick and before Mia started dating Seth, of course. Our last date was a bit of a—disaster."

"Come on, spit it out," Crystal urged Beth to continue.

Beth rolled her eyes but said, "Well, most of you know that I was pregnant before Nick and I got married. Heck, it was a great big surprise that I was in serious denial over for a while." Giving her sister an evil grin, she added, "It all started when Nick and I had sex on Suzy's kitchen countertops. I think we slid all over the place—probably touched every available surface."

Everyone grinned as Suzy's face turned red before

she gave her sister a disgusted look. "You tramp," Suzy mumbled before motioning for Beth to continue.

"Anyway, before Nick came along, I had joined a dating service. I met Seth through it, and we went out a few times casually. After I had found out I was pregnant, I made another date with him just to prove to Nick that I wasn't ready to settle down." Shaking her head, Beth winced. "I know it sounds bad, but it was a confusing, hormonal time. Nick just happened to be at the restaurant where I met Seth, and he proceeded to tell him that he was living with me and that we were having a baby together. Seth didn't waste any time getting out of there. I actually have to give him credit for remaining polite even when his face showed that he was appalled."

"That's my man," Mia said happily. "He can hold it together no matter what the circumstances. And don't feel too bad, Beth. I managed to embarrass myself in the course of dating him as well. My meddling mother bought him for me at a bachelor auction!"

"No shit." Emma gave a thumbs-up, looking impressed. "Heck, I thought I was the only one who had to deal with crap like that from her mother. Mine tried to pimp me out all over our home state of Florida from the time I was eighteen. It was actually earlier than that, but it sounds kind of bad to use the words pimp and sixteen in a sentence, doesn't it?"

"What about now that you're with Brant?" Claire asked.

Twisting her lips into a wry smile, Emma answered, "Oh no, that man can do no wrong where my family is concerned. He could probably kick their cat and piss on the front door and they'd shove me aside while pulling him in and clapping him on the shoulder. My mother is thrilled that I've finally met a man who 'meets all of my needs.' "

"Ugh, tell me she doesn't mean sexually?" Crystal shuddered. "Our mom," she added, pointing to her sister, Ella, "pretends that we were born from Immaculate Conception and frankly that's one of her lies that I'm more than happy to believe."

Ella wrinkled her nose. "You'd all have been my age with the V-card as Suzy calls it if you'd lived with our mother. When she walked in on Declan and me in bed together while we were dating, I didn't think I'd ever recover."

"I'm surprised Declan was able to get it up again after that," Crystal added.

Looking like a woman well satisfied, Ella added, "He NEVER has a problem with that—and I mean never."

Gwen was so wrapped up in the conversation around the table that she jumped when their server put the pizzas that they had ordered on the table. She had been nervous about joining a bunch of strangers for lunch, but she couldn't remember the last time she'd had this much fun or felt such a kinship with a group of women. She loved how they spoke so freely as if they knew that no one at the table would betray their confidences. Even with her earlier worries about her relationship with Dominic, she felt lighter now. Not that she necessarily would, but she could see herself talking to any one of these women about her problems without being judged. She had a feeling that there were many unofficial therapy sessions held during the lunch hour. She had just taken a bite of her pizza when Suzy said, "Gwen, we all want your ass."

"Pardon?" she choked out around the food in her mouth.

Claire nodded her head, looking at her enviously. "I seriously envy your body. I don't know how to say this without sounding—weird—but you have the best backside."

"It's true," Beth added. "If I gain a pound, I just get a fat ass. I've never had that perfect, round Jennifer Lopez butt."

"I even got a tattoo on my lower back as a way to bring some attention to mine. I mean, it's there and all, but it doesn't stand out. I'm not sure why it matters to me though since no one but me sees it," Crystal mused.

"I like my butt okay," Emma added next. "I mean, it's nothing to write home about, but Brant seems to enjoy touching it—a lot."

"I've always been happy with mine, for the most part, until we became friends," Mia teased. "Now, when we're together, I can't stop looking at yours. I've even thought of asking you if I could touch it before, just too see how it felt, but I figured that might give you the wrong idea. I'm totally team penis."

"I'm team penis, too," Suzy tossed in, "but I stare at your ass whenever you're around. I mean, if you were in a room full of women with their boobs hanging out, you'd look wouldn't you? I keep trying to get Gray to admit that he checks out the size of other men's peckers when he's standing next to them at a urinal, but he claims that never happens. He says it's guy code that all eyes are to face forward." Winking, Suzy purred, "I'll tell you one thing, whoever is standing next to my man is going to leave that bathroom with a major case of envy."

"God, yes, mine, too," Gwen moaned, before slapping a hand over her mouth.

Crystal tossed her napkin and crossed her arms as she glared at Gwen. "So, it's big, and he knows what to do with it. You totally suck, and I'm also reconsidering this whole friendship thing with everyone at this table."

Suzy took a drink of her iced tea before zeroing in on Crystal. "Don't you worry, girl—we'll get you a big one of your own. Last time I checked, there was another GI Joe available."

"Gage is really cute, too," Ella jumped in. "Declan says he's a bit of a . . ."

"Man whore?" Emma chimed in. When everyone gaped at her, she shrugged, saying, "What can I say? Brant and I talk about everything."

When lunch was over, Gwen found herself doing something that she rarely did. She walked out of the restaurant first and grinned peacefully knowing that the ladies behind her were looking at her butt with envy. Yeah, what a difference a good group of friends could make.

"So, how long until you find out if Gwen has a bun in the oven?" Gage asked, as tactful as ever.

Dominic settled further into the passenger seat and rubbed his fatigued eyes. It had been a long day of overseeing the security setup at a new customer site. It was already almost midnight, and they had just left Charleston. He really just wanted to close his eyes and catch a nap, but he knew that along with being nosy, Gage was also trying to make conversation to stay awake. "I don't know," he finally answered. "She hasn't mentioned it lately."

"How long does it take to find out?" Gage asked, sounding as if he had no clue. To be truthful, Dom didn't know either. Like most men, other than maybe a doctor, he didn't know that much about how a woman's body worked.

"Hell, if I know," he admitted.

Dominic could hear the other man's brain working as he drove down the unusually quiet interstate road. "Well, if they have a period once a month, then it's probably less than that. How long since the first time you two slept together?"

Thinking back, Dominic replied, "Two or three weeks. She did say something about just having had her period so maybe another week, I guess, before she would know."

Gage grunted in answer before snapping his fingers. "Hey, what about that pregnancy detector thing that they advertise on television? It says you can find out five days early."

Shaking his head in amazement, Dominic said, "First off, put both of your hands on the wheel and watch where you're going, and second, why are you able to quote a pregnancy test commercial line for line? I turn the channel when shit like that comes on. No wonder you're always telling Mac and me to go buy tampons. I thought it was an insult, but you're probably an expert or something, aren't you?"

"Fuck you, Dom," Gage muttered sounding embarrassed. "For your information, I lost the remote to my television one night and was stuck watching commercials and all. You have no idea how many chick products they advertise during the *Victoria's Secret Fashion Show*. All I have to say is that women have a lot of problems to deal with. It's pads or tampons. Razors or some hair removal shit. Hormone pills for menopause, whatever the hell that is, and those damn split ends. And don't even get me started on the wrinkle cream. If they don't use that stuff night and day, apparently their skin will dry up like the Mojave Desert."

Dominic couldn't help but laugh. Gage sounded overwhelmed at what he had learned from one night of commercial watching. "You know, man, you're going to make someone a mighty fine wife someday," he teased.

As was usually the case, Gage chuckled good-naturedly before saying, "Laugh it up, big papa. I'm not the one wondering if I've got a baby on the way. You should have probably already been checking into this stuff. Don't you want to know as soon as possible? I mean what if Gwen thinks you just don't give a shit since you haven't asked her."

Shrugging his suddenly stiff shoulders, Dominic admitted, "Yeah, I guess I'd like to know. It's a big thing, but I'm not sitting around having a nervous breakdown over it every day, and I don't think Gwen is, either."

Gage sounded bemused when he asked, "You're not? I don't think I would have been able to focus on anything else, including more sex, until I knew for sure. I mean, how do you perform, wondering if the baby magic's already at work?"

"Baby magic?" Dominic choked out.

"Hell, yes." Gage removed one hand from the wheel long enough to throw some imaginary dust.

"You know," Dominic began, "if you say stuff like this around women, it's probably why none of them stays around for long."

"Trust me, there's no talk of babies when I'm with a woman," Gage smirked. "They mainly stick to one-syllable words like 'yes!'"

Despite his fatigue, Dominic found himself laughing along with Gage's crude comments. You had to admire a man who was that confident in his abilities between the sheets. After a few minutes, the conversation died down once again, and he pondered the other man's questions. He had been honest when he said that he hadn't asked Gwen when she would know if she was pregnant or not. Maybe a part of him was afraid of rocking the boat. Things had been going so well between them that he was afraid to do anything to change that.

Unlike Gage, he wouldn't freak out if she was pregnant. Sure, it would be a shock, even the possibility had taken some adjustment to get used to, but he'd never been one to run from a challenge. Now that he had been forced to think about it, he found that he did want to know one way or another. He wanted to have a normal relationship with Gwen without either of them stressing over what-ifs. He figured he was probably driving her crazy, trying to monitor what she ate and drank, and her activities . . . just in case.

Worse yet, could she possibly think that he was indifferent as Gage had suggested? That wasn't the case at all. He just didn't have any experience with trying to keep up with a woman's cycle. Hell, men weren't supposed to know stuff like that, were they? It was already completely weird that he and Gage had been discussing Gwen's period. He wanted to be supportive of his woman, but that made his balls shrivel just a little.

He'd never admit this to Gage, but maybe he needed to take one piece of his advice and ask Gwen about when she would be taking a test. If there was a remote possibility that she felt like he didn't care or wasn't interested, then he needed to show her that was not the case. Fuck, what was the world coming to when he was taking advice about women from a man who only exerted as much effort as was necessary to get into the next woman's panties? Mac was going to laugh his ass off about this one.

Chapter Ten

Gwen tried to hide her delight at seeing Dominic waiting for her in the parking garage of Danvers the next morning.

He walked toward her in all of his masculine hotness and opened her door before extending a hand and helping her out. "Morning, babe," he said in a voice that was still slightly sleep-roughened, and oh, so very sexy.

She went into his arms willingly as he pulled her close. The smell of his cologne had her snuggling into the curve of his neck and hoping he didn't catch her inhaling deeply. "Good morning," she finally managed to reply before he pulled back enough to kiss her. The contact was light since they were in a public place, but Gwen felt it all the way to the tips of her toes. "How was your trip?" She knew her voice came out in a high-pitched squeak, but as always, her body betrayed her any time that he was near.

Rubbing her back, Dominic said, "It was good. We got in around two this morning. Needless to say, I'm going to be running on fumes today."

"Poor baby," Gwen teased him gently as she took in the smudges under his eyes. "Didn't you have anyone to cover for you so that you could sleep in for a few hours this morning?"

"I'm fine, babe, just need a big cup of coffee. Plus, if I'd slept late, I would have missed seeing my girl this morning and that just wasn't acceptable to me."

They had just started walking through the parking lot when a hesitant voice behind them said, "Good morning." As they stopped and turned, Gwen felt herself instinctively stiffen as she recognized Ava. The other woman smiled warmly, but her fidgeting hands at her side gave her nervousness away.

"Hey there, Blondie," Dominic greeted her easily. Gwen knew by the quick look that he shot at her that he was afraid she was uncomfortable.

Determined to show him that she was okay, Gwen gave Ava a warm, answering smile before saying, "Good morning, Ava." Then taking everyone by surprise, including herself, she added, "Thank God for our lunch last week or this would be an insanely awkward moment, right?"

Ava's eyes had widened before laughter exploded from her. "I know, right! Like it wasn't bad enough there for the first minute with Dominic looking like he didn't know whether to stay or run."

Dominic looked down at Gwen in disbelief. "You had lunch with Ava last week?"

Nodding, Gwen said, "I did."

"We only pulled each other's hair once before things

turned civilized," Ava joked as Dominic continued to look stunned at their banter.

"Why didn't you tell me?" he asked, and then without waiting for Gwen to answer, he turned back to Ava. "Does Mac know?"

Ava looked a bit sheepish as she shook her head. "No, I haven't mentioned it to him. I know how strange men are about stuff like that. I mean, look at you, we didn't even date and you have that whole jerky feet thing happening."

Gwen looked down to see that he did indeed seem to be shifting nervously. "Don't worry," she patted his arm reassuringly. "Ava didn't say anything bad about you. Actually, she was pretty complimentary."

They had all begun walking toward the doors. As they stepped inside the building, Gwen had her second awkward moment of the morning and it was far worse than the first. Mac stood in the lobby speaking to a man wearing an East Coast Security uniform. Ava smiled brightly as her new husband's eyes landed on her. Mac grinned lazily at her before seeming to realize that Gwen and Dominic were standing just inches away. Gwen saw shock and discomfort flit quickly across his face before he turned to say a few parting words to the security guard. Gwen thought he probably needed a few seconds to regroup. She was going to excuse herself on the pretext of needing to get to her office early, when he returned as if nothing was out of the ordinary.

"Good morning, Gwen." He gave her a genuine smile before turning to Dominic. "Glad to see you made it back in one piece and hopefully without killing Gage."

"It was pretty close a few times," Dominic joked as he took Gwen's hand, clasping it firmly. She wasn't sure if he was trying to give Mac a message or attempting to reassure her, but she was glad for the show of support. They all stood for another five minutes, and she was surprised that the conversation flowed easily. Finally, Mac had to leave to take a call and Ava walked away with him. Dominic dropped a distracted kiss onto her lips and promised to bring her by some coffee in an hour.

When she stepped off the elevator, Crystal was waiting near her doorway with a Kleenex in her hand. Noting the other woman's puffy eyes, Gwen was certain that either her mother or her ex-husband had been at it again. "Hey, Crys," she said gently as she opened her door and motioned her friend inside. Shutting the door behind them, she asked, "What's going on?"

Crystal took one of the chairs in front of Gwen's desk and she perched on the other one. "Just the usual crap. My mom started bright and early this morning telling me what a big mistake I'd made by divorcing Bill. She assured me that he'd probably take me back if I really showed him how sorry I was and that I was willing to change to make him happy. Oh and agree to take his last name again. I had that changed back to Webber as soon as we divorced."

Gwen slumped back against her seat, rubbing her head. "You're kidding? She's completely taking his side?"

Sniffling, Crystal shook her head dejectedly. "Nope, there was more, but that's the gist of it. I'm a colossal disappointment to her. She thinks that I'm going through some rebellion. I swear I'm half-afraid that she will join forces with Bill and they will try to have me committed somewhere for temporary insanity because that's exactly what they both feel has happened. It just hasn't occurred to either of them that they might be the problem and not me."

Handing Crystal another Kleenex from her desk, Gwen asked, "Did you tell Ella yet?"

Crystal looked away but not before Gwen saw another tear trickle down her cheek. "No. Ella has too much going on in her life to worry about me." Gwen didn't know Crystal's sister that well, but from their interactions at lunch, she couldn't doubt that Ella loved her sister and would want to know that she was this upset.

"From what you've told me, Crys, Ella went through something similar when she began dating Declan. She, better than anyone, would understand what you're going through."

"I know she would," Crystal agreed, "but she has a new baby, a wonderful husband, and a life away from our mother. She served her time as the single daughter catching hell. Back then, I was the golden child because I went along with the program. It's shitty, but I admit to sitting back and letting Mom give Ella hell because I was just relieved that it wasn't me. But when Ella met Declan and refused to let Mom control her, it made me realize how unhappy I'd been for years. You would think that getting a divorce would prove that it's over with Bill, but I'm still living in turmoil that I can't seem to escape from."

"Oh, Crystal," Gwen murmured, taking the other woman's hand between her own. "I had no idea that things were this bad for you. I mean, I knew that your mother harassed you, but I thought it was more of a random thing."

Crystal gave her a watery smile full of misery. "Oh no, there's nothing random about it. I mean, I might go a few days between calls or e-mails, but a whole week never passes without some kind of speech about how I've made a fool out of her in front of her church or how disappointed Daddy is in me. Then there are the ones about 'poor Bill' who just doesn't understand why I left him when he gave me the world. I swear, Gwen, a few times I've even thought of just going back to him so she would leave me alone. It's not like I haven't been a Stepford wife before."

"Have you thought that you may have to completely cut your mother from your life until something changes?" Gwen asked hesitantly. She felt wrong about suggesting something so drastic to her friend, but it pissed her off that a mother would speak to her child in the way that she did. It wasn't as if Gwen's own parents were calling and professing their love every day, but they'd always been supportive of her choices, saying that even making mistakes was a part of life. In fact, she'd never appreciated them more than she did at this moment.

"I kept thinking that when enough time had passed, she'd accept that I wasn't going back to Bill. I've tried to show her when she visits that I like the life I have now. I've even tried to talk to Daddy about it when she wasn't around, but that's basically useless. He knows that she's wrong, but there is no way he's going to bring her full attention down onto him. He just says the same crap about 'you know how your mother is.' Well, duh, we all know how she is, but that doesn't excuse her."

"Honey, I think you need to talk to Ella," Gwen suggested. "You know that Mia and I are both here for you, but Ella is your sister. She knows your mother better than we do and might have some suggestions. She would also want to be there to support you in whatever decision you make—don't you think?"

Crystal wiped the moisture from her eyes, and Gwen was relieved to see that she looked better. "You're right," Crystal admitted. "She would want to know. She'll probably be really pissed that I haven't told her how bad it's gotten. She doesn't like being left out of the loop for her own good. Poor Declan has caught a lot of hell for trying to do that even though he meant well. My sister is the quiet, shy one, but when she's really angry, you had better run."

When Crystal stood, Gwen followed her lead. "Want to go down to the lobby for coffee before the day starts?" she asked, thinking she could surprise Dominic with a cup. Since she'd already run into Mac this morning, there wasn't much reason to keep avoiding the East Coast office. Dominic was always taking care of her and just this once, she'd like to give him a little of that back. She'd have to work through lunch to make up for her conversation with Crystal and her coffee delivery, but she was sure it would be worth it.

Dominic was on his way to pick up Gwen's coffee when he met Gage outside of the office. Looking down at his watch, he raised a brow at the other man. "Need a little extra sleep this morning or were you researching more chick products?"

"I knew that conversation was going to come back to bite me in the ass," Gage grumbled as he gave Dominic a dirty look. "No doubt you've already told Mac and anyone else in the vicinity all about it."

"Nope," Dominic smirked, "but the day's still young, my friend."

Shaking his head, Gage asked, "How are you so chirpy this morning? You couldn't have gotten any more sleep than I did. Ohhh, wait. Let me guess. You had a certain hot, little redhead to get you going this morning."

Dominic didn't bother telling him that he'd seen Gwen only when he got to the office. Torturing his friend was far too amusing. "Awww, what's the matter, buddy? No one working the corner near your house this morning?" Lowering his voice to make sure he wasn't overheard, he added, "I hope you're triple bagging it. They've been known to fall off before."

Dominic wanted to laugh when Gage unconsciously readjusted himself as if checking to make sure his dick was still there. Giving him an evil grin, Gage said, "So, did you ask Gwen when she'll know if she's pregnant? You know Kandi probably won't wait for you forever and you don't want to lose such a talented woman do you?"

Even though he wanted to cringe at the thought of the ex-stripper he'd gone out with for a while, he refused to give Gage the satisfaction. Instead, in a voice so sincere that he was proud of himself, he said, "She promised to give me a couple more weeks. She's it for me man, the woman of my dreams."

There was complete silence for all of twenty seconds as Gage stared him down before bursting into laughter. "Stop screwing with me before I've had my coffee."

Gwen locked herself in the bathroom, dropping the two cups of coffee that she was carrying in the sink. She had just turned the corner to Dominic's office, when she'd spotted him standing a few feet away talking to Gage. Not wanting to interrupt, she'd stepped back and stayed out of sight as Dominic had teased his friend. The smile that had been on her face had quickly slid away though when she'd heard Gage say her name. The conversation that had followed had been the all too familiar story of her life—with the exception of a possible pregnancy. Apparently, yet another man in her dating life was bored with her and ready to move on to greener pastures.

Why had she let herself begin to believe that they had something more between them? What had she been thinking? A man who looked like Dominic would always get plenty of attention from women. Not only was he handsome and sexy, but he was also charming and kind. And dear heaven, if a woman was lucky enough to discover how talented he was in the bedroom, then she would likely sell her very soul to keep him. What made her think that she could compete?

Dammit, he had led her to believe that he was just as interested in her as she was in him. Okay, maybe she had been the one to initiate sex, but after that, it had been all him. He'd turned into Mr. Wonderful, and she had fallen for it. Now she was convinced there wasn't a woman around who could hold out when Dominic Brady turned his full attention on them. The ass! This was all his fault. Why couldn't he have left her alone? So what if they had a condom mishap. He could have told her to call if there were any issues and left it at that. Nooo, he had to continue sexing her up at every opportunity and making her believe that he genuinely cared about her. She was well and truly tired of being treated like she didn't matter. Maybe the best thing to come out of the overheard conversation this morning was that she could now turn the tables and be one step ahead. She would be the dumper this time and not the dumpee.

Gwen had fully planned to tell Dominic that she'd overheard him talking to Gage, but now she'd changed her mind. Why warn him so that he could just make up some lie to cover his tracks? No, even if it killed her, she would pretend that nothing had changed until she knew for sure whether she was pregnant. By this weekend, she should be able to take a home pregnancy test to answer that question. Of course, if her spotting from the previous day was any indication, she'd say that she wasn't.

Her sister had called last night to invite her to Peter's birthday party this weekend, so instead of declining as she'd planned to do, maybe she would go. She could take a test there and then call Dominic while she was out of town and let him know. No, wait. That was too nice. She'd text him. . . . Yeah, that was more impersonal with the added benefit of not having to hear him make small talk while he brushed her off.

Now that she had a plan of action, she only had to get through the rest of the work week without breaking down and begging him to stay. She could do this. She had to. Cleaning the coffee mess out of the sink, she took a few deep breaths and squared her shoulders. She just needed to keep reminding herself that he was no different from the rest. Daniel, the man she had dated before Mac, had broken up with her via e-mail with the standard, "It's not you, it's me" spiel. She might have actually bought into that if he hadn't ended it with, "You're a great person, Misty." Needless to say, Gwen had immediately caught on to the fact that her replacement in Daniel's life was Misty. She hadn't bothered to call him out on it. What would have been the point? Apparently, her replacement in Dominic's life was a stripper named Kandi. Just the thought was enough to send a wave of much-needed anger surging through her once again. Ugh, men were pigs!

Gwen stalked back to her office feeling guilty that she had wasted so much time this morning on personal matters. Just as she was reviewing some invoices for approval, there was a tap at her door and a smiling Dominic walked in carrying her morning coffee. Her body went into hyper alert as usual when she saw him before she reminded herself that he was a snake and she shouldn't be swooning over his masculine beauty. God, this was going to be harder than she thought because she was just addicted to him. She had to focus on how it would feel when he walked away from her. "Hey, babe, got you coffee." He smiled as he sauntered over to where she was sitting. She pretended not to notice that his mouth was dropping toward hers as she subtly turned her head slightly causing his lips to meet her cheek instead. He gave her a questioning look to which she just smiled brightly.

"Thanks," she said, picking up her cup. "I really needed this." Before he could say anything she quickly asked, "So, how's your morning going?"

He reached down to tuck a wayward piece of hair behind her ear before answering. "It's fine. Just the usual. How about you?" Oh crap, she was literally melting from the heat in his gaze as she fumbled with a pen on her desk, trying not to think about how much she wanted him to throw her over the desk and take her in every way imaginable. She could feel her body flushing and her nipples pebbling as she repeated to herself that he was now the enemy. Did the man have to smell so good? She was right at the point of plastering her body to his when she was saved by the shrill ringing of her desk phone. She grabbed the receiver like it was a life raft in the middle of the ocean and she was drowning.

If Marta in purchasing thought it a bit strange that Gwen insisted she needed to come over personally to review the new budget for landscaping, she didn't let on. Well, other than the thirty-second pause when Gwen had said that she'd be right there. She really didn't care if she sounded crazy as long as it kept her from licking Dominic's neck and flicking his nipples. Tossing the phone back in the cradle, Gwen jumped to her feet and said breezily, "I've got to go look over some budget numbers. So, I'll see you later."

She had almost made it to the door, when Dominic shot a hand out and pulled her body against his. "Not so fast, Red." Looking at her intently, he asked, "Is everything all right? You seem a bit—strange."

Maybe if I stuffed some dollar bills in my panties and named myself after something edible he'd be happier! Gwen thought to herself. Instead of giving voice to any of those thoughts, though, she simply gave him a confused half smile before answering. "I don't know what you mean. It's just been a busy morning and I'm running late." In his confusion, his grip had loosened on her and she took advantage of the momentary distraction by pulling away and making for the door. "Thanks for the coffee," she threw over her shoulder as she walked quickly down the hallway. When she turned the corner, she glanced back to find him staring after her, looking puzzled and hurt. No, surely she was reading that wrong. The only thing she could have possibly wounded was his ego by walking away from him. It probably wasn't a feeling that he was used to. She had to give him credit, though; he seemed to be determined to stay the course until he knew he was off the hook.

If he wasn't stomping on her heart, she might have admired his resolve. That was something she needed to work on herself because she had been close to folding in her office. She had seriously underestimated the impact that his presence had on her. How in the world was she supposed to hold out for another few days until she could run back to Columbia and hide? At this point, a case of the flu would be like a miracle from above.

Chapter Eleven

Dominic was still perplexed by Gwen's odd behavior by the time he made it home later that evening. He had replayed the scene in her office over and over and still couldn't pinpoint exactly what had been off, yet he knew something had changed since they had parted less than an hour before. First, there was her avoidance of his kiss. He might have believed that her turning just as his lips closed in on hers was a coincidence, if not for the moments afterward. She had kept all eye contact to a minimum and had bounced her pen around her desk as if she was on some kind of speed.

Yeah, he'd been around enough women to know when something was wrong, and she might have said the right things, but her body language was saying something else. What could have possibly happened in the hour that they were apart? He'd barely had time to check his e-mail and say a few words to Mac and Gage before hurrying out to get her coffee. Could it be that Gage was right? Was she beginning to get pissed off at him because she thought he was avoiding the "baby" subject? To him, it didn't change his feelings for Gwen either way. Sure, if she was pregnant, they'd need to make plans for that, but he wanted to be with her regardless. He had assumed that she knew that, but maybe that hadn't been wise. Men were just naturally less vocal than women about their feelings.

He looked at his watch and knew that she should be home by now. He hadn't wanted to risk inviting her to dinner in case she refused so he'd picked up some Chinese on his way. As luck would have it, when he stepped from his apartment to go to Gwen's, he saw Shannon standing in her doorway. As he drew closer, he heard her say, "Sorry about dinner. Any other time the girls and I would have loved to go out, but I couldn't pass up a chance to meet Cameron, with them at my parents' house tonight." As the other woman pulled the door shut behind her, she turned and almost plowed into him. "Eek!" she squeaked before recognizing him.

"Sorry about that, Shannon," he apologized. "Didn't mean to startle you." Pretending he didn't hear what she'd just said to Gwen, he asked, "Where's Maddy and Megan?" He couldn't resist throwing in, "They aren't visiting with their friend, Bastard, are they?"

Shannon dropped her head before giggling softly. "Oh God, I have no idea where they get half the stuff they say. I thought I'd lost the ability to be embarrassed by them long ago, but they just keep proving me wrong."

Dominic reached out to pat her shoulder as he said, "Don't ever try to change them. They are hilarious. If only they could stay that innocent all their lives."

Shannon raised a skeptical brow, saying, "I wouldn't

exactly call them innocent, but I know what you mean. I may cringe sometimes, but I know I'll remember those moments forever." As he smiled and nodded his agreement, she suddenly looked over her shoulder at Gwen's door before lowering her voice. "Did you . . . mess up or something with Gwen?"

He felt his stomach clench as she gave voice to the same question he had asked himself throughout the day. Apparently, he wasn't the only one who had noticed something was amiss. He pondered just making some joke and brushing it off, but instead he found himself saying honestly, "I have no clue why, but I think I have. Did she . . . say something about it to you?" Damn, that question sounded so high school. He couldn't believe he was pumping Gwen's friend for information. He tried to console himself with the fact that she had started the whole thing.

Checking to make sure they were still alone, Shannon moved closer to him, saying, "It's not so much that she's said anything to me. It's just that since you two have been together, she's been all about you in her spare time. Tonight she was waiting for me when I walked down the hallway and seemed almost desperate to have a reason to get out of her apartment. I asked her if she wasn't seeing you tonight, and she started fidgeting like the girls do when they're guilty of something. I felt really bad when I told her that I already had plans. I would have canceled them since Gwen does so much for me, but I really want to see Cameron. Crap," she sighed, "I'm a horrible friend, aren't I? Shouldn't I put her before some guy?"

"No," Dominic blurted out quickly, before adding, "I mean, I know that she understands. And you're doing me a favor because, apparently, I screwed up somehow and I need to fix it. I think Gwen was hoping to avoid me tonight, which she tried to do earlier today, and now she won't be able to. Hey, do you think you could knock on her door? She might not answer for me."

Shannon held up her hand, waiting expectantly for him to fist bump her. He chuckled as he made a new ally before rapping knuckles with the cool single mom. Megan and Maddy were lucky to have her. Knocking on Gwen's door, Shannon whispered to him, "You know, you're all right, Dominic."

He was on the verge of returning the compliment when Gwen slung open her door saying, "I thought you had plans . . ." before she noticed him standing to the side. "Dominic, what're you doing here?"

Shannon pointed to the food bags in his hand. "I saw he had his hands full, so I volunteered to knock for him." Before her friend could reply, she gave a jaunty wave and walked off—quickly.

Dominic pushed past a bemused Gwen and walked straight to her kitchen. He set the bags on the table and made himself at home, pulling out plates for them. "Hey, baby." He smiled as she once again started moving around nervously as she drew near. "I hope you're hungry. I got a little bit of everything. I even made them throw in some extra fortune cookies since I know how much you love those things." He moved to drop a kiss on her lips as he normally would, and he was relieved when she let him without moving away. That was a good sign, right?

"I'm not really that hungry," she said right before the growling sounds of her stomach filled the room. When he cocked a brow at her, she admitted, "Well, maybe I am, after all. I was going to watch a movie tonight, so I'll understand if you'd rather have yours at home."

Dominic's hands stalled in the process of opening the fried rice. He knew a brush-off when he heard one and apparently they were right back to that again. Well, he'd be damned if he was going anywhere before he knew what was going on with her. "Nah, that's okay, babe. I'm fine with anything you want to watch. We can take our cartons to the coffee table and eat while we watch your movie."

"But, you don't even know what it is," she blurted out, looking more than a little rattled.

"Doesn't matter, baby. I don't have to be in control all of the time. If you have something you want to watch, then that's what we'll do. I like most anything." She wrinkled her nose up in a way that told him that she was stumped as to what to do next. He just ignored her plight and started taking their food to the coffee table. "Can you bring some drinks with you, babe?" he called over his shoulder. He was a little concerned about her sudden change in behavior, but he was also amused over her less than subtle attempts to get rid of him. She really should have figured out by now that he was more than a match for her in the stubborn category.

A few moments later, she settled next to him on the floor. Without a word, she picked up the television remote and flipped to one of the women's channels. He managed to choke back a groan. He wouldn't give her the pleasure of knowing that his hair was officially standing up. No self-respecting man watched that shit. As luck would have it, the movie was just starting so he was in for two hours of something called *Monster-in-Law*. "I just love this movie," Gwen enthused from next to him.

"If you've already seen it before, maybe we should watch something new," he suggested, hoping to God that she would agree.

When she turned those big eyes on him, he knew he was screwed. He'd do anything she wanted when she looked at him like that. "Or we can watch it," he relented. "I mean there are probably parts you missed when you watched it before."

"You're right," Gwen said around a mouthful of Kung Pao chicken. "I must have seen this like fifty times, and I always catch something new."

Fifty times? What the fuck? Dominic looked down at his can of Diet Coke and knew he was going to need something stronger. "Baby, I'm going to run to my place and get a couple of beers."

As he stood to leave, Gwen pulled her eyes from the movie and said, "I bought some for you at the market the other day. They're in the refrigerator." She seemed to wince as the words left her mouth as if she'd said the wrong thing to admit that she'd been thinking of him. What was going on with her? Maybe she was having a bad case of PMS, which would pretty much answer his question about the baby possibility. Before they went to bed tonight, if she let him stay, he'd ask her. Not the PMS question because he valued his nuts, but if she'd taken a test. If Gage was right, then she might know by now.

He walked back over to drop a kiss on the top of her head. "Thank you, baby, I appreciate that." *Truer words were never spoken*, he thought as he twisted the top off his Heineken. Hell, maybe he should have brought the whole six-pack back to the table. It appeared that Gwen was already ticked at him over something so looking like an alcoholic probably wasn't going to hurt his case much more. "Hey, isn't that Jennifer Lopez?" He pointed his chopsticks toward the television screen.

"Yep," Gwen nodded, "and she's going to get involved with Michael Vartan. Damn, he's so hot."

All right, this was getting just downright annoying. Now she was lusting after some guy on television? Hello, wasn't he sitting right here? If she mentioned the guy's ass next, he was turning the fucking movie off. He shook his head, thinking how absurd it sounded even to himself that he was jealous of an actor—one who wasn't even that good-looking. Knowing it was petty, he couldn't stop himself from saying, "I've always loved Jennifer Lopez."

Not seeming the least bit perturbed, Gwen gave him a saucy grin, saying, "You just love her big butt. I think we've already established that as your favorite female body part."

When his cock sprang to attention at her comment,

it almost felt wrong to him. He shouldn't be getting hard in the middle of a chick flick, should he? Wasn't that the equivalent of cursing in church or something? As a man, he was supposed to feel only disdain when watching these kind of movies. It was technically not the movie causing the wood, though—it was thoughts of Gwen's ass, bent over the very table they were eating on while he drove into her hard and fast. Yeah, so not what he should think when it was clear she didn't have sex on the brain right now. "You have all of my favorite parts," he joked as she returned her attention to the movie.

When the guy in the movie went jogging down the beach without a shirt, he could have sworn that he caught Gwen panting. He decided he officially hated this frigging movie and breathed a sigh of relief when the first commercial started—until it was a two-minute spiel about not letting your heavy flow keep you from enjoying your life. Immediately followed by something called Summer's Eve for that "oh so fresh feeling." Holy shit, he thought, Gage was right—these commercials were so informative that they were downright horrifying. He hadn't realized that he was scowling until Gwen said in an amused voice, "You know, you don't have to stay if you don't want to."

Leaning back against the couch, he made an effort to wipe all traces of unhappiness from his face. "This looks great, babe, and I'm learning so much. By the end of this movie, I'll be able to hold my own in any feminine hygiene discussion. You're really doing me a favor," he added with a wink.

She giggled before pushing her food away and re-clining backward as well. Dominic dropped his arm around her, pulling her into the curve of his body. She remained stiff for a moment, before allowing her body to conform to his. "Do you guys discuss women's products often?" she asked.

"More than you know," he mumbled under his breath as the movie started again. Within a few minutes of twirling Gwen's hair and watching the movie, he found something happening that he would never admit to his friends. He was drawn to the plight of Jennifer Lopez and her future mother-in-law from hell. At one point, he yelled out, "The bitch tried to kill her with those nuts!" while waving angrily at Jane Fonda's character.

Gwen dropped a comforting hand onto his thigh, whispering, "It's okay. It will all work out in the end. I agree, though—the woman is crazy. I'd just pack up and leave a man before I'd put up with that from his mother." Dominic made a mental note right then to tell his mom to keep the crazy under wraps when she finally met Gwen. He didn't want his family scaring her off.

When the movie ended, he felt like he'd been through an emotional wringer. Why in the world did women watch stuff like that? He'd take an action movie any day where they just blew shit up. It gave you a good adrenaline rush, but you didn't feel like crying when it was over. He'd found himself all tied up into knots while waiting to see if the evil mother was going to stop her son from marrying the woman of his dreams. And to think, Gwen had admitted to watching the movie fifty times. Damn! He'd need a prescription for Prozac by the second viewing. "Um . . . great movie, babe. A tad on the scary side, but entertaining."

Gwen burst out laughing. "What do you mean scary? It's a romantic comedy. I don't think there's supposed to be much suspense to it."

Dominic looked at her incredulously. "You've gotta be kidding. Did you see all of that crap that Mr. Perfect's mother was doing? I mean, poor Jennifer didn't know what she'd be facing each day. And feeding someone nuts who's allergic to them? That's attempted murder! So what if Jennifer got to marry the guy in the end and the mother pretended to be happy about it. You know as well as I do about how long that's gonna last. She'll be up to her old shit as soon as the honeymoon is over, mark my words!"

When he finished his tirade, Gwen was staring at him with her mouth hung open. She swallowed a few times before patting him on the head like a dog. "Um, you do realize that the movie wasn't a true story, right? In addition, there wasn't a sequel, so nothing happened after the honeymoon. You know, because it wasn't real."

Getting to his feet, Dominic started clearing off their dinner from the table, feeling like an idiot. He refused to meet Gwen's eyes as he stacked the cartons of cold Chinese food before taking them to the kitchen. He had just made a first-class fool out of himself, and he was embarrassed and okay, a little pissed off about it. Men didn't handle feelings like that well, and he was no exception. Now thanks to his rant, there was no way she could doubt how taken in he had been by her choice in movies. He knew it was crazy, but he wanted to blame the whole humiliating thing on her. A voice in the rational part of his mind said that she'd encouraged him to go home, but no, he'd been determined to stick it out. It pissed him off even further that he was actually so bent out of shape over such silliness. This sounded more like Gage than him. Heck, he'd said something similar when he'd admitted to watching commercials mainly pertaining to women's products. At least he'd been watching a lingerie show for perverted reasons, though. Dominic couldn't claim the same.

When he stomped back into the living room, Gwen was standing there looking at him warily. "Everything okay?" she asked, as she studied his no doubt closed-off expression. He knew then that he needed to go home for the night. If he stayed here, he'd say something he didn't mean. She didn't deserve to have her feelings hurt because he was acting like a total jerk. He fucking knew that, but he still couldn't shake it off. What was wrong with him tonight?

"It's fine, babe." He forced himself to answer lightly. "Just a little tired from the trip and lack of sleep last night." He pulled her tense form against him before saying, "I'm going to stay at my place tonight. I'll sleep so deeply that I'm likely to snore the bedroom down. Believe me, you don't want that." She laughed, but it sounded strained. He pressed a light kiss to her lips before releasing her and going toward the door. When he reached it, he turned, remembering what Gage had said about him showing interest and concern over the possible pregnancy. It was the last thing he wanted to talk about tonight, but he didn't want her to think that he didn't care—because he did, more than she knew. "So . . . um how much longer until you know something, about, you know, whether you're pregnant or not?"

Dominic saw her freeze at his question. Maybe he was mistaken, but she didn't really look happy or relieved by his question. He was beginning to regret even bringing the subject up, when she finally said, "Probably this week or weekend one way or another."

Trying to sound like he was halfway knowledgeable, he quoted off Gage's statement. "Isn't there some test that tells you early? Maybe you could take one of those. At least then we'd know." When she bit her trembling lip and her eyes looked like they were watering, Dominic felt a moment's panic. This wasn't going at all like he thought it would. To say this hadn't been his ideal evening was putting it mildly. Feeling ashamed of how he had been acting, he put his arm around her shoulders and pulled her in close to him once again. "Did I say something wrong?" he asked. That was a loaded question because he'd probably said nothing right since he'd arrived.

"No, it's fine," she answered hoarsely. "I can pick up a test. I . . . just thought I'd wait to see if I didn't get my . . . period before I did. But, I know you want to know as soon as possible."

"Er—sure," he replied, not knowing what else to say. He hadn't really wanted nor did he need to know early, but the words were out there now, and he thought it was easier to just let it go rather than dragging something out that she plainly didn't want to discuss. Shit, it looked like Gage was right. She had been upset with him for not mentioning it sooner. He wanted to tell her that he hadn't because it didn't change anything at all for him, but nothing he had said was coming out right tonight. He'd just piss her off or upset her further. One thing you learned how to do well in the military was to know when it was time to retreat and that time had come and gone already. He rubbed her back before kissing her on the forehead. "I'm going to head out now. See you at the office tomorrow?"

Without making eye contact, she nodded her head and opened the door for him. If that wasn't a sign that she wanted rid of him, he didn't know what was. "Good night, Dominic," she said softly and a bit too formally for his peace of mind.

" 'Night, babe," he replied as he stepped into the hallway. She had the door closed before he could turn and see her one last time. *You really made a mess out of that,* he thought to himself as he walked down the hallway to his apartment. He probably needed to bring more to the table tomorrow than a cup of coffee. A better mood and some groveling were definitely in order.

Spending two tours in the Marines hadn't allowed for long-term relationships, so in many ways this was all new ground for him. He was under no illusions that this would be the last time he screwed up, but he planned to do his best not to hurt her again. He'd always thought Gage was full of shit since he never stayed with a woman long enough to be qualified to give advice, but it seemed he might have been wrong. He'd no longer disregard his buddy's advice if it sounded even reasonably coherent. Hell, before he opened his mouth again, maybe he should solicit every piece of guidance that anyone was willing to offer.

Chapter Twelve

Going to work feeling like an emotional wreck was becoming a disturbing pattern for Gwen. One that she detested. She'd never been one to bring her problems to the office with her, but now it seemed to be happening a lot this week. She'd stepped off the elevator this morning, hoping to make it to her office without seeing anyone, but she'd had no such luck. Instead, she'd almost immediately run into her beautifully put together friend, Mia. She loved her, she really did, but Crystal would have been preferable in this instance since they both seemed to be having a miserable week. Mia, however, just glowed as a woman who was loved and in love seemed to do. No doubt, she'd had amazing sex before leaving home. God, she could almost hate her.

"Morning chick," Mia said in a singsong voice.

Gwen managed to grunt out, "Morning," in reply before opening her office door. "I've got a ton of work to catch up on today," she threw over her shoulder as she walked to her desk. She hoped the other woman would get the message, but Mia plopped down in a chair as if completely oblivious.

Before either of them could say anything, Dominic walked through the open doorway with a cup of coffee in his hand. As Mia stood, obviously intent on leaving to give them some privacy, he held up his hand, stopping her. "It's okay. I'm just on my way out." He walked over to Gwen, setting the cup in front of her before saying, "Gage and I are heading back to Charleston this morning. Our supervisor that we hired for the new location there has come down with the flu. And to top it off, now his assistant isn't feeling well, either. We just don't have anyone extra in that capacity to send. And I'm likely to be gone the rest of the week."

Gwen felt a wave of relief. She was so confused and distraught over her feelings for him right now that knowing there was no danger of seeing him before she left for her sister's this weekend was a much-needed reprieve. Plus, having him gone would save her from doing something crazy, like wrapping herself around his feet and holding on tight. Who knew that all it took was a hot guy to make her kick her pride to the curb? "I understand," Gwen assured him. Waving a hand brightly, she added, "You go do your thing." *Oh dear God, did I actually just say that?* Gwen groaned inwardly. She sounded like some sixteen-year-old.

To his credit, Dominic's lips twitched only slightly at her cheesy words of encouragement. "I'll do that," he said. "I kind of feel like you'd rather me high-five you instead of kissing you good-bye, but you're not getting off that easy, babe." Gwen heard Mia's murmur of approval as Dominic leaned over and locked his lips on hers. The kiss was short but firm. If it had lasted a few seconds longer, Gwen would have been ready to pull him onto her desk and damn the consequences. Of course, knowing Mia, she would probably be selling tickets to the rest of the office and munching popcorn during the main event. Dominic pulled away and gave one light tug on her hair before starting for the door. He paused there to say, "I'll call you," before walking away.

Before Gwen could say anything, Mia looked down at her watch and groaned. "Crap, I have my morning meeting in ten minutes. That sucks because I have so many questions. We are going to lunch today, and you're not getting out of it! I'll shoot Crystal an e-mail and invite her as well. That poor girl needs something to take her mind off her nut-job mother."

Gwen laughed because there was just no way not to when Mia was in one of her hyper moods, spewing sentences one after another. Plus, if she could manage to put off answering questions about Dominic for a few hours, then she'd happily agree to lunch. "All right, sounds good. Meet you in the lobby at noon?"

"Yep, sounds good. And don't even think about sending me some brush-off text either because I'll come find you," Mia warned before grimacing at her watch and hurrying out much as Dominic had done.

Gwen turned to her computer to begin her morning and try to block out the pangs of loneliness that were already hitting her at the thought of Dominic being gone for a few days. How in the world was she supposed to deal with not having him in her life at all? Surely that was just around the corner.

He had acted so strangely last night at her apartment. She'd thought it was cute that he had been so involved in the movie they were watching. Most men would avoid a romantic comedy, and even though he hadn't seemed thrilled with her choice at first, he'd completely gotten into it after a while. She had thought him completely adorable when he'd been so angry at the mother-in-law for all of the tricks she'd been pulling on her future daughter-in-law.

After the movie, though, it was as if his mood had taken a nosedive. Unlike other nights, he had been more than ready to leave and had made no moves toward spending the night. Heck, it wasn't as if she'd never dated a guy in a hurry to leave so she certainly knew the signs when their eyes suddenly looked a million miles away and they started shifting on their feet as if there were ants in their shoes. It was a first, though, for Dominic to act that way. He always seemed to have nowhere else he'd rather be than with her. She got the feeling at the end of the evening that he'd rather be anywhere else—or maybe just with anyone else. The worst part was that he'd made a point of asking her when she'd know if she was pregnant and had even suggested taking an early pregnancy test. The warning bells of his imminent departure from her life had begun going off like sirens.

Gwen planned to buy a test after work today. She knew her body, though, and she was almost certain that she wasn't pregnant. She'd also had that one instance of spotting. She could have already taken a test, but a part of her just wanted to pretend that she was happily involved in a new relationship with a wonderful man because they liked each other—and for no other reason. Was a condom mishap the only way that she could have a man like Dominic in her life for more than one night? *What a depressing thought.*

She was still brooding when her boss called a few moments later to ask her to work on a new project. Gwen tried to interject some small amount of professionalism into her tone as she asked him questions and made notes. If her mood was any indication, she should be grateful for her job today. Otherwise, she was certain she would be staring at the walls of her apartment and bemoaning yet another relationship. How pathetic; she'd barely dated the man for more than a few weeks, but she knew it would take so very much longer to get over him. God, she hated men—she really did.

"I'm telling you, Crys, you should have been in Gwen's office this morning. Dominic came in to deliver her morning coffee, which by the way is so freaking sweet, and then he was all, 'I know you want to high-five me, but I'm kissing you.' And, boy did he ever. My lips were practically tingling as he locked his mouth on hers. After that, if I hadn't had meetings stacked up, Seth Jackson would have had a surprise visitor this morning. The whole thing made me seriously horny."

Gwen rolled her eyes and knew she should be mortified, but she giggled anyway. Crystal's face was the color of a tomato as she fanned herself. "Like that's anything new—you get that way from walking by the produce stand down the street."

Wiggling her brow, Mia grinned. "Hell, yeah, I do. All those cucumbers just waiting for a new home."

At Crystal's puzzled look, Gwen started to choke on a bite of food and almost asphyxiated before getting herself under control. "Mia, geez, get a grip on your body. You don't really use those . . . No, don't answer that!" Gwen added quickly.

"You can use them for—that?" Crystal asked with rounded eyes.

"Crys, don't ask questions you don't want the answers to," Gwen warned while shaking her head. The last thing she wanted to hear was an in-depth explanation of Mia's experience with produce.

"Whatever, you prude," Mia smirked. "Since you don't want to talk about me, let's get back to you. What is going on with that military stud of yours? You seemed upset this morning, but he certainly walked into your office and laid claim to you as if nothing was amiss."

Gwen felt the smile that had been on her face begin to drift at Mia's question. A part of her just wanted to brush the whole topic off and act like everything was fine, but the other part needed the support of her friends so she found herself on the verge of tears in the blink of an eye as she admitted, "I think he wants out."

Mia blinked in surprise before asking, "Out? As in breaking up?"

"That's the one," Gwen said shakily.

Looking confused, Crystal asked, "But I thought you said he was—you know, affectionate this morning in her office?"

Before Mia could answer, Gwen said instead, "He was just coming by to tell me he was going out of town. A few things happened yesterday that lead me to believe that he plans to move on—soon." Mia motioned for her to continue. "Well, yesterday morning I decided to take Dominic coffee since he always brings me one. I was almost to his office when I saw him speaking with Gage outside the doors. I didn't want to be rude so I took a few steps back and waited around the corner for them to finish talking."

Always the sweet one, Crystal patted Gwen's arm and said, "That was very nice of you; I'm sure he appreciated that."

"He never knew it," Gwen continued morosely, "because I heard Gage ask him when he was going to find out if I was pregnant or not so he could go back to his ex-girlfriend, Kandi."

"Kandi?" Mia shrieked loudly before popping her hand over her mouth. "Shit, sorry, but that sounds like a stripper name or something."

"It is," Gwen moaned into her hands. "He dated a stripper before me and from what he told Gage, she is the love of his life and he plans to go back to her as soon as I give him the all clear. Maybe she hates kids or something and won't take him back until he knows for sure that he's not going to be a father."

"No fucking way," Mia deadpans. "That's something you'd read about in a book, but never happens in real life. Are you sure you aren't mistaken? Maybe he just said something that sounded like that?"

Throwing her hands in front of her in exasperation,

Gwen asked, "How many words rhyme with Kandi? I don't think I could have heard that wrong."

Taking her question literally, Crystal began saying, "Well, there's Mandy, Randy, dandy, Sandy . . ."

"You are so not helping, Crys," Mia said, stopping her. Turning back to Gwen, she asked, "You said there were a couple of things that happened yesterday. What was the other?"

Gwen told them all about their movie evening and his strange behavior afterward. "And then he asked as he was leaving when I'd know if I was pregnant or not. He went so far as to suggest an early pregnancy test. That was too much of a coincidence after what I heard that morning—don't you think?"

When instead of having a good explanation for his behavior, Mia simply said, "Damn," Gwen knew she hadn't jumped to conclusions at all. "But, he seemed so into you this morning," Mia added weakly, looking mystified by the whole thing. "I just don't think it's that black and white. You should talk to him. He doesn't seem the type to have a woman on the side while seeing another. You hear plenty of rumors at the office about the players and his name has never come up. Now, Gage—he's a different story."

When both Gwen and Mia looked at Crystal, she blushed and shook her head furiously. "I'm not involved with him. Plus, I saw him Monday afternoon in the parking garage kissing some girl. He's cute and going out with him would drive my mother crazy, but he's just too much for me."

"And Mark DeSanto isn't?" Mia said incredulously.

Crystal's pink cheeks had now become a bright shade of red, Gwen noted curiously. "Who's Mark De-Santo?" she asked, glad for a reprieve from her pathetic love life.

"Oh, honey," Mia let out a very unladylike wolf whistle. "Come on, surely you've heard of the DeSanto group that is partnering with Danvers? Mark DeSanto is the owner."

Snapping her fingers, Gwen nodded. "Of course, yes. I've never actually met him, though. Is he cute?"

"Hot as the fires of Hades," Mia gushed. "He's young, probably in his early to midthirties, with dark hair and a kicking body. Apparently, he's taken some office space in the Danvers building now that they're doing so much business together." Pointing to Crystal, she added, "I caught our girl here drooling over him in the coffee shop this morning. She poured half a container of sugar in her cup, watching him add cream to his a few feet away. Show her the picture, Crys."

Gwen gaped at her innocent-seeming friend. "You took a picture of him?"

"Thank God for cell phones!" Mia enthused as she motioned for Crystal to find the picture.

Instead of looking embarrassed now, Crystal looked almost proud of herself as she hit some buttons on her phone, before handing it to Gwen. "He's the most beautiful man I've ever seen," she sighed dreamily.

Gwen found it hard to argue with Crystal's assessment as she stared at the phone. Whereas Dominic was all rugged masculinity, Mark DeSanto was polished perfection in a fitted suit that looked expensive even on camera. His black hair was the only part of his appearance that wasn't immaculate. It was tousled as if he'd run his hand through it several times that morning. Somehow, that only added to his appeal. "Wow," Gwen murmured, as she looked her fill before returning the phone. She might be totally infatuated with Dominic, but there was no way any woman wouldn't look twice at a man like that.

Mia grinned. "I know, right? That man is a walking sexual fantasy."

"But doesn't Seth dress the same way?" Crystal asked as she cradled her phone to her chest as if it were the actual man himself.

Mia smacked her lips in obvious appreciation. "You bet your ass he does, and I love it. There is nothing quite like a little game of bad CEO to get me going."

As Crystal opened her mouth to speak, Gwen cut her off by saying, "Crystal, honey, didn't we cover the part about not asking questions like that? I get that you're ready to spread your wings and fly, but you might want to think twice about being educated completely in just one day."

Mia snorted, sticking her tongue out. "You're no fun at all, Gwen. I'm just trying to help her land that bad boy. Because I've heard the rumors, and that's exactly what he is."

"He's innocent until proven guilty," Crystal defended her new crush.

"Or until he ties you up," Mia quipped.

Crystal looked over her shoulder uneasily, clearly hoping that no one was listening to the conversation at their table. "Can we just talk about Gwen's problems? I want to be able to stare at Mark without knowing stuff like that—at least for now."

"We don't have to do anything about my issues right now. Dominic is going out of town, and I'm heading to my sister's for the weekend so I won't see him for days. By the time that I do, I'll have taken a pregnancy test and—then he'll probably be gone." Giving Crystal a weak smile, Gwen asked, "Hey, do you think I could stalk Mark with you? I might have a lot of free time again soon."

Mia placed her hand on top of Gwen's in a show of support. "If Dominic is really that kind of person, then good riddance. It's better to find out now. I have to say, though—I didn't really get that vibe from him. The few times I've seen you two together, he seems so into you. I bet he blows your phone up the whole time he's away. Trust me, men don't bother to call if they're trying to get rid of you."

Crystal, who was once again staring at her phone, added without looking up, "Yep, Mia's right. He'll call you every day, and you'll see how much he misses you, and then you'll feel silly for doubting him."

"You need to give the girl some space, bro. You live just doors away from each other so you're always around. How's she ever gonna miss you if she keeps tripping over your lovesick self?"

Dominic scratched his head as he pondered Gage's words. It seemed that talking to him about Gwen on their road trips was becoming a strange routine for him now. He was so confused by her hot and cold behavior the last few days that he'd needed some advice. Mac would have been his first choice seeing as he was actually the married one, but Gage was here and Mac was back at the office. "I didn't stay at her place last night so it's not like I'm always there."

"Yeah, but you left in a girlie huff over watching some sappy movie with her. Dude, did you really lose it over the evil sister and start yelling?" Gage asked incredulously.

"It was the guy's mother, not his sister," Dominic added weakly. "And I didn't exactly lose it, more like mildly pointed out how crazy Jane Fonda was."

"The fact that you'd even know Jane Fonda as anything other than Ted Turner's ex says more than enough."

Doing a full body shudder, Dominic added, "And you're completely right about the kind of commercials they play during shows aimed at women. I think that's one thing that about pushed me off the deep end. And come on, that advertisement for the herpes medicine where they make it sound all glamorous? That's just gotta be misrepresentation."

"You got that shit right," Gage agreed. "Any kind of itching downstairs is never going to be a fun event. I saw that commercial, too. Held my dick the whole time it was on."

"So, you really think I'm just too available where Gwen is concerned? Fuck, did I really just ask you that? This is starting to sound like a Maury What's-his-name show." Dominic grimaced.

Gage chuckled as he shook his head. "You got it all

mixed up. Maury's show is cool. They are always throwing punches and beating each other up. I believe you're thinking of Steve Harvey. He has all of those dating shows on the dos and don'ts."

Dominic rubbed his face before looking at his friend. "Man, how much television do you watch? Apparently your usual 'hit it and get it,' dates allow you far too much free time."

"They did," Gage agreed, sounding surprisingly serious about Dominic's joke.

"Did?" Dominic asked, raising a brow in inquiry.

Was it his imagination or did Gage look flustered when he quickly amended his earlier statement. "Do . . . I meant do. No need to linger, right?" he added with an easy grin. "So, back to Gwen. Just give the girl a little space. If you're planning to call her ten times a day while you're gone—don't. Show her that your whole world doesn't revolve around or depend on her—in other words, try to pretend that you have a life."

Looking doubtful, Dominic asked, "Have you actually been in a relationship before that I don't know about?"

"Nope," Gage replied.

"Then why should I be taking advice from you? Hell, you don't know any more than I do," Dominic sighed.

"Probably not, but I think we've already established that I watch more television. It's amazing what you can pick up from those shows. You could always ask your sister if you want another opinion."

"No way," Dominic spat out. "You better not tell her,

either. You caused a long laugh at my expense in front of Gwen over Kandi. Why in God's name would you be telling Meredith about me dating a stripper?"

"Oh, stop whining," Gage laughed. "I love your sister. She's one of the few people who gets my sense of humor. I'm telling you, if she wasn't already married, I'd be your brother-in-law by now."

Dominic dropped his head back against the passenger seat. "And to think, I didn't believe it possible for me to be more depressed today. Thanks for proving me wrong. Next time, we're driving in separate cars."

"You're the one who needed to talk about your problems, dude. If you want me to keep helping you, then you could attempt to be a little more civil." As they pulled into the parking garage of their destination, Gage parked the truck and turned to him before opening his door. "Remember, no smothering Gwen this week. Be chill. Let her come to you—for once."

Chapter Thirteen

Gwen stared at the three pregnancy tests that she had lined up on her bathroom counter. Two were showing only one line and the other clearly said, "Not pregnant." She felt a pang of disappointment even though she had no desire for a baby right now. Something about seeing the negative tests just seemed so *final*. She was already feeling a little dejected—or maybe the better word would be rejected—after not hearing from Dominic since he'd left two days earlier. It was now Thursday night, which meant after work tomorrow, she was planning to drive the two hours to visit her sister.

She wasn't sure why, but somehow she'd seen this whole thing going differently a week ago. She imagined herself taking a pregnancy test, and then collapsing on the couch with relief when it was negative. Dominic would open a bottle of wine and they'd relax together, happy to have dodged a bullet. Then they'd have hot, crazy sex—with no condom mishap—before moving into a regular relationship.

Instead, Dominic had been out of town and hadn't called her once. She was left to take a test alone and have the celebratory glass of wine solo, as well. She pondered calling him to let him know the good news, but she couldn't bring herself to do it. Actually, she didn't even care about the wine anymore. So, after a quick shower, Gwen was in bed by nine o'clock. As she curled her arms around the pillow that still smelled of Dominic's musky scent, Gwen knew she had to accept the fact that he would likely leave her life before the smell of his cologne faded from her feather pillow.

As Gwen drove down her sister's street, she took a few deep breaths to pull herself together. The last twenty-four hours had been an emotional roller coaster. With the negative pregnancy test, the arrival of her period to drive the point home this morning, and Dominic's continued radio silence, she was well on her way to an epic pity party. She had decided last night to tell him the news when he returned, but she had since changed her mind. So, when she pulled her car to a stop, she grabbed her cell phone from her purse and quickly brought up his name. Instead of calling, she decided to send a text. It was more impersonal, and it seemed that their relationship had declined to just that level over the course of this week.

So, without any fanfare she typed, *"Took test—not pregnant."* Her fingers hovered over the keys for another moment. It felt wrong to send such an abrupt message, but what was she supposed to say? *Do you like me? Check yes or no. Where are you? Why haven't you called?* Yeah, those were just a few of the questions that she'd like to have answered. Instead, she quickly hit the SEND button, then proceeded to sit in the car in front of her sister's house for an additional ten minutes, waiting for a reply.

She was getting her overnight bag from the backseat when her phone chimed. *"Good deal . . . Thanks for letting me know."* Following the one sentence reply was a smiley face. In an uncharacteristic display of temper, Gwen took her phone and threw it against the oak tree in her sister's yard where it promptly separated into a few extra pieces.

"Okay, who's the man this time?" asked Wendy dryly as she stood staring at Gwen from the front steps.

Gwen wanted to throw herself at the tree next. Not only had she given her sister something to relentlessly question her about, but she'd also destroyed a phone that would eat a chunk out of her checking account to replace. Maybe it was childish, but she blamed both of those things on Dominic. What an ass. "It's nothing," Gwen mumbled as she walked past Wendy and into the house.

Before she could make an escape to the spare room that she normally used when visiting, Wendy took her arm and steered her toward the kitchen. Motioning toward a barstool, she said, "Sit," to which Gwen promptly complied. Her sister tended to treat Gwen like one of her students, and she'd long ago gotten used to taking orders from her. As Wendy's husband, Peter, had said more than once, it was easier to go along with the program where Wendy was concerned. After buzzing around her well-organized kitchen for another few minutes, her sister settled onto the stool across from her with two cups of coffee. Gwen took a sip from the mug placed in front of her and waited for the inquisition to begin. "So, what's with the tantrum in the yard?"

Fiddling with the handle of her cup, Gwen said, "It was hardly a tantrum. I was just blowing off some steam after a hectic day at the office."

Wendy lifted the busted iPhone from the counter. "These things cost about eight hundred bucks to replace, so I hope it was worth it."

Gwen winced, thinking the price was even worse than she had imagined. She'd paid only a couple hundred dollars when she'd taken out the plan last year. "It's just—things aren't going too well with this guy I've been seeing."

Wendy rolled her eyes and huffed inelegantly. "When are things ever going well on that front, Gwenie? You keep picking the same losers over and over again and then expect a different outcome. Honey, when are you going to learn from your mistakes?"

Instead of being pissed off at her sister's words, Gwen found herself tearing up. Dammit, the last thing she wanted was for Wendy to see her sobbing over some guy again. But Dominic had been different. Maybe they hadn't officially known each other long, but she'd been drawn to him from the first moment she'd seen him. Love at first sight might seem far-fetched and cliché, but that was how she felt when she was with him. "This wasn't the same, Wendy," she choked out on a sob. "I care about Dominic and he—I thought he felt the same. I mean, even though it started with the pregnancy thing, we really clicked. He was so—"

"WHAT?" Wendy screeched. "You're pregnant? Oh,

fluck, Gwen! How could you let that happen?" Even in the depths of her despair, Gwen couldn't help but notice that Wendy still couldn't say a proper curse word. Maybe it was for the best since she was around a bunch of impressionable kids all day.

Before she could answer her sister's hysterical questions, Peter walked into the kitchen and froze as he took in the scene before him. Gwen could only imagine how she looked with tears rolling off her like a fountain; Wendy's face was so red, she looked like she would combust at any moment. "Bad breakup again, Gwen?" He made a bad attempt at a joke as he grabbed a water bottle from the refrigerator.

"No, this time she's gotten herself pregnant!" Wendy snapped. Peter's mouth dropped open as he stared at them both in shock.

"I'm not pregnant," Gwen finally managed to get out. "Dammit, Wendy, will you stop jumping to conclusions!"

Throwing her hands up in the air, Wendy shouted, "Well, then why did you say that you were? And please tone down the potty mouth while you're at it!" Peter, to his credit, after having been down this road with his wife before, lowered his head and hurried from the kitchen without saying another word. Gwen was sure that the reason their marriage worked so well was that Peter was secure enough in his masculinity to basically let Wendy be in charge at home.

Gwen had to wonder as she looked at her sister, why she always came directly to her for a shot of tough love. Maybe because she knew without a doubt that her sister loved her and would slay a village to protect her. Wendy just had a hard time relating to Gwen's love life since her own course to happily ever after had been so smooth. She and Peter had met in high school, dated throughout college, and then gotten married when they had both obtained their degrees. Their romance had been orderly and followed the exact path that they'd laid out. Gwen's on the other hand had never been smooth for more than a few months, it seemed.

It was far too easy to see why Peter had assumed she was here over a man. Because she had sat on this same barstool many other times as she bemoaned yet another failed relationship. Wendy had stated after her last breakup that she couldn't understand why Gwen kept allowing history to repeat itself. The thing was, Gwen had no idea what she was doing wrong. It wasn't like she was picking bad boys each time, knowing they'd screw her over. She dated men who, for the most part, were gainfully employed, educated, and stable. For some reason, they just never wanted to stick around—with her, that was. Several had gone on to marry shortly after leaving her and were now minivan-driving super dads. Heck, maybe she was a required course for men to take before they got married.

Wendy gestured impatiently for her to explain her latest dating disaster. Slumping her shoulders because she knew that her sister hated bad posture, Gwen told her about the first night with Dominic. She left out the fact that they'd had sex for pretty much the entire night. In this instance, it was better for Wendy to believe that she had lost her common sense only that first time and not her morals and inhibitions along with it. "So, everything had been going so well between us up until the last week. I mean, I tried to hold back and not get attached to him. . . ."

"But you are," Wendy added quietly. "Honey, didn't you think it might be a bad idea to get involved with someone at work? You're going to have to see him every day. Think about how awkward that's going to be now."

Rubbing her watery eyes, Gwen asked, "So, you think it's over?"

"Isn't that why you're here, Gwenie? You know that both Peter and I love you and we're thrilled when you come to visit, but we'd sure like to see you happy sometimes when you're here."

Laying her head on the bar, Gwen relaxed as she felt Wendy begin to stroke her hair soothingly. They may be only a few years apart, but her sister had always been a mother figure in her life. Their mom was wonderful, but Wendy was the one Gwen turned to for advice and support. "I know I haven't been with Dominic for long, but I—I love him, and more important, I love who I am when I'm with him. It's like he only sees the best parts of me and nothing else. I've never been involved with a man who made me feel so good about myself."

"You've never told me that you loved someone you were dating before," Wendy said, sounding surprised. "I always thought that was strange, considering you were so upset when the relationships ended."

"I think I was more upset over the fact that the same

things kept happening to me than actually saying good-bye to the person I was dating. I know a woman shouldn't define herself by a man's opinion, but after a while, you have to start thinking that there is something wrong with you. I mean the whole 'It's not you, it's me' thing really doesn't hold much water when it's used more than a couple of times."

"But it *was* them," Wendy huffed out. "You're beautiful, smart, funny, and have a big heart. Probably the only truthful words those jerks said to you was that it was them. A real, worthy man would kill to have you. These little wimpy shoot-heads of the past can take a flying leap off a tall building!"

"Shoot-head?" Gwen smirked. "Is that the same as shithead?"

Wendy picked up a placemat from the bar and threw it at her. "Yes, smartie. If I let myself become comfortable with tossing around curse words casually, before I know it, I will have dropped the F-bomb on some unruly student in my class and then my husband will be forced to fire me. Do you think I'd really give the man that much satisfaction?"

"Point taken," Gwen agreed. For a moment, she let herself imagine being in a small classroom with Maddy and Megan all day. Of course, they'd more than likely be the ones doing the cursing.

Straightening her spine in what Gwen knew was her war pose, Wendy cracked her knuckles before saying, "All right, let's figure out what to do about this guy who you're in love with. You say that everything was great until the last week. Can you think of anything that was a turning point? And if your answer pertains to anything between the sheets, I don't need to know details—well, unless they're really good ones. . . ."

"I heard that," Peter yelled from the other room. Both Gwen and Wendy covered their mouths as they giggled.

Gwen didn't need to think about it. She knew when things had changed with Dominic. "Well, it started off when we watched *Monster-in-Law*."

"Oh, I love that movie," Wendy sighed. "You mean, he actually watched it? That's a love story, so why would that have put him off?"

"I don't know. Even though he grumbled a little at first, he seemed to really get into it. He was yelling at Jane Fonda's character and shouting warnings to Jennifer Lopez. It was so unbelievably cute that I could barely concentrate. Then after it was over, it was like he was embarrassed or something. He couldn't leave fast enough, which is unusual because he normally wants us to spend the night together, at either his place or mine. I think that was the first time that he clearly wanted to go—alone."

Shaking her head, Wendy said, "I don't think that's really a big thing. Everyone has an off night occasionally and just wants to be alone. Did you make a big deal out of it?"

"No. I was surprised, but I don't think it showed. But, before he left, he made a point of asking me when I was going to take a pregnancy test and recommended that I go ahead and buy one of those early ones. Oh, and there was the conversation I overheard between

him and his friend Gage. He was telling Dominic that
he needed to find out if I was pregnant so he could get
back together with his ex-girlfriend while she was available. Dominic agreed, saying she was the woman of
his dreams. I couldn't believe he would say something
like that after how great things have been between
us."

"Maybe they were joking, Gwen. You know how
men can be sometimes. I wouldn't put too much stock
in a conversation you probably only caught pieces of."

"Well, considering he hadn't mentioned a single
word about taking a test up until that point, it just
seemed to fit with what he'd said to Gage."

"And he hasn't called or texted at all while he's been
out of town, except for the one that caused you to de-
stroy your phone?"

"No, that's it." Feeling utterly confused, Gwen confessed, "I just don't understand it. When I tried to keep
some distance, he just kept pushing through. He took
my seniors water class with me for God's sake, more
than once! Can you imagine another man doing that?
Why would he go to that much trouble—not to mention embarrassment—if he was just biding his time until he could make a clean getaway? Before this week, he
texted me during the day several times just to see how
I was and he always called when he left work. In my
past relationships, even if I didn't want to admit it,
something made me not fully trust them. It's almost as
if I went into the relationship knowing that it would
end badly. With Dominic, the fear was there from experience, but the overall feeling was different. I tried to

guard my heart, but there was just something from the first moment I saw him that was unique for me. I was dating his friend, Mac, who I liked a lot, but I couldn't take my eyes off Dominic when I saw him around the apartment complex."

Lowering her voice, Wendy whispered, "He looks that good, huh?"

"And then some," Gwen sighed. "But, that's not even it. He has a great personality and presence, bigger than life. He's the type of person that people just gravitate toward. You feel like you're the only one in the world when you have his attention. I swear, a bomb could drop nearby and he wouldn't break eye contact. He certainly wasn't checking out other women, either. My friend, Shannon, the single mother, is just gorgeous, but other than being polite, I never saw him give her a second look."

"Well, he sounds wonderful," Wendy admitted. "I hate to say it—maybe he's just that good at convincing others that he is. Hey, are you still on speaking terms with Mac?"

"Um—I guess. It's not like we had a big fight or anything. Why?"

"Well, maybe you could talk to him about Dominic. They are friends, right?"

Wrinkling her nose, Gwen said, "I don't think that's a good idea. I can only imagine how awkward that would be. Mac's a really nice guy, but he and Dominic go way back. He probably wouldn't want to be put in the middle of whatever is going on with us."

"Just a thought. I know this sounds like no advice at

all, but I think you should just play it by ear and see what happens next. Normally, I would tell you to walk away and not look back, but if you love him, then maybe you shouldn't write him off yet. On the other hand, don't take any crap from him. You deserve a man who makes you his priority. Please don't settle for less than that. I swear, he better not be like Chris or I'll take you both out."

Grinning, Gwen thought back to one of her weirder breakups. She'd dated Chris for six months before he broke up with her. "Oh, come on, he had an original excuse at least."

"Yeah, I'll give him that. How many women have heard the old, 'My mother wants me to break up with you so that I can focus on my job and securing my future'?"

"I guess his mommy was right," Gwen mused, "because I heard he got married three months later."

"I never liked him anyway," Wendy admitted. "He actually told me all about his prostate exam in great detail! Who does that? Even Peter guards that like some kind of secret man ritual."

Giggling, Gwen stood and hugged her sister, more thankful than ever to have someone who never gave up on her. Maybe she should run Peter off so she and Wendy could be old spinsters together. "Thanks for listening, sis. Now, please promise me that no matter how much I beg, you won't let me replace my phone this weekend. I don't want to break down and call or text him and it certainly wouldn't hurt for him to wonder what I'm doing like I have him this week."

Throwing up her hand for a high five, Wendy sang

out, "Ohhh yeahhh, baby! I'll lock you in your room this weekend if I have to. By Monday, you will be well rested and ready to take on the world. Oh . . . no e-mail, either. I'll hide my laptop. Let the man see that you've got a life with or without him. You know, I've always said that if you act like a doormat, then that's exactly how people will treat you."

Peter, obviously deciding to brave another trip into the kitchen, tossed out, "It's true, kiddo. I hate to turn on my brothers-in-arms, but I've got friends who go through one woman after another. The common theme seems to be that they have no respect unless there's some kind of mystery or a chase. If the woman is too available, they quickly lose interest and move on."

"Pigs," Wendy grumbled under her breath.

Peter threw an arm around his wife's shoulders, pulling her in for a side hug. "Honey, I wore out the soles of my shoes chasing after you." Wendy rolled her eyes, but Gwen could see the faint tinge of pink on her sister's cheeks. "I fell in love with this woman way back in junior high," Peter continued, "and she wouldn't have anything to do with me. I had chased her for a solid year before she agreed to go out with me in our freshman year of high school. I embarrassed myself by spending most of my time thinking of ways to keep her while she spent her time doing things that didn't involve me at all." Dropping a kiss on Wendy's nose, Peter admitted with a wry grin, "It drove me absolutely crazy. I knew I'd do whatever it took to marry her, and I jumped through hoops for years until I finally wore her down."

In an uncharacteristic show of affection, Wendy pulled

Peter's head down to her level and kissed him. "I loved you all along, baby. I just needed to know that no matter what, you were in it for the long haul with me."

As her sister and brother-in-law seemed determined to relive their love, Gwen thought it was a good time to slip away to her room for a much-needed nap. As she settled back on the bed in the guest room, she thought over Wendy and Peter's advice. She had to admit, in the past, when she felt that things were beginning to deteriorate with a man, she panicked and did everything she could to keep him. Could it be that by doing that, she was actually dooming herself to yet another failure? Sadly, Wendy was right; she hadn't truly loved any of the men she had previously dated so why had she wanted to keep them? Was it more of a fear of failure than the actual desire not to lose the person?

She didn't want to lose Dominic, but this time she was going to try something new. She was going to do the exact opposite of what she'd always done and see what happened. She would take each day as she normally would, enjoy Dominic's company when the opportunity presented itself, and just stop overthinking every little aspect of their relationship. Did she really want to keep someone who didn't want to be with her? The answer to that was no, not anymore. If she was still single when she was eighty, it was a better alternative than being with someone who didn't love her in the way that Peter loved Wendy. She was tired of being a distant second and third to everything in a man's life. If Dominic didn't feel the need to make her his priority, then he wasn't worthy of her. Maybe she had made her other relationships worse by trying to hang on and make them work, but if the other person had truly valued her, then it wouldn't have been necessary to begin with.

It was in no way their fault, but Gwen had always envied the relationship between Peter and Wendy. She thought it was a big reason that she'd felt compelled to attempt to save each of her failing romances. Her sister was always so content and happy with Peter even before they got married. Gwen wanted the same and kept searching for it in each new man that she met. And each time it ended, she kept thinking that if she could just be what the other person wanted and needed, then she would have her Prince Charming, too. She had felt like a failure as a woman for years, when in reality, maybe she had yet to meet the one man who was meant for her. She had been trying to shove a square puzzle piece into a spot meant for a circle and growing more and more frustrated when it didn't fit.

As much as she had come to care for him in such a short amount of time, Gwen had to accept the fact that Dominic might not feel the same way as she did. All she really knew for certain was that for once, it was up to him—the man in her life—to show her that he was worthy of her. Although it felt somewhat terrifying to let go of her need to make him into Mr. Right, she knew that if the pieces were to ever fit, then he had to want to solve the puzzle himself.

Dominic had been by Gwen's apartment more times than he could count after getting home from Charleston Friday night. On his second round of knocking at her door, Shannon had come out of her apartment and told him that Gwen was visiting her sister for the weekend. He'd stood there with his mouth hanging open, shocked that she hadn't told him she was going out of town. Suddenly, another voice said, "Does Gwen not love you no more, Domino?"

He tried to hide his wince when he looked up to see Megan standing beside her mother. He hoped that Shannon would come to his rescue, but the only thing she said to her daughter was, "Honey, it's Dominic, not Domino." He guessed he should be grateful she called him something close to his name unlike poor Baxter, or Bastard as Megan called him. Now both females stood apparently waiting for him to answer the original question.

"Er—you'd probably have to ask Gwen that question," Dominic finally said as he started edging backward.

Relentless as always, Megan moved closer as he tried to put some distance between them. "Did you do something stupid and make her mad?"

He looked over the little girl's head, silently beseeching Shannon for help, which she ignored. Dammit, what was this, "give Dominic hell" day?

Finally, Shannon said, "Megan, we don't call people stupid, remember?"

Megan put her hands on her hips, full of attitude, as she huffed, "I didn't say Domino was stupid. Grandpa says that people do stupid stuff sometimes like Daddy. It's not like calling them dumb or nothing, Mommy."

Shannon raised a brow, but otherwise didn't comment, leaving the burden of conversation once again on

Dominic. He felt a moment's sympathy for Shannon's ex because apparently he wasn't the most popular man in the world if Megan's recollections were any indication. "I try really hard not to do um—stupid things, Megan, and I really hope that I haven't upset Gwen in any way." Crooking his finger and motioning the little girl closer, he leaned down to whisper in her ear, "Because she's really pretty and I want to be her boyfriend."

Megan started giggling, bringing a smile to both her mother's and his face. He was still smiling when he walked back toward his apartment before he heard Megan throw over her shoulder, "Good luck, Domino." Somehow, those three words sounded almost ominous.

He had his cell phone out and was dialing Gage before he got his door shut behind him. When the other man answered, he blurted out, "She went to visit her sister this weekend and didn't even let me know."

Sounding puzzled, Gage asked, "Who?"

"Gwen! Who else would I be talking about?" he snapped impatiently.

"Ohhh, gotcha. So, what's the big deal?"

"Didn't you hear me? She just took off without telling me anything. Finally, our neighbor let me know when I was pounding on her door for the second time in an hour."

"Dude," Gage sighed, "I thought we talked about this? You were supposed to let her make the moves for a while. I mean, you know there is no reason that you have to stay glued to her side since the baby scare is resolved, so you can chill out and see where the chips fall. You feel me?"

Dominic dropped onto his couch, fighting the urge to fling his phone. "I know this may come as a surprise to you, but I actually like being with Gwen. I'm in love with her, and I don't want to lose her."

"Oh, come onnn," Gage groaned. "You barely know her. It's really not like you to lose it like this."

"Exactly. Doesn't that tell you that she's different for me? I've never come close to saying those words to a woman I was dating before. I was gone on her before we even got together and nothing's changed that."

"All right, all right." Gage hastened to adjust his plans. "We're still on the right track here with the whole giving-her-space thing. If she took off without letting you know, then she's probably trying to tell you that very thing, right?"

Dominic pondered his words before reluctantly saying, "You might have a point. Otherwise, she surely would have told me that she was going away. I mean I've had my phone on me, and she hasn't called or texted."

"Please tell me you haven't been blowing her phone up?" Gage sounded as if he was bracing for the answer and expecting the worst.

"Just once," Dominic admitted. "I didn't want her to be trying to answer her phone if she was driving."

Sounding relieved, Gage said, "Okay, that's good. We can work with that. Now you know that she's not home, so you sit back and relax. Let her come to you when she gets back. Don't leave like a thousand sticky notes on her door or tons of texts on her phone. If she didn't call your ass, then there's a reason, and you just need to respect her wishes. I know this is a tall order, but try to get it together. Women like a little bit of a challenge, you know, just like men do."

"Makes sense, I guess. I just sit here and do nothing. Maybe I better make a beer run," Dominic added as he got back to his feet. He wasn't sure if a Corona—or twelve—would help, but it sure as hell couldn't hurt. He'd always been a man of action and this sitting around shit was going to be torture.

Chapter Fourteen

As if her legs were a complete traitor to the rest of her body, Gwen paused outside of Dominic's door when she got home Sunday evening. Her phone was still broken so she hadn't talked to him all weekend. Even though she missed hearing his voice, there was some relief in knowing that there was no reason to stare at her phone every five minutes, hoping he'd called or texted. Maybe life was better before cell phones.

Her hand was literally twitching and wanting to knock on his door. She stood there for a few moments, chewing her lip before squaring her shoulders and moving down the hallway to her apartment. She had put the key in and was pushing the door open when she heard a commotion behind her. Whirling around, she saw Dominic burst from his apartment, causing his door to fly back against the wall with a loud whack. She stood gaping at his disheveled appearance. His short, spiky hair looked as if he'd slept on it the wrong way. His clothes were rumpled, and he had a crease in the side of one cheek. Yep, from the looks of it, he'd been sleeping and woken abruptly. "Hey," she croaked out, and then wanted to cringe at how high her voice was. Ugh, if saying one word could make you sound desperate, then she'd nailed it perfectly.

"Hey . . . babe," he replied softly, as he seemed to drink her in. She'd noticed his hesitation over the use of his usual endearment and tried not to make a big deal out of it. He'd been asleep, and probably wasn't thinking too clearly yet. "Did you . . . um, have a good time at your sister's house?"

Blinking in surprise, she tried to figure out how he knew where she'd been. She didn't think he'd ask Mia or Crystal, so it had to be Shannon. Was it evil that she hoped Megan and Maddy gave him hell? "I did." She nodded. "Wendy and Peter are great. She's a bit bossy, but you never have to worry about her holding back." Gwen hadn't really meant for that last line to be a dig at him, but when he flinched, she had to wonder if he'd taken it that way. Maybe a guilty conscience.

Looking very unlike the usual confident Dominic that she knew, he stuck his hands in his pockets and studied the floor before abruptly asking, "Have you had dinner yet?" When she shook her head no, he asked, "Can I . . . I mean, do you want to go—with me to get something?" Looking at his clothes with a grimace, he added, "I can change clothes in just a few minutes."

Gwen was tired and still hurt over his week of silence, but he was making an effort. Wasn't that what she wanted? If he hadn't wanted to see her, he could just as easily have stayed in his apartment, but he hadn't. And dammit, he looked so adorably hopeful that she didn't have the heart to play hard to get tonight. Her stomach, which always seemed to betray her, growled loudly right before she agreed, causing them both to laugh. "I guess that's a yes then," she joked. "Just let me take my suitcase inside and freshen up. I'll come to your place when I'm ready, okay?"

Maybe it was her imagination, but he looked thrilled as he hurried toward his door. "Great, I'll hurry, babe." As he disappeared through his door, Gwen followed suit more slowly. She couldn't help but marvel at how much things had changed between them in a short amount of time. The old Dominic would have kissed her senseless by now. God, she missed that easy connection that they'd had from the beginning. Now it was almost as if they were going on their first date. Had things changed that much because there was no longer the possibility of a baby? And what about the conversation she'd overheard between Gage and Dominic about Kandi?

Running a hand through her hair, Gwen fought the urge to knock her head against the door until either her thoughts had cleared or she passed out. One day at a time, right? She'd promised herself and Wendy that. So now, this was day one and it was time to sit back and see where things were going to go.

Oh my God, I'm a complete failure at this, Gwen thought as she listened to the door close behind Dominic. Slumping back against her pillow, her mind wandered to the previous night as she tried to figure out where she'd lost control.

Since they both loved Italian food, Dominic had

taken her to a new place in North Myrtle Beach called Nino's. They'd ordered the lasagna for two and after that . . . things had gotten strange. Gwen had been at her bungling best, and Dominic hadn't been much better. Between them, they had managed to knock over a glass of wine, and then the bottle before Dominic stuck his elbow in his antipasti salad followed by Gwen dropping a huge bite of her lasagna onto her white top.

When they left, they were both splattered in food and wine, and she was certain the restaurant hoped they'd never come back again. She didn't know if she'd ever felt that socially awkward before. She should have known it was a sign of the evening to come when she rolled her silverware from her napkin and directly onto the floor where it made a loud bang.

Even the conversation had been sweet and shy. They had each talked more about their families and their teenage and college years. He had opened up about his time in the military with Mac, Gage, and Declan. He had said that it had been very hard being away from his family, but that he'd mostly enjoyed the time he'd served and the brothers that he'd grown to love. Gwen came away from the meal with new insight into the man who had come to mean so much to her.

When they'd returned home, she and Dominic had stood outside her door looking everywhere but at each other. It seemed that the good night kiss stress that usually came after a first date was back, which was absurd since they'd slept together numerous times. If it was possible to turn back the clock on a relationship, then they seemed to have done it. She cleared her throat nervously while Dominic actually scuffed his foot back and forth. To have something to do with her hands, she'd shifted to unlock her door. When she turned back to say good night, Dominic had given her a shy grin, and then she had no idea how it happened, but before she realized what was happening, she was in the entryway of her apartment with her mouth crushed against Dominic's and her legs around his waist.

Things had moved even faster from that point. Buttons had ripped and a trail of clothes was strewn through the hallway as they stumbled into the bedroom. There was no sign of their previous awkwardness as their bodies came together like perfect matching halves. The first time had been frantic and fast, but the second had been a slow, gradual buildup as they explored each other thoroughly. Thankfully, all condom systems were go, and there had been no malfunctions of the latex.

Dominic had left just a few minutes ago while she was still half-asleep. As far as taking things slowly went, she wasn't sure how to rank the previous evening. She didn't think she'd made the first move toward sex last night—but she couldn't rule it out. After being afraid that she was losing him, it had felt so good to reconnect on any level. In hindsight, she knew that probably hadn't been the wisest decision. It was hard to be objective though when a man like Dominic started touching and kissing you. Yeah, she'd never stood a chance.

Gwen had another hour before she needed to dress for work so she was drifting off when she heard a chime that sounded like a text alert. She grumbled under her breath, wondering who it could be this early.

She fumbled around on her nightstand until she found her phone. She'd had Dominic wait for her in his truck last night while she ran into her cell phone provider and replaced the one she'd destroyed. There was no way she wanted him to see the broken phone. When she finally managed to hit the button to light the screen, it showed no missed calls or texts.

Just as she was wondering if she'd imagined the whole thing, the sound came again, only this time it was clearly coming from the other side of the bed. Huffing as she crawled to reach the other nightstand, she found Dominic's phone there. He'd obviously forgotten it while trying to dress in the dark earlier. The phone chimed and the screen lit. Trying to convince herself it was because there might be some kind of emergency and not just because she was nosy, Gwen picked up the phone and saw a couple of texts on the screen. The first one was the most recent and was from Gage telling Dominic to stop for coffee and doughnuts. Gwen was smiling until she got to the next one from a contact called simply K. *Got something special planned for you and Gage. Back in Charleston this week?* As Gwen reread the message, suddenly it hit her—Kandi! It had to be from the stripper. What was she doing in Charleston? Maybe the entire work emergency had been a lie.

She could blame what she did next only on a severe case of woman-scorned anger. Clicking on his phone once again, she was surprised to find that it wasn't password protected. A part of her had hoped that it would be because there was no way she could stop herself from flipping through his call history and text messages now.

Feeling like a teenager checking up on her boyfriend, Gwen thumbed through the phone finding nothing at all suspicious except the text message that had made her invade Dominic's privacy. When her fingers brought the message up, she paused for a second before hitting the DELETE button. A warning popped up asking if she was sure . . . Oh crap, she shouldn't do it, should she? The phone was practically telling her to stop. It wasn't as if she was removing Kandi from the picture simply by deleting her message. What purpose did it even serve other than to do something completely childish? She was old enough to know better. She'd simply give the phone back and let that be it. She wouldn't break it as she did hers or confront him about the message. No, she was an adult. "Oh, fuck it." She cringed as she hit YES on the warning and watched the offending text disappear. Gwen dropped his phone like a hot rock, when a chime sounded from the other side of the bed. "Are you kidding me?" she murmured to the empty room as she crawled back to her phone.

"Hey, babe, I think I left my phone at your place. I'm already on the road so could you bring it with you to the office?"

She began to laugh hysterically as she sat on her heels clutching her phone. It wasn't even eight in the morning and already she'd lost all of the relationship maturity that she'd promised both Wendy and herself. Now, thanks to her trigger-happy finger, she couldn't just simply tell Dominic that she'd seen the message from K— who was quite possibly Kandi. Shit, why had she deleted it? Realizing that he was probably waiting for a response from her, she typed out, *"Okay, I'll bring it."* Maybe she should have added, "Don't worry; I've already looked at everything on it."

Falling backward onto the bed, Gwen kicked her feet against the mattress in frustration. Surely, Kandi being in Charleston with Dominic was no coincidence and she hadn't gotten one call while he was gone. And then, being the forgiving and desperate person that she was, she'd fallen into bed with him promptly last night. Yes, she had vowed to be mature and let Dominic walk away if he wanted to, but she was getting damned tired of being the girl that NEVER got the guy! She'd even tried to make herself into someone she wasn't because she felt she was the one who needed to change to make things work.

In theory, there was always something about a person that wasn't perfect and could be improved upon, but you couldn't and shouldn't have to change the core of who you were for anyone. That was what she was finished doing. She had no problem fighting for her man—she might not be able to work a stripper pole, but she brought plenty to the table and one of those things was honesty.

Jumping to her feet, she headed to the shower. She was tired of not knowing where things stood with Dominic. She would deliver his phone and confess what she had done. Really, how much worse could things get? At this point, being officially dumped would be rather anticlimactic, to say the least. She was walking into the bathroom when the phone chimed again. Freezing, she muttered under her breath, "You have got to be kidding me," as she stalked back to his phone, thinking it was another text for him. She sagged in relief when she found nothing on his screen. Thank God, she didn't think she could handle seeing a sext from Kandi at this point.

Grabbing her own phone, she found a text from Wendy. *"Make sure you take that test we discussed first thing in the morning."*

It took Gwen a moment to understand what her sister was saying. Then it hit her—another pregnancy test, just to be certain. Geez, why had she even mentioned that to Wendy? She would have her taking a damn test every day for the next month, even though she'd already taken at least twenty of them just days ago. *"Well, good morning to you too,"* she typed out sarcastically.

"Good morning, Gwen. How are you today, my dear sister? Now take the darn test already!"

Gwen laughed despite herself. Wendy could do sarcasm just as well as she could. Glancing at the clock, she knew she didn't have time for a debate so she quickly typed back, *"I'm going to do it now—just for you!"*

"Let me know! Love you!"

Gwen sent her a quick reply and then retraced her steps to the bathroom. She rolled her eyes, but still pulled out one of the remaining pregnancy tests that she'd stashed in her cabinet. She grumbled as she made short work of peeing on the stick, before setting it on the bathroom counter and getting in the shower. As much as she loved her cell phone, Gwen could only think that life would surely be better if they didn't exist. There would have been no text from Kandi for her to find and no nagging from Wendy. She could have started her day relaxed and happy instead of suspicious and grumpy.

Technology, ugh, sometimes she hated it.

Chapter Fifteen

"Hey, where's the coffee?" Gage asked as Dominic walked through the office door.

"Do I look like your maid?" Dominic quipped as he dropped into a chair in front of the security feeds.

"But I texted you to bring some coffee," Gage huffed as he punched some buttons on his keyboard. "If you'd let me know you weren't stopping, I'd have done it myself."

Dominic brought up the feeds for the next customer's property before saying, "I left my phone at Gwen's so I didn't get your message." Dominic heard the familiar squeak of Gage's chair as he leaned back in it.

"You totally went right after her last night, didn't you? How long did you make it before you ran to her apartment? Ten minutes?"

"Oh, shut it," Dominic grinned. "I knew from Shannon that she was supposed to be home Sunday evening, so I just—kept an eye out for her."

Gage surprised him by sitting up straight and asking, "Shannon? As in your neighbor, right?"

Shaking his head at Gage's abrupt question, Dominic said, "Yeah. That's what I said. You know the one with the crazy kids that I've mentioned."

"Damn, Dom, give them a break. I'm sure they're not that bad. Kids will be kids and all that stuff. I bet Shannon has really done a good job with them, all on her own. You gotta give single moms some serious respect; you know what I'm saying?"

Dominic turned from the monitor he had been watching to stare at his friend. "Man, what's wrong with you today? You're like an emotional wreck or something." Instead of laughing at his insult, Gage did something even more out of character and actually blushed. He was still trying to figure it out when Mac walked in carrying coffee and a bag.

"Morning. Ava guilted me into stopping to pick this shit up for you two," Mac grumbled as he plopped the bag and cup carrier down on the desk.

Recovering from his earlier snit, Gage chuckled, saying, "Bro, you are so whipped. I wonder what else I can have her suggest for you to do."

"She didn't say I couldn't stir yours with my finger," Mac threatened as he held Gage's cup suspended.

"I will so go tell her," Gage whined until Mac reluctantly handed him the cup he'd been holding hostage.

Mac took a chair next to Dominic and pulled a doughnut from the bag. "We need to eat fast because Seth Jackson called me while I was on the way to the office. A couple of his brothers are going to be in town today from Florida and he wanted to know if we could squeeze in a last-minute meeting this morning at the Oceanix Resort."

Looking at his watch, Dominic asked, "How last-minute are we talking?"

Mac popped the last of the doughnut in his mouth. "We need to be there at nine."

"But that's only thirty minutes from now," Gage scowled as he snagged a doughnut.

Dusting the crumbs from his shirt, Mac said, "Yeah, Seth said he'd understand if we couldn't make it. Apparently, there was some mechanical issue with their company plane, and the brothers ended up landing here instead of Charleston. Since we've been trying to get a meeting with them, Seth thought it might be a good opportunity."

"We can make it." Dominic nodded as he got to his feet. "I'm going to run a cup of coffee up to Gwen and see if she's here yet with my phone. How about picking me up out front in fifteen?" Dominic heard Gage making the sounds of a whip cracking as he walked toward the door. Just as he was opening it, he heard him shout; then a loud thud sounded. Fucking Gage. When would he learn to keep his chair firmly on the floor? No doubt, Mac had flipped him backward.

Dominic was still grinning when he walked out of the cafeteria and almost plowed into Gwen as she was walking through the lobby with Crystal. "Whoa . . . morning, babe. Sorry. You were almost wearing your coffee."

When he leaned down to give her a kiss, she phone-blocked him. Or rather, she somehow stuck his cell phone in his face, before his lips could connect with hers. "Good morning," she replied in a voice that sounded unusually shrill. "Here's your phone," she added unnecessarily since he already had it in his pocket. She was nervously chewing on her bottom lip, glancing between him and a curious Crystal. "Um—I . . . Do you have a minute?" she finally asked.

He was just opening his mouth to answer, when he saw Mac's Tahoe pull up in front of the door. "Sorry, babe. I've got to run," he said, pointing to where Gage was now on the sidewalk, flagging him. "We've got a meeting across town. If I don't see you today, though, I'll stop by when I get in this evening." Not wanting to risk getting stiff-armed on the kiss again, he rubbed her shoulder briefly before hurrying toward the door.

Gage was still standing on the sidewalk, so Dominic stepped around him and slid into the front passenger seat before motioning the other man to the back. As they pulled away, Gage leaned between the seats, saying, "I thought we talked about the space issue. It looks like you practically pounced on the woman as soon as she walked in the door. I mean, I know you blew it last night with your whole stalking routine, but it's not too late to reclaim a piece of your manhood."

"No doubt," Mac began idly, "I'm gonna hate myself for asking, but what in the hell are you two talking about?"

Before he could answer, Gage jumped in. "I've been helping him out with Gwen. She was all freaked out because our boy here was stuck to her like a second skin. She was beginning to push him away, and I told him to step back and give her some space. Like, be the man and ignore her. I mean that's second nature to most of us born with a penis. Well, actually, I'm questioning even that on Dom because he lost all of his manliness by crying over a girlie movie that he insisted on watching with Gwen last week. The poor girl took off without telling him a few days later. Hell, she probably drove to the nearest truck stop just to feel the testosterone again. Then she comes home last night and he's standing outside her apartment door, trying to look through the peephole. He'd already banged on her neighbor's door to find out where she was."

Dominic frowned as Mac looked at him with a mixture of pity and surprise. "Bro, is that true? I mean, I can overlook the stalking thing because I've probably been guilty of that with Ava, but what's this about crying during a movie? Don't you know if you feel that coming on, you get up and go to the bathroom? That's usually the one place women won't follow you."

"I didn't cry!" Dominic snapped. "I just pointed out that Jane Fonda was trying to kill her soon-to-be daughter-in-law and that the girl should jump ship before she had to put up with that for life."

Wrinkling his nose in confusion, Mac asked, "Are you talking about Ted Turner's ex? What's the movie got to do with her?"

"Thank you!" Gage crowed.

"Fuck you both." Dominic glared at his friends. "I might have embarrassed myself slightly by making a few comments during the movie, but I wasn't even remotely close to crying like asshat here is trying to insinuate."

Mac chuckled for a minute before saying, "All right,

I'm gonna let that part go for now. But I have to ask you, man, why in the world would you be taking relationship advice from speedy dick back there? His idea of a long-term commitment is buying the woman dinner first."

"Hey!" Gage protested. "I've had girlfriends before. I mean, come on, I've dated way more than either of you have so don't you think I probably know more about women?"

"Relationships?" Mac laughed. "Have you ever gone out with a woman without sleeping with her? And if that miracle actually happened, did you ever attempt to see her again or did you go ahead and delete her from your phone?"

Dominic turned in his seat to find Gage once again looking around nervously as he had in the office earlier. "Of course, I have," Gage snorted. "I'm just not sitting around crying over my feelings all of the time like you two."

"We're not talking high school here," Dominic added. "We've been friends for over ten years now, and I've never known you to actually date anyone. You seem to have an unlimited supply of women more than ready to sleep with you, though, which is completely baffling to me."

"Why are you busting my balls?" Gage huffed. "Unless you've forgotten, we all spent eight years surrounded by mostly men. None of us were exactly doing much dating back then. And Mac might have finally snagged a woman and gotten married, but Dom, you're not doing too hot in that area. Plus, I don't recall a single long-term relationship that you've been involved in—your mother and sister don't count, by the way."

"You're right." Dominic seemed to surprise Gage when he agreed. "I had girlfriends at times before I joined the military, but like you said, that doesn't happen too much while you're enlisted. Gwen is a completely new thing for me, which I knew she would be. Being married to Uncle Sam was all of our lives for too long. Hell, I hate to admit it, but I'm afraid I'm screwing up with her because I've been out of the dating game for too long."

"You've dated since we got out," Mac added. "Why the sudden panic over a woman?"

Dominic ran a hand over his head in frustration. "Because I'm in love with her and it has me second-guessing everything I've ever known."

"But you've only been going out a few weeks," Mac choked out. "That's pretty fast, bro. Are you sure it's not just something of the physical nature? We all spent a lot of time without a woman in our lives—well, other than . . ."

"One-blow wonders?" Gage added from the backseat.

Mac winced at the other man's description. "I wasn't going to put it like that, but you know, casual hookups. It would be too easy to lose it over the first woman who you have some kind of connection with."

Dominic released a heavy sigh, wishing this conversation had never gotten started. "Mac, I'm not some teenager who lost his head after having sex for the first time. I've been hung up on her since I first saw her at our apartment building. I went to a senior citizens water dancing class for God's sake! What does that tell you?"

"Well, fuck," Mac said, sounding stunned. "You do love her, don't you?"

"Ain't no doubt about it," Gage added. "No man does something like that unless he's already given his dick away. Big props to you on going that far, though, bro. I thought it was bad when I waxed her legs the other night."

Laughter filled the vehicle when Gage's last comment hit him. "Dude, whose legs did you wax? We better not still be talking about Gwen."

"Shit, no, not Gwen," Gage sputtered out. "I . . . I meant I've done that in the past. Not like recently or anything."

Looking at Gage in the rearview mirror, Mac snorted, "I call bullshit on that. You're seeing someone, aren't you? Hell's bells, you got a woman, Gage?"

Dominic turned completely in his seat to stare at Gage incredulously. "You do, don't you? That's why you've been wigging out this morning. I knew something was up. It's Crystal, isn't it? You finally get her to take pity on you?"

"No, it's not Crystal," Gage replied, surprising them all. "I . . . um just ran into this girl one day and then we seemed to keep running into each other. I mean, it happened before I even realized it was a thing. One day we were laughing when we almost collided in Walmart and then I was eating with her at McDonald's." Seeming truly perplexed, he asked, "Can you imagine me doing something that innocent with a woman? And I had a good time, too. There are a couple of issues with her that I have no idea how to deal with, though."

Forgetting his own problems, Dominic was intrigued. The only woman he'd ever heard Gage say more than a few sentences about was Kandi and that was just because the other man was obsessed with the thought of a stripper threesome. "Why haven't you said anything about seeing someone? Hell, I've given you plenty of opportunities while we've been talking about Gwen. And what are the issues with her? Fuck, she's not married, is she?"

"No, man, she's not married. She's just different than my usual type."

"Doesn't accept dollar bills in her underwear?" Mac asked.

"Ha-ha." Gage rolled his eyes. "I believe you're talking about Dom's past girlfriends." Looking relieved, he added, "Oh look, we're here. I hate that this conversation will have to wait, but what're ya gonna do, boys?" With that, he flopped back against his seat, and Dominic thought it was probably the first time Gage had been more excited to work than to goof off. Strange— who was the mystery woman that Gage had gotten involved with? Shaking his head, he decided that he had enough confusion and mixed signals in his own love life without worrying about his friend's.

"That's a total waste of a manicure." Gwen looked up to find Suzy smiling down at her. She'd decided to have lunch at one of the outdoor tables that were scattered into the beautiful landscape around Danvers. Her mind was on the previous night with Dominic when Suzy's voice pulled her from the daze that she had fallen into.

Holding up her half-chewed nail, she gave a sheepish grin before dropping her hand back to her lap. "Yeah, between popping my fingers and chewing on them, I'm a lost case. It just makes me grateful that I never understand what they're saying at the nail place when they fix my mess."

Indicating the bench, Suzy asked, "Mind if I sit with you? I've already walked off my nervous anxiety and now I'm just tired."

"Sure," Gwen replied, even though company was the last thing she wanted. She'd really enjoyed her lunch with Suzy and the other girls, but they were still somewhat like strangers to her. Good manners dictated that she at least attempt a few minutes of small talk before making her excuses and leaving, though. "So, nervous anxiety, huh?" Boy, did she know that feeling well. "Bad day at work?" Gwen only wished her problems centered on Danvers and not what she had discovered earlier that morning.

"Nope, nothing work related." Suzy took a deep breath and said, "I just found out I'm getting a baby. Or Gray and I are."

Gwen felt like all of the air had left her lungs. This wasn't the explanation that she'd expected by any means. "You're pregnant?" she managed to squeak out.

"No." Suzy shook her head. "My husband and I have been on a waiting list to adopt a child . . . and I just got the call. A birth mother has selected us."

Gwen gaped at the other woman, trying to process her words. "Oh, my . . . Wow!" she whispered. "I . . . um didn't know you were trying to adopt. I remember someone asking you if there was anything new on the baby front at lunch the other day, but I just assumed . . ."

"No, I'm not trying to get pregnant—anymore." Then looking completely at peace, she added, "This is our path—what we're meant to do right now. I just . . . never expected it to happen this soon." Turning to fully face Gwen, she admitted, "I'm excited, beyond excited, honestly. But, I'm scared to believe that this will actually work out. We've gotten our hopes up too much in the last few years. I want to run to Gray right now and tell him, but then a part of me is afraid to see his happiness dashed if this isn't our baby."

"Oh, Suzy." Gwen squeezed the other woman's hand in hers and then felt about two inches tall about how upset she had been over her problems. Compared to what Suzy and others were struggling through, she was lucky. She may have things to figure out in her life and plans to make, but she would survive, even if she had to do it all on her own. Well, and with Wendy kicking her ass every step of the way.

They had been quiet for a few minutes before Suzy seemed to compose herself and Gwen could see a little of her usual spirited personality return. "So, what're you doing sitting here looking like you're heading for a firing squad? Work or man problems? Those are usually the two things that take over our lives."

There was no way she could tell Suzy, of all people, why she was sitting here staring off into space as her thoughts and stomach churned. She'd been that way since she'd left her apartment that morning and it hadn't improved as the day had passed. She had seen Dominic only briefly, while walking in the building that morning, but he'd been gone in the blink of an eye. She had to talk to him tonight, but she wasn't sure what she was going to say. He was likely to be angry with her, and dammit, she was angry with him and the world one minute, then ready to cry the next. What a screwed-up mess. "I . . . It's nothing," she finally said in answer to Suzy's questions. "Just one of those days, you know?"

"You're pregnant, aren't you?" Suzy asked quietly.

Gwen spun around so fast she almost fell from her bench. "How did you know? No one else knows—shit." She sagged as she realized what she'd accidentally admitted. "Oh, my God, I'm so sorry. I know you couldn't possibly want to hear that."

Suzy took Gwen's hand, offering comfort. "Gwen, it's okay, really. It took a while, but I'm in a good place now. There is no way I could begrudge you or another woman that happiness. And right now, you look like you're in desperate need of a friend. It's Dominic's?"

Gwen nodded, and then found herself confiding in someone she barely knew, but it seemed that fate had brought them together today to give the other the support they needed. "Yes, it's Dominic's. I . . . just found out this morning. I mean, I took a test—a bunch of them last week and they were negative. We knew it was a possibility because we had a condom . . . mishap. I only had my period for a couple of days though and it was, just different. I had mentioned it to my sister before I left her house on Sunday, and she suggested I take another test just to be certain. I just laughed it off because I hadn't been having any symptoms or anything. Well, this morning as I was getting ready for work, she texted me a reminder and since I had purchased like twenty of them last week, I went ahead and took one, just so she'd drop it. I didn't even bother looking at it until I was out of the shower and—it had both lines showing. I completely freaked out and took every last test I had left and they all indicated 'Pregnant.'"

"Oh honey, congratulations," Suzy said, sounding nothing but sincere. As if noticing Gwen's tight expression, she asked, "Are you not happy about it?"

Gwen felt horrible at Suzy's question. She didn't want the other woman to think that she didn't want the baby after she'd been unable to have one of her own. "It's not that," she assured her. "I'm just not sure what to do next. I told Dominic last week that I wasn't pregnant, and he just seemed to brush it off like it didn't matter. I think he was relieved because he has feelings for someone else, a stripper named Kandi, and now this is going to mess up his plans—to end things with me and move on."

"Wait a minute," Suzy stopped her. "He is seeing you and a stripper? Dominic? Are you sure? Everyone talks about him like he's the best thing since sliced bread."

"I don't know for sure," Gwen admitted. "It's just that I overheard a conversation between Gage and Dominic about how Dominic could go back to Kandi if he found out I wasn't pregnant. Then I saw a text on his phone this morning from Kandi wanting to know when he'd be back in Charleston. While he was there, he didn't call or text me other than to say, 'good deal,' when I told him I wasn't pregnant."

"Oh no, he didn't!" she muttered. "That's just wrong. Wait, but you said he left his phone at your place. Does that mean he spent the night there, I mean after that bonehead text?"

"Um, yes, he did," Gwen admitted sheepishly. "When I got home from my sister's Sunday afternoon, he came out of his apartment while I was getting my keys out. He seemed kind of nervous and asked me to go out to dinner. I agreed because I didn't know where things stood between us after not hearing from him. Then our dinner was really awkward, but kind of sweet. Like a first date."

"And then he looked so good when you got home that you went all in for the wild monkey sex and still don't know where things stand with him?"

Feeling dejected, Gwen sighed. "Yep, that's it pretty much. I mean he's never seemed like some kind of player, but I have no idea if he really cares about me the way I care about him. You know?"

"You need to talk to him," Suzy advised sternly. "Tell him to grow a pair and let you know what's going on."

"But what if he just says something he doesn't mean because I'm pregnant? I mean, I will tell him, of course, but it would be nice to know if there is something between us outside of that."

Suzy gave her an understanding smile. "Then you have the whole state-of-the-relationship talk first. Tell him you're in love with him and see what he says in return. You'll know how he feels before he even opens his mouth, though. Men have a hard time with the whole poker face thing."

"But, I didn't say I was in love with him," Gwen denied weakly. "I'm not sure I know what I feel."

"You love him." Suzy smiled. "It's there, written all over your face."

"But how can I be in love so soon?" Gwen protested. "We've only been together a few weeks. That's crazy."

"I'm going to tell you something I have never even admitted to my husband. I was in love with Gray Merimon from the first moment I saw him. He terrified me because I knew he was going to be my life—my future. I fought it as long as I could, but he had me at first sight. My stomach dropped, my breath caught, and my body came to life. I loved that man before he ever finagled me into our first date, and I'll never love anyone the way I do him. So, to me, it's very easy to see how you can be in love with Dominic. And if he's the kind of man everyone says he is, then the feeling is going to be mutual." Suzy had just finished her sentence when her cell phone began ringing. She pulled it from the pocket of her leather jacket and smiled. She answered the call with, "Hey, baby," causing Gwen to smile and get to her feet. She mouthed, "Thank you," to her new friend and walked away, giving her some privacy. She was still a bundle of nerves, but she had a direction now. She would talk to Dominic tonight and by the end of the evening, she planned to know how he felt about her one way or another.

Chapter Sixteen

Dominic left his apartment after a quick shower, intent on going to see his woman. He turned after locking his door and found Gwen already walking toward him, looking uneasy. He searched her eyes, trying to find a clue as to what was bothering her when laughter close by drew both of their gazes down the hallway. Dominic did a double take, thinking he was seeing things. No, surely that wasn't— *What the fuck?*

"Shannon?" Gwen whisper-shouted but her neighbor paid her no attention. Probably because she had both arms, legs, and her mouth wrapped up in—Gage? When the couple either ignored or didn't hear Gwen's voice, Dominic cleared his throat loudly, still trying to make himself believe what he was seeing. Shannon was the woman—the someone different—Gage was seeing?

Finally, they were forced to come up for air—either that or the truck backfiring in the distance got their attention—and they slowly disengaged their lips and stared at each other like lovesick fools, completely oblivious to rest of the world. Dominic stepped up next to Gage and asked, "Gage, man, what're you doing?"

Gage and Shannon jerked apart and both began talking at once. Dominic couldn't make sense of anything they were saying and was glad when Gwen finally asked, "But what about Cameron—the doctor?" Then she turned suspicious eyes to Gage before putting her hands on her hips. "This is Gage—he works with Dominic. He's not Cameron, and he's not a doctor!"

"Bro," Dominic began, ready to kill his friend over lying to Shannon. "That's not cool at all."

Shannon, sounding exasperated and a little embarrassed said, "Guys, I know who Gage is."

Slapping a hand against his forehead, Dominic muttered, "Gage's middle name is Cameron."

"Huh . . . ?" Gwen asked, still looking confused.

Gage pulled Shannon snugly into his side. "I ran into Shannon when I was visiting Dom. Then it seemed like we just kept running into each other. Walmart, Walgreens, and finally, when I saw her again at McDonald's, we both started laughing. I told her I worked with Dom, and we just started talking. She invited me to eat with her and the girls, and it just kinda went from there."

"So, why didn't you say anything—and what's with you going by your middle name?" Dominic asked, now more curious than anything.

"Shannon and I wanted to take things slow without others knowing for a while. I mean she's got Megan and Maddy to consider and all." Looking embarrassed, he admitted, "I introduced myself to her as Cameron. I was concerned . . . that since she lived in the same apartments as Dom that she might have heard my name before. I really liked her and wanted a fresh start.

When we kept seeing each other though, I finally told her the truth."

"But Shannon," Gwen sputtered. "You can't date him. He sleeps with a lot of women. Mac told me all about Gage's strict 'no stay zone.' He just—you know, does it and then moves on. You can't let someone like that around your kids."

Dominic could see both Gage and Shannon stiffening at Gwen's harsh words. Okay, so maybe there was some truth to them, but he didn't want to see either of them lose a friend over this. In the end, both Gage and Shannon were adults, and it was their decision. So, he put a reassuring arm around Gwen's shoulders and said, "Babe, I think we need to leave this up to them."

"Gwen, I love you, I really do," Shannon began, "but you need to let me worry about my girls. I'm their mother, and I always do what's best for them."

Dominic felt Gwen's back go ramrod straight at the bite in Shannon's voice. He thought they were probably only minutes away from some hair pulling. He noticed Gage looking equally as nervous as his gaze darted between the two women.

"How is it best to lie about who you're seeing to everyone you know? I mean if you went to those lengths to keep us from knowing . . . are you certain about what you're doing?"

Shannon took a few steps closer, now almost nose-to-nose with Gwen. "Oh yeah, and you're so much better? Let's see how great your decisions are after you have your baby!"

"WHAT?" Gwen shouted, looking appalled. "How did you . . . ?"

"You told me to let myself in this morning to get the new shoes you'd bought for Maddy. Megan had to use the bathroom. I saw all of those pregnancy tests lined up on your bathroom sink. So, don't you two be lecturing Gage and me about hiding things. Looks like you're doing a bit of that yourselves." Finally, the anger left her voice, and she just sounded hurt as she added, "You told me you weren't pregnant. You lied to me about that."

"Looks like you're not the only one," Dominic said in a daze. Dropping his arm from Gwen's shoulders, he put some distance between them before turning to stare at her. She looked almost green as she stared back with something that could only be described as guilt on her face. "You told me . . . the test was negative. Why—why would you lie about that?"

Gwen reached for his arm, but he stepped back quickly before she could make any physical contact. "It was," she assured him in a shaky voice. "They were all negative, but then this morning they showed positive. I—I was going to tell you tonight."

Dominic had no idea what was going on, but as he looked at the three sets of eyes focused on him, he just knew he had to get out of there and find a place where he could think—and breathe. Before he knew it, his legs were carrying him down the steps. He heard voices shouting his name, but he never stopped, never paused. He grabbed his bike keys from his pocket, grateful he had picked them up at the last minute. He'd thought that he and Gwen could go to the beach and talk. Now, he just wanted distance from the thoughts racing through his head.

"Gwen, I'm so sorry," Shannon cried as Gwen sank to the floor when it became apparent that Dominic wasn't coming back. "I didn't know! I thought he knew you were pregnant."

"I just found out," Gwen said hoarsely. "I wasn't lying. It was negative last week."

As Gwen sat there trembling in shock with Shannon's arms around her, Gage stepped forward. If he was offended by Gwen's earlier words, he didn't show it. Instead, he held a hand out to her. "Come on, ladies, let's take this inside. Megan and Maddy will be home soon from their grandparents' house and there will be a lot of explaining to do if they find us out here."

Gwen stood and turned toward her apartment, but Shannon held firm to her arm. "No, sweetie, come to my place. I don't want to leave you alone. I'm so sorry I said that. I can't believe I did that to you," she cried harder.

Gage motioned them toward the doorway of Shannon's apartment but didn't move to follow them. He grabbed Shannon's hand. "I'm going to go, baby—let you two talk. Call you later, though. You good?"

Gwen turned to see her friend smiling at Gage, her eyes soft and filled with something that looked a lot like love. At that moment, she hoped with all of her heart that Gage proved everyone wrong and had just been waiting for the right woman all along. She'd never known Shannon to even date since finally breaking free from her disaster of an ex. The man hadn't had a faithful or truthful bone in his body. Gage might have gone through a lot of women, but if Dominic and Mac had been friends with him for all of these years, then he was a good guy—he had to be.

"I'm good," Shannon murmured right before Gage trailed a finger down her cheek before dropping a kiss on her lips.

Both Gwen and Shannon collapsed side by side onto her couch. "I owe both you and Gage an apology as well," Gwen said. "I don't know why I said all of that. I love you and the girls to death, but your personal life is none of my business. I'm sorry, Shannon. I truly am."

Shannon scooted closer and dropped her head against Gwen's shoulder. "We really outdid ourselves this time, didn't we? I swear, I thought for a minute there we'd start throwing fists or something. I really care about Gage, and I guess I'm a little overly sensitive about our relationship. He's the first man that I've connected with in such a long time, and I'm afraid of losing him."

"How long?" Gwen asked, curious as to how she could have missed Gage coming and going from Shannon's apartment.

"A couple of months," Shannon admitted. "He just officially met Megan and Maddy a few weeks back for the first time." Blushing, Shannon added, "I think you remember them telling you all about it at the zoo that day."

"Ah yes, the whole 'don't—stop Cameron' thing. I

thought that all came out of nowhere." Feeling a little hurt, Gwen said, "I can't believe you didn't tell me."

"I hated keeping it from you, of all people. I just didn't want anyone knowing in case I'd made yet another mistake. When you're a single mom, people seem to have a lot of opinions about what you should and shouldn't be doing, especially where men are concerned. I didn't want everyone rolling their eyes and talking about me. Trust me, I've been there, and it's not pretty."

Gwen winced. "I guess I validated all of those fears with my little tirade, didn't I?"

Shannon chuckled. "You kinda did that for a moment, Rambo. I'm just gonna let you blame it on your crazy pregnancy hormones and not hold it against you."

Gwen instantly sobered at the mention of what she'd been trying to wrap her mind around all day. Her hand lifted to rest on her flat stomach, still in disbelief that any of this was really happening. Well, the part about the man leaving her was actually pretty easy to believe. She might not have been pregnant during her other relationships, but she was certainly familiar with seeing the guy's back as he walked away. "I really didn't know, Shannon. I took a test on Friday and thought I had my period, but it only lasted less than two days. Wendy told me I should test again after I admitted to not having a regular period. I swear I didn't really have any reason to think that I might be pregnant. I had the tests leftover and you know Wendy, the drill sergeant. I knew I'd never hear the end of it until I double-checked. I almost passed out when I saw that second line. Then I guess you saw all the tests lying around my bathroom. I lost my mind there for a while and was just frantically taking the rest of them. Now Dominic seems to think I've been lying to him about it."

"Well, he kind of deserves some crap after his comment to you. What was it again?" They both repeated, "Good deal, thanks for letting me know," at the same time. "Come on, that was kind of an asshole reply, wasn't it? Seems so out of character for him, though."

"Boy, this is one of those times you'd like to get drunk with your girlfriend, isn't it?" Shannon mused. Before Gwen could reply, the front door opened and she heard Maddy and Megan's voices reverberate down the hallway. Raising a brow, Shannon said, "I can't offer you booze, but if you need a distraction, I got two who will more than do the job for ya."

Chapter Seventeen

Dominic peeled the label from his second beer as he stared at the large screen television in the bar without really seeing it. He wasn't even sure what he was doing here. He'd been feeling a cross between anger and betrayal, helped along by a good ole fashion case of panic when he'd taken off earlier. The whole crazy relationship between Shannon and Gage had been surprising, but kind of entertaining, until the whole revelation of the pregnancy. Now *that* he had not seen coming. Hell, they really hadn't even discussed it since Gwen had texted him while he was in Charleston. He had been sitting next to Gage, who immediately advised him not to make a big deal out of it. So, he sent that stupid, fucking text, using Gage's words. Damn, he'd regretted doing that, but he didn't want to bring it up to Gwen on the slim hope that she had not thought it strange.

The question on his mind tonight was why she had said she wasn't pregnant if she was? Clearly she was if Shannon saw the positive tests. Gwen claimed she had just found out that morning, but that was days after she said the test was negative. *What the hell?*

"Damn bro, couldn't you have picked a bar a little closer? The traffic was hell getting here." Dominic jerked around in surprise to see Gage standing behind him. He was at Flannigan's, which was miles off the beaten path. He hadn't actually had a destination in mind; he just drove until he was ready to stop. "I tracked your phone," Gage added at his questioning look. "You know we have that enabled on all of the company phones, just in case."

"Shouldn't you be with your new girlfriend?" Dominic asked sarcastically as the other man settled on the stool beside him. He waved a bartender over, signaling for a beer before speaking.

"Nah, she had her hands full with your very upset girl. Why'd you take off like that? I mean, that's like something I'd do."

"Why would she lie to me about that, Gage? I get that she might have been upset about it, but she plainly told me in that text that she wasn't pregnant. Then just a few days later, I find out that she is, but she hasn't said a word to me. She should have known I wasn't going to lose my shit or anything. Hell, we both knew it was a possibility. Do you think she just wasn't going to tell me at all?"

"Come on, man, you live next door to her and work in the same building. I don't think she intended to keep it from you. That would be damn near impossible. I think you're overreacting. Gwen's not the type of woman to be trying to play you. That doesn't even make sense. She said it was negative the first time."

"Well, if it was a closed case, then why was she taking another test? She had to have suspected that something wasn't right. Women don't just randomly take pregnancy tests whenever they feel like it, do they?"

"Hell if I know, Dom. You should go on back home and talk to your little mama." Gage started laughing. Fuck. He wasn't ready to talk to Gwen yet, and if Gage was going to be tossing out baby jokes all night, he was going to need something stronger than beer.

"Holy shit," Dominic groaned as his head threatened to explode. Hell, he could even see the white light coming for him. This must be what death felt like. He could think of no other explanation.

"Getting up today, princess?" an amused voice asked as he writhed in pain.

Rolling onto his back and blinking until he recognized Gage, Dominic had his answer. He was in hell and Gage was his executioner. The asshole had turned on every light in the room, along with opening the blinds. Come to think of it . . . where was he? He was obviously on a couch, but not his. "What the fuck, man?" he grumbled as he tried to sit up.

"You know, if Gwen could see you now, she'd be rethinking her feelings. Frankly, dude, you look like roadkill, and you smell even worse. I knew when you passed out in the bathroom at Flannigan's last night that things weren't gonna be pretty this morning, but I wasn't expecting it to be quite this ugly. And FYI, you owe me a visit to the chiropractor because I almost threw my back out carrying you to the truck."

"Where's my bike?" Dominic asked, picturing it trashed or stolen.

"I had one of the guys pick it up last night. He dropped it off at your place. Told him to bring the keys by the office this morning."

His head was hammering relentlessly as he tried to focus his sluggish thoughts. "How much did I have to drink last night?" he croaked out. His mouth felt like sawdust.

"I think it'd be easier to ask what you didn't drink last night," Gage smirked. "I tried to cut you off, but you listened to your other friends over me."

Flopping back, Dominic asked in confusion, "What other friends?"

Gage took a loud slurp out of the cup he was holding, making Dominic's hair stand on end before saying, "Oh, you know, most of the bar. After you buy a few rounds of drinks, you get a lot of new buddies. I'm gonna say, though, I don't think you should invite them over for Sunday dinner anytime soon because when you were falling in the urinal, I was the only one with your back—and a wad of paper towels. When I call your ass for a favor in the future, you better not hesitate or question me. Trust me, you owe me big."

"And Gwen?" Dominic asked. He'd probably drunk dialed her all night.

As if knowing what he was getting at, Gage pulled a phone from under the chair cushion in the corner. "Don't worry; I took this from you early in the evening when you started trying to bring your contact list up. I knew no good was going to come of that. I hid it when we got home because I was afraid of what you'd do if you woke up. That's one way in which you didn't make an ass out of yourself last night." Gage laughed as Dominic weakly flipped him the bird. "Oh, guess what. I saved the best part for last."

"What?" Dominic asked, not sure he wanted to know if it was worse than what he'd already heard.

"We have to go to Charleston this morning. You know how fun those road trips are when you're hungover."

"You can't be serious! They can't all still be sick down there. We just got back." His stomach was threatening to revolt at the thought of being anywhere near an interstate today.

"It's the Oceanix—Charleston. We're meeting Asher Jackson there. He wants to show us around the resort and get a feel for what we can do for them. He was impressed when we met yesterday and is ready to make a change. His contract with his present security company is up for renewal next month so time's an issue. It's a big operation, and we'll need to know what we're looking at staff-wise like yesterday before we put a proposal together. We're talking big time here, brother, if we pick up that chain."

"Fuck," Dominic hissed, feeling like an idiot for getting wasted, especially during the middle of a busy workweek. He never did crap like that. Hell, he was just too old for it, not to mention the pain it caused. "I've got to go home to shower and change."

"We don't have time. I let you sleep as long as possible. Go hit my shower. I left some clothes out in there. We're pretty much the same size."

With no time to argue, Dominic got to his feet and

staggered down the hallway toward Gage's bathroom. He'd been to his friend's apartment countless times, but he went straight to the door on the left and opened it to find—the laundry room. He couldn't imagine that this day could get any worse.

Chapter Eighteen

Gwen went from feeling sorry for herself to just being pissed as the red display on her bedside clock showed seven in the morning. She couldn't believe that Dominic hadn't showed up or called last night. What happened to all of the support he had promised her a few weeks ago? It seemed that now when it was crunch time, he was nowhere to be found. On the few occasions that she'd allowed herself to think of the "what-ifs," she certainly hadn't imagined Dominic taking off. For God's sake, the man had brought her a bottle of folic acid and obsessively Googled information about early pregnancy. That just didn't seem like the actions of a man who would panic.

She was still spitting mad when she slammed out of her door an hour later. She debated stopping by Dominic's apartment but figured he would already be gone to work by now. And truthfully, she refused to chase him down. It wasn't as if he didn't know where she lived. When and if he was ready to act like an adult and have a rational discussion, he could come to her. If she had to raise the baby alone, then she would. Heck, she could move back to Columbia where she'd have her family. She had options, but what she didn't have was the will to chase another man who didn't want any type of commitment. She wasn't after a marriage proposal, but being a father was a huge commitment and as of yet, Dominic showed no signs of being ready to make it.

As she was walking to her car, she saw that Dominic's truck and his bike were still in his parking spaces. So, he was still home, after all. It was unusual for him to be this late going into work, and she felt a moment of worry before she shook it off. He certainly wasn't concerned about her, that much was painfully obvious.

Of course, as luck would have it, she ran into him outside of the coffee shop in the lobby for the second morning in a row. She had no idea how he had arrived before her. He was still a few feet away, wearing dark sunglasses, but she could tell by the stiffening of his spine that he had spotted her. Beside him, Gage waved, seeming relaxed and thankfully not hostile over their confrontation the previous day. She was debating making a run for it when Dominic said, "Gwen, we need to talk."

She dropped her eyes to the floor, counting to ten as she tried to control her temper. What she really wanted to say was, "Oh, so now you're ready to talk?" When she looked back up, she noticed something strange. His pants were several inches too short. He was wearing his usual work attire of cargo pants and a company shirt, but none of it appeared to fit. His muscular chest, arms, and shoulders were always visible, but the shirt he was wearing outlined every taut inch of his upper body. Come to think of it, the pants were also formfitting. Heck, she had to pull her eyes away from his crotch. Those pants were like a spotlight on his impressive length. Oh God, she was staring. Gage was giving her a knowing grin, but she couldn't tell if Dominic had noticed, thanks to his sunglasses. "I . . . er . . . have to get to work. Maybe we can talk this evening."

Dominic raised a hand, rubbing at his temple as if he had a headache. "I don't know what time I'll be back. We're going to Charleston as soon as Mac picks us up."

"Charleston?" Gwen hissed out before she could stop herself. "You seem to be going there an awful lot lately." She couldn't remember Mac going that often when they'd been dating.

"We live for that place," Gage joked before pointing to Mac's car pulling up out front. "Gotta go, bro. You know how cranky McKinley gets when we keep him waiting."

"I'll call you tonight unless it's too late when we get in. I really don't know. But we need to talk." They stood staring at each other for another moment. It felt weird not to at least touch in some way as they usually would. Dominic finally gave her a brief smile before walking off, still rubbing his head. *I bet Kandi can make him feel better today*, Gwen thought cattily. Maybe the other woman liked her men to wear clothes that were too tight. There was no way Dominic would be working a stripper pole in those pants, though. The seams would blow out within the first ten seconds.

Gwen kicked her foot against the tile floor in the lobby. This was the second official day of knowing she was pregnant, and so far, nothing had changed. She didn't feel any different and she had no idea where things stood with the father of her baby. Yeah, her life was going so well. It made her long for the days when her hardest decision was what flavor of Ben & Jerry's to buy for her evening at home.

"Dom, either you packed on twenty pounds overnight or your clothes seriously shrank in the wash, man." Mac grinned as he looked at Dominic's too tight shirt.

Gage, always one to volunteer too much information—except for his relationship with Shannon—stuck his head between the seats of Mac's Tahoe, saying, "He got wasted last night and passed out at my place. We didn't have time for him to go home and change this morning."

Mac shook his head as if not believing what he heard. "You got drunk? And on a school night? That's not like you. What's up?"

"Well, Gwen is . . ." Gage began until Dominic put his hand up in the other man's face.

"Mind if I talk here, Chatty Cathy?" When Gage waved a hand for him to go ahead, Dominic pinched the bridge of his nose before saying, "Gwen's pregnant."

Mac darted a look his way before pulling out into the Myrtle Beach traffic. "But I thought you said that she wasn't. Didn't you tell me that?"

"He did, but then shit got real yesterday outside his apartment and he had a bomb dropped on him," Gage piped in again.

Dominic's head was killing him and his body felt like a bus had hit him. He was ready to kill someone, and Gage was setting himself up to be a perfect target with his loose lips. "Shit got real all right, when I saw your boy back there sucking my neighbor's face."

Mac's hands twitched on the steering wheel, causing them all to yell in alarm before he quickly righted the Tahoe. "Gage, what the hell man? You caused this mess? Please tell me you didn't hit on Gwen!"

As Gage bristled indignantly in the backseat, Dominic continued, "Gage has been involved in a secret little affair with our neighbor, Shannon. As in the single mother, with two kids."

"Maddy and Megan's mom?" Mac blinked. "Gage, that's who you're in a relationship with? That's just—well, hell, I don't even know what to say."

"Messed up?" Dominic offered. "Can you imagine the shit that will come out of their mouths now with Daddy Gage in the house?"

"Hey listen, you nosy assholes," Gage snapped, sounding seriously pissed off, "that's my girl and her kids you're talking about."

"Actually, we're talking about you and not them," Mac pointed out. "Come on, brother, we all sprout the F-word like it's our national anthem. Plus you've screwed your way through most of the women in South Carolina and more than your fair share overseas. How are you managing to keep your mouth PG-rated and your dick in your pants?"

"It's not as if I'm incapable of being faithful to someone," Gage defended. "I've just never found anyone who I wanted to be with—like that. But Shannon, she's different. She makes me want to be better. She . . ."

Dominic opened his mouth and pretended to gag. "I swear to God, if you say she completes you, I'll have Mac pull over and throw you out of the car."

"Just because your life is a mess, big papa, don't take it out on me. Shannon and I have it together more than you and Gwen do right now."

"Our boy appears to have a small point there, Dom," Mac threw in. "You're one of the calmest fuckers I've ever known. You stood behind me in Afghanistan more times than I can count with an M4 assault rifle in your hand, and I never thought twice about it. You're complete ice under pressure—usually. Since you've been seeing Gwen, you've been all over the place. I mean, case in point, you're wearing Gage's clothes, which he probably went commando in without washing because you pulled a drunk. I've seen you drink a whole bottle of tequila and still be able to walk a straight line so I can't imagine what put you down that hard."

"Don't forget the part about lying in piss—that was freaking disgusting," Gage added.

Mac shuddered. "I don't even want to know the details. I'm just saying that I'm a little worried about you. I thought you were crazy when you started spouting words of love so soon, but I believe it now. Only something that life altering would have you so far off your usual mark. I have no idea what's going on with Gwen and the pregnant or not pregnant thing, but you need to straighten it out. I told you in the beginning that she's a good woman, and I don't believe for a minute that she's trying to bullshit you. I do think that you two have some serious miscommunication going on and a part of it is probably your listening to advice from everyone else instead of just figuring the shit out on your own like you normally would."

"That's directed at me, isn't it?" Gage grumbled.

Mac ignored the question and continued. "Avie told me that you helped her out a lot while we were both trying to get ourselves together. That's who you are, brother. You don't overreact, freak out, and second-guess yourself. You told me after Gwen and I broke up that you'd wanted her all along. All right, guess what. She's there. She's having your baby. Are you waiting for an engraved invitation or what?" As Gage started laughing, Mac looked in the rearview mirror, adding, "And I don't even know where to start with you. Single mother? You better be good to her, Gage, or I'll kick your ass myself."

"Fuck," Dominic groaned and slumped into his seat. "You're right. I've been losing my shit, and I don't even know why now. What's wrong with me?"

Mac let out a full belly laugh. "Love may be patient and kind, but it also grabs you by the balls and takes you on the head trip of a lifetime. Welcome to it, my friend."

Chapter Nineteen

Gwen stood in the doorway of her refrigerator, eating chocolate pie straight from the pan. She could practically hear the five pounds that she'd gain settling on her already big butt. Tonight, though, she didn't give a damn. She'd already had phone sessions with both Mia and Crystal and even Suzy had stopped by this afternoon at the office to check on her. The other woman was practically glowing, apparently now over her initial anxiety and excited to move forward with adopting. All three women seemed certain that things would work out with Dominic, but Gwen wasn't so sure. She hadn't heard from him all day. It was now nine in the evening, and she'd eaten everything in her refrigerator. She alternated between never wanting to see him again, which was unrealistic since they were having a baby together, and begging him to talk to her, which would be humiliating after the way he'd taken off yesterday.

She was still brooding with a spoon stuck in her mouth when her doorbell rang. Freezing in place, she wondered if she'd wished for the sound so much that she'd imagined it. But a few seconds later, she heard it again. Tossing both the pie and the spoon into the refrigerator, she smoothed her hands down her hair and grimaced at her lounge pants and tank top. If it was Dominic and he wasn't here to break things off, he would probably consider it after seeing her disheveled state. "Screw it," she said to the empty room. "If he doesn't like it, what do I care?" She stalked to the door and looked through the peephole. Dominic stood there, looking as if he had no plans to leave anytime soon. Squaring her shoulders, she jerked the door open and felt her body completely betray her as she stared at him. He was still wearing his too small outfit from earlier. There were dark circles under his eyes, and he was sporting some scruff on his face. Despite her best intentions, her nipples hardened, pushing against the thin material of her top. Of course, she wasn't wearing a bra and if the widening of his eyes was any indication, he'd noticed.

When she didn't move to let him pass, he cleared his throat nervously. "Hey, babe. I . . . um . . . just got home. Can I—can I come in?"

Dammit, she wanted to say no. To strike a blow for women everywhere who'd been hurt by a man, but she found herself moving to the side and waving him forward. Heat gathered between her thighs as she noticed the way the tight pants he was wearing outlined his butt. Her body was fast turning traitor and her mind was barely holding her libido in check. "Wh-what are you doing here?" she managed to spit out around the knot in her throat.

He sank down on her couch before dropping his

head in his hands. "Baby, I think I've lost my mind lately. You started pulling away from me, and then Gage told me I wasn't showing enough interest in the pregnancy possibility and was not being supportive. Then I made a fool of myself over that Jane Fonda movie, and Gage said I acted like a pus— um, girl. Then I was supposed to give you the space that you needed because I was coming on too strong and scaring you. You told me you weren't pregnant and I typed out this whole text in reply about it not changing anything and how I felt about you, but Gage said I was being a pus— um, girl again and going too fast. I tried not to push you, but when you got home from your sister's, I couldn't stay away from you. Of course, I had to go to Charleston AGAIN. Next, I come home to find out about Gage and Shannon and you're not pregnant, but now you are. Then I got drunk and passed out in some nasty bathroom before Gage carted me home and made me wear his more than likely dirty clothes. The pants are so tight they've crawled up my ass all day. Gage said I was complaining like a pus— girl again. Mac pointed out that I could shoot an M4 assault rifle but couldn't tell the woman I'm crazy about that I love her and I needed to stop acting like a pus— girl." He grimaced, shaking his head. "We say that word too much, don't we?"

Gwen's head was spinning as Dominic finished with his rapid-fire explanation. She was trying to process his words when it hit her. Her heart seemed to pause before taking off. "You—you love me?"

Dominic got to his feet, looking completely exhausted and pale, but his eyes were filled with emotion. He stopped just inches away from her and took both of her hands in his. "I used to think I was a cool person. Nothing ever shook me. I'm the original 'Plan B man.' Then you came along, and I just lost it. I prayed that Mac and Ava would finally get their head out of their asses and be together because I had wanted you from the beginning. You were dating my best friend, and I hated it. I waited too long to ask you out and fate handed you to Mac. Finally, though, you came to me and you were nothing like I'd imagined, baby—you were so much more. I thought I fell in love with you the first time I saw you with Megan and Maddy on the playground outside, but I knew I loved you the first time I held you. I've made a lot of mistakes trying to tell you—and show you—how I felt when all along it should have been one moment and those three words." He released one of her hands and raised it to cup her face, stroking her cheek. "I love you, Gwen. God, I love you so much, baby."

Gwen felt tears begin to flow from her eyes as she heard the words that she never thought she'd hear from a man other than her father. She knew at that moment that every heartache in her life had led her to this moment—to Dominic, who loved her unconditionally and who was surely meant to be the father of her child.

His eyes were now watery, as well, as she turned her head to kiss his palm. "So, you're saying this is all Gage's fault?"

He looked embarrassed as he said, "The only excuse I have for listening to him is that I was terrified of screwing up and losing you. I was constantly second-guessing myself and Gage always seemed to be around at those times. Hell, when a man's desperate, everything starts to sound like a lifeline."

"You might want to rethink that the next time." She winced, causing them both to laugh before she sobered. "I love you, too, Dominic. I was so drawn to you after our first night together that I was running scared. I'd been hurt in the past, and I knew that those feelings would pale in comparison to loving and losing you."

Dominic pulled back only to lower his hand and place it reverently over her stomach. "I was surprised at how disappointed I was when I got your text that you weren't pregnant. I mean I'd never allowed myself really to believe that it would happen. But then when the possibility was gone—I had a hard time coming to terms with it. I didn't say anything to you about it because I didn't know how you were feeling and I was afraid of pushing you farther away."

"I was sad as well," Gwen admitted. "I knew I should probably be relieved because I hadn't planned to be a mother at this point in my life, especially after only dating someone less than a month, but my heart still had a hard time accepting it. I'm a little scared and a lot nervous because I don't know how this is going to work, but I want this baby—with you—more than I've ever wanted anything in my life. Oh, my God," she suddenly gasped. "But what about you and Kandi?"

"Kandi?" Dominic asked, looking dumbfounded.

"I saw the text she sent you, about Charleston," Gwen blurted out. "She said she had something for you and Gage and were you going to be back in Charleston."

"Baby, I have no idea what you're talking about. I haven't spoken with Kandi since I ended it. Plus, why would I see her in Charleston? I never saw a text from her. Hell, she's not even in my contact list anymore."

Gwen dropped her head against his chest and confessed to seeing the message from K and deleting it. "Then who is K?" she asked hesitantly.

"K? Just the letter, right?" When she nodded, he began laughing. "Babe, that's the owner of the department store in Charleston that we've been setting up security for. She has some long name, but everyone calls her K. She is a seventy-plus-year-old sweetheart who cooked for Gage and me when we were there. That's probably what she was talking about. She wanted me to let her know when we would be back so she could cook us another meal."

"Oh," Gwen whispered, completely embarrassed. "Can we please forget everything I just said and pick up where we left off?"

Giving her a soft smile, Dominic hugged her to him tightly and dropped a kiss on the top of her head. "You got it. As for your being scared, we'll take it slow, baby. I have no idea what I'm doing, either, but I don't think we have to have all of the answers right now. We'll move in together, get married, and make a life and a family together."

"Whoa," Gwen stuttered in surprise as she pulled back. "This isn't the nineteen fifties, and I'm not looking for a shotgun wedding simply because I'm pregnant. A lot of people have children together without being married."

Dominic grinned down at her, and Gwen felt her body turning to mush. God, how could he do that with just one look? "I didn't say today, babe. Give me some credit. When I propose, it'll be so romantic that the word no won't even be a possibility. You'll be screaming yes at the top of your lungs." With a wicked wink, he added, "Both before and after the proposal."

Gwen could feel the heat steal over her cheeks as he reinforced his statement with a grind of his hard length against her core. His cocky statement might not be so far-fetched because she was biting her tongue to keep from moaning "Oh, yes," right then. She couldn't imagine ever being able to say no to him.

Maybe they were starting their life together completely backward—putting the cart before the horse, as some would say. However, as Dominic kissed a line down her neck, whispering words of love and desire, Gwen had to believe that some of the best-laid plans were the ones that were—well, not planned at all.

Epilogue

It had taken Dominic exactly a month to wear her down and convince her to move in with him. Then it took him another couple of months after that to propose to her.

Even though she'd been expecting it, Gwen could still remember how surprised she'd been when he asked her to marry him. They had invited both of their families up to Myrtle Beach for Thanksgiving. She had wanted to wait until she was through her first trimester before telling everyone about the pregnancy. Of course, that had proved to be impossible. Dominic had practically been bursting at the seams to tell his family and there was no way that she could keep the news from Wendy. And most of Dominic's friends already knew, so in the end, they'd gone ahead and shared the news, trusting that all would be well.

Wendy had been thrilled, and her mom and dad, although more than a little surprised, seemed happy for her as well. Dominic's family had been over the moon. His sister, Meredith, had been back to visit several times. She was desperately hoping for a girl in the family since she had two boys. She claimed all the testosterone was giving her hives and the women needed to level the playing field in the Brady family.

Their apartment had been beyond full with both families. They had just sat down to Thanksgiving dinner when Dominic stood. Gwen was surprised that he'd decided to give the holiday thanks and prayer, when suddenly he was on his knee and pulling her chair away from the table. Truthfully, she'd heard nothing but white noise for the first few seconds until he popped open a jewelry box and a breathtaking, princess-cut emerald and diamond ring winked at her. Finally, his words started penetrating the shocked bubble that had surrounded her. "Our love has been unique, unexpected, and amazingly beautiful—just as you are. Baby, almost any ring would pale in comparison to you, so I tried to find the one that I thought would be a perfect fit, just as you are for me." Smiling to herself at the memory, Gwen admitted that he'd been right that night four months ago when he'd confidently told her that she'd scream yes, because she had—and then she had again later . . . when they were alone. A fact he had pointed out to her with much smug glee.

They had also had their first ultrasound the previous day. The doctor had wanted to do it earlier than usual due to the spotting she'd had before her pregnancy had been confirmed. They were relieved to find out that everything was fine and she was measuring exactly where she should be. It had been emotional for them both. And whoever said that tough, military men didn't cry, was wrong. Tears had trickled down Dominic's face as they'd seen their little bean's heartbeat flicking on the screen and his or her little hands and feet kicking and moving. It was still too early to know the sex, but Dominic was sure it was a boy. He swore he saw a penis on the screen although the doctor had assured him it was actually an arm. So, the jury was still out on that. Gwen secretly thought it was a boy, as well. It was just hard to imagine a macho man like her fiancé not having the dominant Y chromosome in his child. She knew that secretly, though, a little girl would own him; he'd never stand a chance.

"Ready, baby?" Dominic pulled her from her musings as he rubbed her stomach tenderly before dropping a kiss on her upturned lips. She was just beginning to get a very tiny baby bump, and he couldn't keep his hands off it.

She had been resting as he'd insisted. Maddy was in her first school play, and they were meeting Gage, Shannon, and Megan at school to see it. Yawning as she stood from the chair she'd been curled up in, she answered, "I'm ready, babe." He put a protective arm around her shoulders and led her out of the apartment. He had been pushing her to look at houses, but for now, she wanted to stay where she was comfortable. Frankly, she was just too tired at this point to tackle the big task of moving.

"Thank God they didn't give Maddy a speaking part in this play, right?" he joked as they found a parking space at the school. "I can only imagine how epic that would be."

Gwen laughed, agreeing. "I know. Poor Shannon would be terrified. I think the girls are even worse with

Gage practically living there. You know, it seems that we were all wrong about him," she admitted. "He is crazy about Shannon and a natural with the girls. I've never seen her happier than she is now."

"Yeah." Dominic nodded as they walked through the entrance to the auditorium. "I'm still surprised by that. The guy talks about her nonstop. He's the last person I would have ever imagined in a serious relationship, much less with kids involved. He's still a goof, but Shannon has grounded him. I don't know, despite all his joking around, he always seemed like he was kind of lost. I thought it was because he never had much of a relationship with his family."

"Maybe he was just waiting for her," Gwen suggested softly as she curled her arm around Dominic's waist.

"Maybe he was, baby," Dominic agreed, looking at her with so much love in his eyes that she knew they were no longer talking about Gage.

Before she could reply, Shannon came rushing up. "Hey guys! We saved you a couple of seats beside us. Oh, my God, you aren't going to believe it, but my brother Mason brought his boyfriend, Cash! I thought my father was going to swallow his tongue! My mother gave him a few digs in the side, and he actually stood up and shook Cash's hand and was passably friendly. I left Megan to keep them distracted."

"Good times," Gage smirked as he clapped Dominic on the shoulder before hugging Gwen. "Hey, little mama, looking good." Gwen laughed while Dominic removed his arms from around her.

Rolling his eyes, Dominic said, "Hands off, bro. I think we've discussed this." Both Gwen and Shannon giggled because this conversation happened every time they were together. It was perfectly innocent, but Dominic was the ultimate alpha male where she was concerned and Gage loved to get under his skin.

Shannon took Gage's hand, pulling him down the aisle, while Dominic and Gwen followed. "Come on, Romeo; let me get you in your seat before Dom takes you out." Soon they were all settled in the four end seats with a few minutes to spare until curtain time.

Megan was already restless and fidgeting when a little girl about her age walked down the aisle. Megan burst out of her seat and ran to hug her. "Caroline!"

As the girls talked, Shannon leaned over telling Gwen, "Caroline has a sister in Maddy's class. I think she has one of the speaking parts."

Beside her, Dominic was saying to himself, "Caroline?" as if trying to figure something out. Gwen gave him a questioning look before a little boy walked up and pulled Megan's hair, causing her to scream.

As Gage made to grab for Megan, who now looked completely pissed off, Shannon stiffened, saying, "Oh no," under her breath. It hit Gwen at the same time that Dominic started chuckling under his breath.

It was as if everything suddenly went into slow motion. Megan, bent on revenge, grabbed the little boy's arm and yelled loud enough to be heard in the next state, "I'm going to get you, Bastard!"

Shannon gasped in horror and every mouth around them dropped open in shock. Gage leaned around the women to give Dominic a high five. "That's my girl." He grinned proudly.

"Our kid cannot be friends with anyone named Baxter—are we in agreement?" Dominic smirked.

Gwen started giggling as she snuggled into his arms. "I agree," she whispered against his neck, "but you'd better prepare yourself. With Megan and Maddy as honorary aunts, I'm scared to think of what our child will pick up along the way."

She continued to laugh as her words turned him to stone. "Holy—" he began before she elbowed him in the side. He finally relaxed, dropping a kiss onto her head. "I've got this, babe. I'll just run interference whenever they're visiting. No problem."

Gwen choked back a reply, not wanting to burst his bubble yet. The poor guy would find out soon enough that, in life, you had to pick your battles and she was sure that Megan and Maddy could get the best of him anytime they chose. But God, you had to love the man for trying.

Acknowledgments

As always, a special note of thanks to my agent, Jane Dystel, and my editor at Penguin, Kerry Donovan. None of this would ever be possible without you both and I appreciate all that you do.

Also, thanks to Jenny Sims for all your help.

To Tabitha and Kim, who help me get started each day with good coffee and great conversation!

A huge thanks to all the readers and bloggers who continue to embrace the Danvers series. It always touches my heart at how much you love the characters that I've created. Thank you for making them as much a part of your lives as I have.

To my special friends: Amanda Lanclos and Heather Waterman from Crazy Cajun Book Addicts, Catherine Crook from A Reader Lives A Thousand Lives, Shelly Lazar from Sexy Bibliophiles, Christine with Books and Beyond Fifty Shades, Marion Archer, Lorie Gullian, Stacia from Three Girls and a Book Obsession, Shannon with Cocktails and Books, Sarah from Smut and Bon Bons, Andrea from the Bookish Babe, Jennifer from Book Bitches Blog, Tracey Quintin, Melissa Lemons, Chantel Pentz McKinley, Nicole Tallman, Stefanie Eldrige-O'Toole, Tara Thomas, Lisa Salvary, Monique Harrell-Watford, and Jen Maxner.

Don't miss the next book in the Danvers series!
Continue reading for a special preview of

THE ONE FOR ME

Available from Signet Eclipse in February.

There were some days that just sucked, Crystal Webber thought to herself as she used one hand to rub her aching head and the other clutched at her cramping stomach. Why in the world had she come to work this morning? True, she hadn't felt quite this sick when she'd left home, but she had been nauseous. She'd attributed it to skipping dinner the night before since she had fallen asleep on the sofa hours before her usual bedtime.

Now, though, she could no longer avoid the fact that she was ill. Her boss had gone to lunch, so Crystal sent her an e-mail explaining the situation before getting rather shakily to her feet. She quickly grabbed the edge of her desk until the room stopped spinning. "You can do this," she mumbled under her breath as she put one foot in front of the other. She was grateful that she had been promoted a few weeks before to assistant to the director of marketing at Danvers. Otherwise, she would be struggling to make it through the cube farm where her previous desk had been located, where there was little to no privacy and someone would have certainly noticed that she was weaving as if she'd had one too many drinks. Right now she couldn't take the time to stop to explain anything to her coworkers. Thank God, things were quieter on the management side of the hallway.

She was relieved when the elevator doors opened as soon as she hit the down button. The next few moments passed in something of a daze, and she had no idea that she'd actually made it to the sidewalk outside Danvers until she was blinded by the bright sunlight. As her eyes blinked quickly to adjust, her stomach rolled alarmingly. She was so focused on the realization that she was going to be sick before she got home, she hadn't even noticed someone standing beside her until a hand touched her arm.

"Are you okay?"

Crystal jumped in shock, then whirled around to see Mark DeSanto looking down at her with concern-filled eyes. *Please, no.* Fate wouldn't be so evil as to place the man she'd stalked and lusted after for months in her path today of all days.

Using the last reserves of her strength, she pushed her shoulders back and gave him a bright smile. "I'm fine," she replied in a voice that sounded weak, even to her own ears. He gave her a skeptical look, and then the unthinkable happened. Her body went into a full revolt, and almost in slow motion, she threw up on a pair of shoes that had likely cost more than her Volkswagen Beetle. Words of apology flashed across her mind, but before she could give voice to them, her world dimmed and then turned black. As consciousness slipped away, all she could think was that she'd met the man of her dreams face-to-face, and she wasn't going to live long enough to do a damn thing about it.

Mark DeSanto stood in shock as he held the limp body of the woman who had just moments before ruined his favorite pair of Tom Ford shoes. He wasn't a vain man, but he knew the effect that he had on most women. Hell, he'd had more than a few swoon at his feet, but the whole throwing-up thing was completely new. Now he held a stranger in his arms, with no idea what to do with her. It wasn't as if he could just lay her on one of the nearby benches for someone else to find—could he? No, he discounted that option, regardless of how appealing it sounded.

When he'd seen her staggering, he should have turned the other way and left her to be someone else's problem. But, as if drawn by some unseen force, he had found himself reaching out and touching her arm, wanting to see the face that belonged to the enticing body, even though he usually preferred tall blondes or redheads.

The woman he'd followed through the doors of Danvers, though, was one he'd caught glimpses of in the hallways and lobby of the office many times in recent months. For some reason, he'd never gotten a good look at her face. He'd recognize her ass anywhere, because that body part was usually facing him as she walked in the opposite direction. She was petite, but she had curves in all of the right places. Today her long brown hair hung in loose waves, which stopped just inches from her delectable backside. She was wearing a black skirt, which reached her knees, but the slit in the middle had shown shapely thighs as she walked. When she had lifted a small arm, rubbing her neck, the top she wore had edged up, and Mark was surprised to see a tattoo on her lower back. Yeah, completely not his type, but damn did he want to see her face.

She seemed to be everywhere he was lately, and he was ready to meet his mystery woman so that he could move on. Anything beyond that was doubtful. He didn't like to muddy the waters where he worked—that wasn't to say he'd never made an exception, but he tried not to.

When she'd jerked around to face him, he'd felt a jolt of electricity shoot through his body. He wasn't a man given to romantic foolishness, but there had been songs written to describe women like her. Wide eyes that looked almost violet in color. Plump pink lips that made a man's cock sit up and take notice, and the kind of flawless peaches-and-cream complexion that some women tried to achieve through thousands of dollars' worth of cosmetics purchases.

He had still been gaping at her as she assured him that she was fine before she further shocked him by vomiting and promptly passing out. She had been seconds away from her beautiful face meeting the unforgiving concrete when he'd caught her. As he stood with her light weight in his arms, a black Bentley sedan pulled to the curb. His driver, Denny, who was also his cousin on his mother's side of the family, got out of the car, gawking as if unable to believe what he was seeing. As far as the employer-employee relationship, theirs was very informal. They'd grown up together, and although Mark's family had money from the DeSanto side, Denny's did not. Denny had proposed that he become Mark's driver and assistant years ago when Mark had taken over the family business. It had worked well for both of them. Denny was paid more than probably anyone else working in a similar position, and Mark trusted him implicitly.

"I'm almost afraid to ask what you did to that girl, but if I'm going to become some kind of accessory, then I guess I need to know," Denny sighed in resignation.

Mark shook his head helplessly. "I have no idea. She was weaving as she walked. Then she got sick and fainted."

Denny wrinkled up his nose as the smell of the vomit finally reached him. "Shouldn't we do something with her? I mean, do you think she's drunk?"

"How the hell am I supposed to know?" Mark snapped. "I didn't smell any alcohol, and it's barely midday. Also she just left Danvers, so it seems unlikely."

"Then we need to get a doctor. She obviously has something wrong with her," Denny pointed out.

Rolling his eyes, Mark said, "You think? Open the car door so I can get her inside." Denny jogged ahead and had the door ajar when Mark reached him. "Here, you're going to have to hold her for a minute. Then you can hand her to me."

Denny held his hands up, trying to back away. "She's

got puke on her. Can't you just get in with her? There's no need to ruin both of our clothes."

"Oh, for God's sake, Denny, I'll buy you a new suit. Just take her for one second." Mark wouldn't have believed how hard it was for two men to juggle such a tiny woman if he hand't witnessed their spectacle. Finally, as Denny gently handed her off to him and shut the door, Mark slumped against the leather seat with her curled against him. Since he had no idea what her name was, he rubbed his hand along her leg as he said, "Angel, open those eyes and look at me so I'll know you're okay." He continued to say variations on the same thing. He had almost given up when she shifted in his arms.

Suddenly, the violet eyes that had captivated him earlier were looking at him with something close to awe. He was too stunned to react when she lifted her hand and stroked it down the side of his face. "Oh, Mark . . . can we please have sex this time before I wake up?" she asked before dropping her head back to his chest. If not for the soft snore that her mouth emitted, he would have been checking her for a pulse.

He was chuckling at her words, when it hit him. She'd called him by name. His angel wasn't deliriously asking for sex from a stranger. She wanted him. He had no idea who she was, but for the first time in a very long while, he was interested in knowing more.

He'd become so jaded where women were concerned that he rarely cared enough to ask their names anymore. They were just strangers passing through his life for a few hours. This beauty seemed different, and as soon as she was conscious and coherent, he intended to find out who she was. She'd already accomplished something that no one in years had. She was in his arms, and regardless of the circumstances, something about it felt strangely right.

About the Author

Sydney Landon is the *New York Times* and *USA Today* bestselling author of *Weekends Required*, *Not Planning on You*, *Fall for Me*, *Fighting for You*, and *Betting on You*. When she isn't writing, Sydney enjoys reading, swimming, and being a minivan-driving soccer mom. She lives in Greenville, South Carolina, with her family.

CONNECT ONLINE

sydneylandon.com
facebook.com/sydney.landonauthor
twitter.com/sydneylandon1

Also available from *New York Times* bestselling author

Sydney Landon

THE DANVERS NOVELS

Weekends Required

Claire Walters has worked for Jason Danvers as his assistant for three years, but he never appreciated her as a woman—until the day she jumps out of a cake at his friend's bachelor party...

Not Planning on You

Suzy Denton thought she had it all: a great job as an event planner and a committed relationship with her high school sweetheart. But life is never quite so simple...

Fall For Me

All her life, Beth Denton battled both her weight and her controlling parents. And now that she's declared victory, she's looking for one good man to share the spoils of war...

Fighting For You

Ella Webber has spent years uncomfortable around the opposite sex, but as soon as she meets the handsome Declan Stone, she's smitten. But can she persuade Declan that they're a perfect match?

No Denying You

Working for uptight workaholic Brant Stone is more than Emma Davis can bear. But when the tension between them explodes, hate will turn into lust, and then to something much more...

Always Loving You

Ava Stone has spent her entire life looking over her shoulder. But when she's forced to rely on the one man who has never let her down, can he break through the protective walls she's needed for so long?

Available wherever books are sold or at
penguin.com

sydneylandon.com